Adriatic Tales: Island at the Edge of War

Roger Malone

ISBN 9781708338312 (Paperback)

This book is a work of fiction. References to historical events, real people, or real places are used fictitiously. Other names, characters, places and events are products of the author's imagination, and any resemblances to actual events or places or persons, living or dead, is entirely coincidental.

Front cover image: Korčula, ca. 1487, from *Beschreibung der Reise von Konstanz nach Jerusalem* by Konrad von Grünerberg, courtesy Karlsruhe, Badische Landesbibliothek (Cod. St. Peter pap. 32, fol. 13r).
Map illustration of Korčula and the region courtesy of Doriana Berkovic.
Cover and book design by author.

First printing 2020

Printed by Kindle Direct Publishing

Follow Roger Malone…
…on Twitter: @RogerAMalone
…on Instagram: malone.author
…on Facebook: Roger-Malone-114496966607084

*To Luka and Alex, the two stars
that travel with the Cheshire moon*

Table of Contents

Acknowledgements

Adriatic Tales: Island at the Edge of War was inspired and supported by many things and people, directly and indirectly, as all creative works are. The narrative of the Ottoman attack on Korčula is drawn primarily from *Defense of Korčula from Turkish Attack in 1571*, a first-hand account of the assault written in Latin by Antun Rozanović and translated into Croatian by Reverend Ivo Matijaca and then into English by Nikola S. Batistich, "a proud descendant of one of the defenders," to mark the 400th anniversary of the attack. While Rozanović becomes Father Anton in my story as a historic character, Father Anton's motivations, dialogue, and actions are pure conjecture and fiction. Indeed, all the characters are complete and shameless fabrication.

Along the way to completing this manuscript, I benefited from the kindness of strangers who took the time from busy schedules to answer random emails from out of the blue about a specific fact or idea. I appreciate their help. I am also thankful for a small group of friends who read early versions of this story and offered comments, ideas, and encouragement – Damir, Doriana, Idil, Jennifer, Richard, Sebastian, and Slavenka – as well as Caroline, Cody, and Peter, who offered helpful advice once the publishing phase began. And I am eternally grateful to my wife, Jasmina, and my sons, Luka and Alex, who had to live with me during all this and were among my harshest critics and my greatest cheerleaders.

And, of course, Toots.

While I endeavored to be as historically accurate as I could in this tale and sought help when I recognized a question, there will likely be errors found in these pages. The faults are all mine.

A convenient conceit: place names

Place names in Croatia, like everywhere, have changed over the centuries, largely reflecting swings in political or military might or the speaker's heritage or allegiance. And often, places went by different names at the same time, much like, say, Wien, Vienna, and Beč today. In an original draft, I tried to be true to the relevant 16th Century names for the places visited by the characters in this story. The exercise was enjoyable, but the result was confusing. It also robbed readers familiar with Croatia's coast and islands the pleasure of recognizing immediately their favorite haunts. For everyone's convenience, with some exceptions, I reverted generally to modern, English place names.

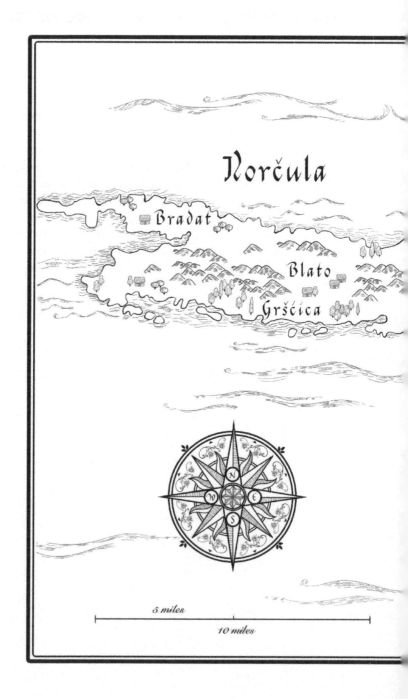

Pelješac

Orebić

Pupnat   Korčula
      Žrnovo

Hvar

Korčula

Lastovo   Mljet

Dubrovnik

A feast in troubled times

Sometimes, even an islander doesn't see the approaching tempest. And as a young olive grower guided his donkey cart across Korčula in mid-summer 1571, for instance, he was oblivious to the small fleet of Ottoman galleys roaming listlessly across the choppy waters where the Mediterranean and Adriatic seas meet. Under the command of a famed corsair, the ships pushed vaguely northward beneath large lateen sails and into Venetian waters. The officers and crew were fresh from quick victories along the Albanian coast and were probing beyond the Republic of Ragusa for new conquests. By oar and wind, they pushed toward the southernmost islands claimed His Serenity of Venice.

One of those islands was Korčula, a thin swath of land venturing into the deceptively calm waters of the southern Adriatic. The rocky, forested island – a few scattered villages toward the west and a small town on the east – rested uneasily amid a maelstrom of geopolitical ambitions bearing down from all points of the compass. Jutting out into crystal waters at the fault line between a changing array of great powers, Korčula over the centuries posed an enticing target for attackers great and small in search of conquest and booty. Spain, Austria-Hungary, Genoa, Venice, and the Ottomans had all fought in these waters at one time or another, and the fighting wouldn't be over for several generations.

In these times, many islanders on Korčula were nervous. A bloody raid by mainland brigands on the island's biggest village had raised fears in the countryside. Though forays by thieves of all stripes weren't uncommon, the attack on Blato was especially brazen. And in the walled town of Korčula, which shared its name with the island, the Italian elites and merchants were panicked by

1

rumors of an imminent war between the newly allied European powers and the Ottomans. While some tried to dismiss the stories as fear mongering, many of those with the means fled north across the sea, some as far as Venice, the master of the island.

As August passed its midpoint, however, islanders tried to put their fears behind them and focus on the upcoming Feast of the Assumption of the Blessed Virgin Mary. As a group, they had mixed success.

Damir was gold-star successful. The teenager from the tiny western village of Bradat was blind for the moment to the political tempests of his time. As he rode a cart laden with olive oil across the serpentine paths that etched Korčula from east to west, Damir relished his first taste of adult freedom. The seventeen-year-old was on an unexpected solo adventure, bringing the family's oil across the island to town for the feast.

Sitting tall and proud in his wooden cart and urging his tired donkey over the rutted dirt trail, Damir smiled to himself in anticipation. Normally, he'd be making this trip with his father. This year, though, the fates had contrived to send him on the journey alone. So, on Sunday, as his friends would be gathered in the dusty square of Blato to celebrate the feast, Damir would be reveling in Korčula … without his father … alone. Or, as he desperately hoped, not entirely alone.

For the past five years, Damir had climbed into the rickety cart with his father every August to rumble the 30 miles or so across the island and deliver the last of the family's special olive oil to Father Anton at Saint Mark's Cathedral in the town of Korčula. That alone was already the highlight of the year. A respite from endless days in the orchards moving dirt and stone, harvesting and pressing the tiny olives. Very few people from the western villages ever journeyed far from their homes. Those who did were mostly cartmen and farmers delivering the grain, produce, and fruit grown in the Great Field around Blato to the warehouses of Korčula.

But by tradition, Damir's father and his fathers before him brought casks of olive oil each year to the mid-summer's feast. And now, Father Anton himself insisted on the annual pilgrimage, saying that fresh-baked bread dipped in the Grgić family's olive oil offered a brief glimpse of the happiness that awaited good Catholic souls in paradise. Damir liked that, even though to him it was just olive oil, the product of a year's drudgery in a dusty village where a new goat was considered excitement.

Of course, the olive oil wasn't exactly his family's oil. By rights, it belonged to the Nikoničić family, nobles who owned a small palace in Blato and much of the land on the western tip of the island. The land was mostly steep, rocky, and not especially fertile, a striking contrast to the bountiful plains of the Great Field. But olive trees grew well there, and noble families from Korčula had established vast estates amid the karsts that surrounded the many bays on that end of the island. Most of the olives from these plantations were brought to Blato, where villagers crushed and pressed them until thick, green oil oozed into pine buckets. The oil was stored in casks, and most eventually reached Korčula, the only real town on the island. The church kept some of the oil, the rector some more, but the bulk was loaded along with wine and other goods onto ships bound for mainland towns north of Korčula – Split, Zadar and others. Some made it as far away as Istria.

Damir's family had been working the Nikoničić land for generations. The lord even delighted in telling the story about how one of Damir's forefathers, a young man named Pero, taught the island to make olive oil centuries earlier when a plague left the year's harvest in Italy across the sea rotting in the fields. Demand for the oil was so great that everyone in the southern Adriatic began growing olives. It took years to establish the orchards, and eventually trade in olive oil enriched the noble families of Korčula further while giving the peasants more work. To offer thanks for their good fortune, the noble families built chapels not only in Blato, but also in scattered sites across the western hills, including one dedicated to Saint John on a small islet in Gradina Bay, Damir's bay. The chapel, already in disrepair by Damir's time, looked westward toward an unseen Italy behind the horizon.

And as a personal reward from the Nikoničić family, Pero was allowed to keep some of the harvest each year and make his own olive oil. The tradition passed down through generations. On years when the family met the Nikoničić quota – which thankfully were most years – the Grgić family pressed some of the excess into their special oil. They couldn't sell the oil they made, at least not openly, but they could barter with it and earn favors. The five casks in Damir's cart were all that remained from last year's harvest. The oil, flavored with a hint of rosemary, lavender, and other local herbs, had been aging for almost nine months, and when Father Anton taps into the casks it will be like pouring nectar directly from heaven. Or so the priest said. For Damir, though, the oil and its rustic scent was omnipresent in his house and far from exotic.

The days around the Feast of the Assumption usually witnessed some of heaviest traffic along the bumpy trail that ran from the western end of the island, twisting around the spiny peaks of the mountains that crossed the island and on to the eastern tip and the walled town. Each year a dozen or so men and a few lucky boys from Blato and the surrounding villages would hitch oxen and donkeys to carts and bring figs, grapes, grain, wine, and other fruits of their labor to the townsfolk. The journey itself was almost part of the festival as the travelers formed and reformed makeshift caravans, camped together along the way, exchanged gossip, and told tall tales.

As Damir guided his timeworn cart around a sharp bend near Žrnovo, he remembered the first time he made the trip with his father. He was just twelve, a boy, and, like now, the first day shifted frequently between a blistering August sun and the cool, scented shade of the pine and cypress forests. They had stopped that night near a ragged peak, where if you climbed the rocky slope a few lengths you could see across both sides of the island – Hvar to the north and the unending Adriatic Sea to the south. Of all the brilliant watery vistas along the trail to Korčula, this would become Damir's favorite. The sun was setting that night years ago, making the undulating waters on both sides of the island a fiery orange. In Damir's mind, his island had become a cool, green paradise surrounded by the burning sulfurs of Hell that the priests had described. But Satan couldn't reach Damir or his family here. They were safe between their high hills and among gnarly olive trees.

That night when he was a mere child, Damir and another village boy clambered down the rocks and joined the others around a campfire. Ivan, an old cartman from Blato, was commanding the audience.

"…hundreds of ships? And what did the people of Korčula do?" Ivan asked no one in particular as he poked a stick into the fire, sending a fury of sparks skyward. "I'll tell what they did. Most just sat on their asses and watched from the town walls. Sure, a few took their galleys out and joined the other Venetians against the Genoese dogs, and what did they get for their troubles? Defeat! That's what they got. And the sailors who weren't killed were taken prisoners, thrown in some jail somewhere. Where's the glory in that? Where's the sense?"

"But tata says no one's ever seen so many galleys fighting in one place before or since," protested a young man, resting in the shadows at the edge of the fire's warm glow. "The banners, the cannon fire … galleys crowded into our channel…"

"True. True," Ivan agreed, "but for most of those there, it was still no more than a show, like the little plays the priests put on before the feast, where the Blessed Virgin is lifted up into heaven. They do that with ropes, you know. Fun to watch, yeah, but who lies there on his death bed, coughing out those last bloody breaths of life, telling his grandkids about a show they watched?

"Now, the Neapolitans, they were an enemy worth fighting, and when Aragon came to Korčula, that wasn't a show. That was blood and cannon and sword."

Most of the men around the campfire knew Old Ivan, his body bent with age, would eventually get around to his grandfather's stories about Federico of Aragon and his battle with Count Viario in Korčula. Most of them had even told the tale countless times to their own children. But it was a warm night, and no one complained about hearing the it once again. The stars crowding low overhead offered the ideal background for stories of a legendary past. Indeed, the two boys perked up at the mention of blood and cannon. "Tell us, cartman, what happened?" Damir begged.

"It was in my deda's time, a good century ago." As Ivan recalled his grandfather's tales, he prodded the fire again, sending a new cascade of sparks heavenward. The glow traced over every hardened wrinkle in the old peasant's face, for a moment mimicking the island's own rugged landscape. "Naples was at war with Venice, and as usual we were caught in the middle.

"It was August, like now, and some greedy princeling son of the King of Naples – Federico, he was called, of Aragon – had just rampaged over tiny Vis. They said that at night, from the hills around Vallegrande, you could see the island's fires across the sea to the west. The whole island was ablaze. Everyone knew the

Neapolitans would be coming to our dear Korčula next, so deda and some other young lads from Blato made ready to march into town and help defend it. Everyone told them they were stupid, and they were. But like young Božidar, they marched away anyway ... for the adventure.

"When Federico got to Korčula, he brought a huge army that easily outnumbered the defenders. They pitched their tents from one side of the island to the other, but," here Ivan, his face red in the firelight, leaned closer to the two boys, "they didn't reckon with Giorgio Viario, the Venetian count who ran the island back then. Naples may have had the numbers, but we had the walls and the spirit of all the saints on our side. The attack came right around Saint Bartholomew's Day, and old Bartol wasn't too pleased, I guess.

"Ships in the harbor fired at Korčula, and soldiers under the gold and red stripes of Aragon advanced toward the southern wall. Thousands, they said, charging and screaming. Deda said the Neapolitans kept coming at the wall with their bows and cannon, with catapults launching stones, and each time the army was pushed back. The ditch outside the main gate was filling with their soldiers, some dead, most lying there moaning in their own gore. Deda was firing a hand cannon near the gate. He'd hold it up, while a buddy lit the fuse. Boom! By the end that cannon was hotter than a forge, he said, and deda swore by the saints that they destroyed two or three catapults just themselves."

Ivan paused and made a snorting kind of sound. Most of the men were already asleep, but the two boys were riveted to the cartman's story.

"Count Giorgio was brave and led his men well. He also had a couple of tricks down his codpiece." Again, the snorting. "Before they closed the gates, he had some of the strong village men hide in the hills around Korčula, and they did what they could to poke the enemy in the eye, blocking paths and fighting when a good opportunity came up. And after a couple of days, the count had the town boys ring every bell in every church for no reason whatsoever, and then do it again. The Neapolitan soldiers outside the wall didn't know what was happening, and their captains must have thought some Venetian ships and soldiers were on the way because they packed up their tents and ran back to their ships. The town was saved, and Saint Bartholomew's Feast that year was the happiest anyone could remember."

"I don't believe you," said a snub-nosed boy who had come with one of the farmers. "Nothing ever happens on Korčula. It's just working the fields, gathering the grain, sleeping, and doing it all over and over and over again. That's just a story."

"Don't believe me, do you? What would your tata say to that? Not believing your senior. In my day, we'd never put up with that." Ivan vaguely swung the stick he'd been using to stir the fire in the direction of the boy. "Tell you what. If you don't believe me, when you get to Korčula, just after you get through the main gate, under Revelin Tower, look at the small plaza on the left. You'll find some banners and spears hanging there that were dropped by the Neapolitans when they scattered. Someone etched some words about the fight into the wall there, too. Get a priest to read them to you."

A movement in the dense undergrowth lining the path brought Damir back to the present. He stopped and listened as the rustling moved leisurely closer. Probably a wild hare, he thought, but maybe a jackal. People said the Venetians brought jackals over from Africa to harass Ragusa when it owned the island a long time ago. However they got here, they were all over the island. Damir saw one once, at dusk at the edges of a freshly mown field. Its course coat was reddish brown with black flecks, and the dog-like jackal ran with its small head low to the ground. Usually, you don't see them, though. You just hear them barking and howling at night.

Damir pulled a knife from the carry sack lying next to him on cart and unsheathed the blade. He listened as the animal rustled among dry twigs and leaves. He gingerly climbed off the cart and stepped to the edge of the trail, facing the rustling. He looked up and down the trail and saw no one. He was alone. He bent his knees and stood ready, sweaty fingers clutching the knife. Whatever was in the thicket had stopped moving.

It was probably a hare, Damir told himself, adding for effect that jackals didn't hunt during the hot day. They hunted higher in the hills and in packs, too, so it was absolutely a hare. Damir played with the idea of chasing it down. A quick pounce, and hare meat would make a great dinner. He could probably even trade some of it for wine once he got to Korčula. He looked at the knife and the dense maquis. He hadn't moved for several minutes.

In his concentration, he was startled by renewed rustling in the thicket and jumped back against the cart.

"Hah!" he cried, feigning a step toward the noise, and the animal bounded away unseen.

It was just as well, he thought. Anyway, he couldn't leave the cart and the casks unattended on the road as he went off hunting hare or whatever. He climbed back onto the driver's bench and called to his donkey to pick up the pace. If his family had a horse, he'd be in Korčula already, he thought, settled in and maybe loitering near an inn on the western edge. But few families could afford a horse. Even with the old donkey, though, Korčula was only a couple of hours further. Maybe less if he stopped looking for unseen hares. Soon, Damir would reach Saint Nicholas, the Dominican Monastery at the far edge of the town's western bay, and from there it was just a short push along the shoreline to the town's southern gates and through a tower they called Revelin.

Serenaded by the rhythmic clops of his old donkey and squeaks of his cart, Damir forgot about roadside noises and became lost in a reverie of the feast that awaited him. Tonight would be meager, just some bread his mother had packed and water. But tomorrow... Tomorrow the whole town would gather in celebration of the Virgin Mother's assumption, and after the masses and the pantomimes the town would lay out a banquet of cool wines, steaming pigs roasted whole on a spit, and salty fish straight off the fire. Figs would be plentiful, too. And, of course, the townsfolk would be begging for his olive oil, the best on the island. And as his father often said, there was always a *ruined* cask in the batch that was unfit for the church, but just good enough to share at a plentiful table.

And then there was Iskra. Damir froze at the memory of her. He met her last year at the feast, and they spent some time together in an empty courtyard behind her family's inn. Damir wondered whether she would remember him. Would she even want to remember him? How was he different from the sons of shipbuilders and stonecutters who made up her world? Damir was tall, more than six feet, and muscular from tending the orchards. His brown hair, bleached from working among the trees all summer, hung to his shoulders. His face, sun-kissed and rough. As he took inventory, nothing seemed to set him apart from the town boys – except one thing. Iskra talked about his eyes, light blue like his mother's. She joked that he must have some Hapsburg blood in him and started calling him *plavica*, little blue. But, he wondered, was that enough for her to remember him? For his part, he remembered her in flashes of images, textures, and impressions. Dark hair. Long hair. Keen brown eyes. Soft skin and soft lips. A worldliness and wit you didn't find in village girls. A warmth that stopped his breath.

Damir, lost in memory, suddenly found himself at the wall that hugged Saint Nicholas' Monastery. He guided his cart around the bend and marveled as usual at the panorama that opened across the small western bay. It was late in the day, but the summer sun had not yet set. He stopped the cart to admire the view of Korčula, a young man sizing up his future and trying to see through the walls into a small inn at the western edge. Korčula was a mighty fortress, splendid to Damir's eyes. Its stone houses were built around a small rise at the tip of a peninsula that jutted toward the mainland. The town was surrounded by high, limestone walls, pierced by a dozen towers with arrow slits and cannon emplacements. A ditch ran across the slender isthmus, the only land entrance to the town. A single drawbridge crossed the ditch at Revelin Tower, the southern gate.

How could Federico of Aragon have hoped to take this beautiful gem, even with all the armies of Naples? Damir had heard that the walls of Dubrovnik were even bigger and more imposing. He could not imagine that. Even though it was the capital of the Ragusa Republic, he felt it could not possibly be more splendid than Korčula, a white Venetian diamond set against a sapphire sea.

Damir waved at the fishermen rowing their boats out from the bay that splashed between the town and the monastery. None waved back, and Damir continued along the waterfront trail, watching wistfully as the boats rolled over the small swells in the bay. The life of a fisherman must be so much easier than that of an olive picker, he thought. Further out, boats that left earlier had already unfurled their weathered, triangular sails and were riding a gentle Maestral wind that was still blowing from the northwest. The breeze would soon calm, though, leaving the fishermen to the mercy of their oars and strong backs. The small fleet would be back well before morning. If the sea were generous, their holds would be brimming with tuna, yellow tail, sea bream or some other prize catches, all to be gutted and scaled in plenty of time for the feast later that night.

Tired from the long journey, Damir's donkey slowly tugged the cart toward Revelin Tower. It reluctantly climbed the last hillock, past the village of Varos. Venice had prohibited any buildings outside Korčula's walls, but the rule wasn't enforced with any enthusiasm. Varos, a community of shipbuilders, had sprouted along the waterfront of the eastern bay. Every house, workshop, and warehouse was illegal in the eyes of His Serenity in Venice, but no one on Korčula cared, least of all the new local rector.

Although it was late as Damir approached the drawbridge and the south gate was about to close, a small group of townspeople – men, women, and children – was leaving town carrying lanterns and overfilled bundles. They rushed past Damir with scant notice.

Raiders from the mainland

As Damir drifted toward Korčula amid his musings, the tranquil dusk that greeted him was in sharp relief to the violence that had visited the island just a few weeks earlier. Even on an island accustomed to periodic attacks from mainland thugs, the raid on Blato was exceptional. Korčula was never truly at peace, and violent attacks were a part of the texture of life on the island. Most were endured and forgotten.

For generations, the waters around Korčula played stage for the rival powers around the seas. Continental kingdoms from Spain to Hungary fought and bargained for control over the lucrative shipping lanes that passed near the island, as well the island's valuable stone quarries and forests. Korčula, to be sure, was rarely more than a minor token in these larger struggles, but a token that changed hands often and was occasionally battered in the transfer. Control of the small island passed from one royal house to another in rapid succession for hundreds of years, and the doges of Venice were among the many who coveted it to help secure dominance in the region.

Indeed, at one point, His Serenity paid Crusaders on their way to Palestine to conquer Zadar, a Hungarian stronghold on the mainland, and open the southern islands to easy conquest. But it wasn't until 1409 that Venice finally secured its grip on Korčula, buying it along with a vast swath of Dalmatia for 100,000 ducats from the king of Naples, who was looking for allies against Florence at the time, before turning again against the Venetians.

Almost 200 years later, the giants of Europe and Asia were again stirring the southern Adriatic waters and bringing long-simmering conflicts to a head. Indeed, when Ivan the old cartman was still a young laborer in Blato, the Ottomans had reached as far as Vienna. Even though they were pushed back, the Turkish Empire still had control over much of the Balkan hinterland, and fleets that prowled the Mediterranean made periodic forays into the southern Adriatic.

Although Vienna held against the siege, the European powers feared and resented the lingering threat posed by the continued Ottoman presence. But for decades, their own continental rivalries blocked concerted action. The Hapsburgs in Vienna, holders of the titular crown of Croatia, guarded the oscillating land border with the Ottomans, which stretched across the northern Balkans and lingered much too close to Vienna. Still, their agents in the northern Adriatic harassed Venetian ships for plunder when the opportunity arose, and in turn His Serenity would regularly blockade northern garrison ports. Across the channel from Korčula, the Republic of Ragusa sat restively between the Hapsburgs, the Venetians, and the Ottomans, contriving to maintain its autonomy and neutrality while protecting its rich commercial interests. Fiercely independent, Dubrovnik sent annual tributes to the Ottomans, who numbered the republic among its vassals, and kept trade and diplomatic ties with the European powers, especially Venice and Rome.

Amid this turmoil, groups of lawless men and women roamed the region almost without restraint. Not pirates by desire, most were villagers and townspeople stripped of their fields, pastures, and markets by the dangers of living in the borderlands between the Ottomans and the Hapsburgs. Desperate, these raiders would prey on undefended villages, taking livestock, stores, and captives in deadly, rapid forays. The bigger villages on Korčula were inland, next to fertile fields, but since the island was never more than five miles wide, no village was entirely out of reach of these seaborne marauders. Blato, with villas and peasant homes hugging the hillsides around the Great Field, was an especially tempting target.

And on an early August night, a group of seven small barks rowed into a long, narrow cove called Gršćica south of Blato, their lateen sails like shark fins quietly drifting toward prey. It was well after midnight when they weighed anchor in the still cove, and about a hundred men jumped from the ships and waded to shore. The men, Hercegovians from the mainland with pistols and swords, formed wordlessly into three groups. The night was calm and the marauders had rowed their barks the last few miles to Korčula. They took time to rest as their captain talked with a man who boarded from a rocky spit near the western end of the island. The two men argued as they paced along the edge of the forest, the captain waving a torch wildly.

"It's night, and I'm not from this part of the island," the stranger rasped in their third pass along the tree line. "Hellfire, find the accursed path yourself if you can. Just give me the money for getting you this far, and I'll go home."

Finally, they stopped at the far end of the cove, and the shouting stopped as well. The two disappeared briefly into the trees. When they reappeared a few minutes later, the captain gave the order to form ranks. In single file, the brigands followed the captain and the stranger up a steep trail that ran through the karsts toward Blato. They hiked wordlessly, stopping at sudden sounds within the dark woods and continuing once they were sure that they had startled animal and not a sentry. The crew that was left guarding the ships watched as the torched procession zigzagged along the hillside and slowly reached the crest.

Like islanders across the southern Adriatic, the people of Blato had heard stories that gangs of thieves from Pālješac and further inland were becoming more aggressive. The villagers were not overly concerned, however. A thin line of steep mountains protected them from the sea, both north and south, and while an occasional band of robbers found its way along the hidden trails, Blato was usually spared the worse of the raids.

When the Venetians came through a few months earlier gathering crew for galleys, parents lamented their conscripted sons, but much of the talk orbited around rumors of a giant fleet the European families were amassing near Sicily, and little notice was taken of the village's heightened vulnerability. One of the Venetian soldiers described galleys bigger than any seen before with scores of cannon that fired from the side, not the bow. The people of Blato could not imagine such monstrous ships. They argued about whether the soldier was telling tales and protested meekly as their children were being taken, but nothing was said about how to protect the village with so many young men gone.

And so, as the brigands' torch-lit parade marched closer to

Blato, the village's night watch was largely depleted. Those who remained took turns at sentry, with the best men watching the routes from the north, toward the mainland. The two dullards assigned to the southern approach were hardly the best and were sleeping as the raiders passed through a narrow gap in the mountains that opened onto Blato. Finally, within sight of the prosperous village, the raiders rushed forward, and the sudden noise woke the southern sentries. Half asleep, the Blato men saw through blurry eyes scores of men charging down from mountains, torch light flickering off swords and pistols. The sentries hesitated a moment, unsure whether to believe their vision, and then fled screaming into the nearby woods.

Although the sentries did little to slow the advance of the raiders, their shouts were enough to rouse villagers in the nearest homes. Slowly at first and then with greater urgency, the alarm spread toward to the village square and beyond. Frightened families quickly gathered what they could carry and followed the sentries into the woods. With surprising speed, the village began emptying into the surrounding forests and fields.

But the raider captain also dispatched his men quickly and efficiently. His company was divided into three groups, with the smallest remaining near the pass to guard their retreat to the ships. Another, the strongest fighters, rushed forward, ready to confront any defense the village might muster. The final and biggest group were the hunters and gatherers. They combed through the village, searching homes, warehouses, and churches for plunder and captives.

They needn't have been so cautious, however. The villagers had neither the time nor the men to assemble a defense, much less a counter-attack. There were individual acts of resistance, like the man with a boar spear who charged into a band of three brigands trying to carry away his mother. He saved his mother, killing the raiders, but was fatally wounded when other brigands arrived. But most escaped … or tried to. One villager scurried up a tree, only to become a target for archers when he was discovered. The arrows pierced him repeatedly through his nightshirt until he fell to the ground, dead.

For the most part, however, the marauders were interested in plunder and not death. A frightened elderly couple found in their beds was left undisturbed, and a newborn abandoned in the chaos was given to a woman who was allowed to flee into the woods. Throughout the raid, the captain ambled among the bedlam issuing orders and maintaining a level of discipline.

"Break down that door!" he shouted, sending men to a small granary. "Let's make quick work of this!"

With little fight from the villagers, the raid was over well before noon. Captives – about fifty – were herded into a small clearing near the southern pass. As they were tied together, sacks of grain and produce were stacked nearby in a disorderly pile. A few cows and goats were also added to the assembled booty.

The captain looked around and took measure. Seven of his men were dead, and four villagers. And for that, he thought, the captives might bring as much as four hundred ducats in ransom. Probably less from a village like Blato, though, and more likely he'd end up accepting more grain or livestock for their return rather than coin. The old man cursing his guards…, they would probably have to bribe his family to take him back. After paying suppliers, even four hundred ducats wouldn't stretch far when divided among his crew, he calculated. The sail makers at Neum had gotten greedy lately, so that will eat deep into their profits. He scowled as he looked across the sacks of food and tethered animals. That might last a month at his village, he decided. Blato was not nearly as rich as he had been led to believe, and his guide's payment would reflect that. He signaled his men to start the march south toward the ships. If only it were safe to tend their own fields again, he thought wearily.

On the morning of the raid, Damir and his father were several miles west of Blato, inspecting olive groves around their village. Early that morning, a mother and her two young daughters from Blato came out of the woods, leading a goat and carrying sacks of figs. The three collapsed in tears when they reached the two men and described the onslaught of horrid bandits who flooded into their village. Damir and this father took them back to Bradat and tried to calm them wine and bread. Soon, a few others from Blato staggered in as well. No one was sure what to do next, but everyone knew it was useless to go back and fight such a huge gang.

The day lingered, and eventually there was nothing to be done except return to Blato and hope the bandits had gone. Now rested and less panicked, the refugees turned fretfully back to the path

15

through the woods, joined by Damir, his father, and a few of the men from Bradat. They lumbered through the olive groves and pine forests without talking and listened for any noises ahead. The men carried their long knives in sweaty hands.

As the small group approached Blato from the northwest, they were joined by others who had fled the attack. A few wept softly as the group clustered at the far edge of the Great Field, staring across the expanse with ashen faces. From there, Blato looked normal, though eerily empty. A single plume of dark smoke rose from somewhere behind the closer houses.

"Look!" someone cried, pointing. "The curs must be gone!"

Near an outlying row of houses, a few people – a small family by appearances – were slowly weaving between little vegetable gardens before they hastened around a corner into the heart of Blato. The group with Damir was encouraged, and some of the townspeople began scurrying across the field, anxious to see their homes and find family and friends. Damir and his father were among the stragglers moving more tentatively through the stalks and over the furrowed ground.

The village greeted Damir as it had never before. The commercial and social heart for half the island, Blato had always welcomed Damir with bustling streets and promise. Fieldworkers and craftspeople hurried importantly among its stone buildings throughout the day and gossiped noisily over herbal teas and wine after sunset. But today, Blato was almost lifeless. Broken crockery and upturned barrels lined the broad streets that wound along the hillsides. The raiders had smashed open doors on some homes and buildings, leaving pools of broken wood and splitters. The few people Damir spotted on the streets, mostly in groups of twos or threes, darted quickly into homes, leaving the lanes once again forlorn.

The tenor changed immediately when Damir arrived at the walled square in front of the Church of All Saints. The unnatural solitude was replaced by crowded activity. The square, generally the site of festivals and feasts, had become an open-air mortuary, hospital, and gathering point. As the morning's refugees returned, after checking their own homes they gravitated toward the square and joined a circuit that moved counterclockwise around its interior.

First, along the shaded western wall, they passed the wounded. Bloodied men and women lay or sat on the tiled pavement as nuns from the village monastery bandaged their wounds and offered water. Most had suffered a single blow from a sword, spear, or arrow, but a few lay almost lifeless on the ground, their clothes and skin stained dark scarlet. As the returning villagers passed the makeshift clinic, they scanned the faces of the injured with a mixture of hope and dread. Next, in an isolated corner, they would stop and exchange whispers with two men standing over four forms lying on the ground in a corner wrapped in dingy linen stained deep red. Though they had already heard the names of those who had died in the raid, it didn't seem real until they heard the same names spoken softly by these men.

And finally, the villagers would pass before the carved church façade and reach the eastern wall, where knots of family, friends, and neighbors awaited. Guilt and relief seeped into the quiet conversations. Men and women crossed themselves at every mention of the dead and wounded. To Damir, the people in the square seemed to move in slow motion, a clock running backwards in no hurry. Steps were measured, and the background sounds were a blend of hushed conversation and gentle moans.

As he and his father left the square, the ethereal aura of Blato shifted yet again. Men with buckets sloshing with water ran from the well just behind the church up a sloping street into the northern quarter. The olive growers followed the line of men whose faces were darkened with soot and found two abutting houses engulfed in flames. Their stones walls held, but wooden rafters gave way and roofs collapsed. One burly woman, a miller judging from her clothes, was trying to bring organization to the chaos.

"Start in from the sides or its going spread all over Blato," she yelled. "You there, make sure that goat shed is soaked!"

There were no extra buckets or tubs, and Damir and his father could do nothing more than stand with the others as they watched the chain of water bearers fight the flames. When it was clear that the fire was tamed, Damir broke away and wandered aimlessly back into the southern neighborhood. More families had returned and were going through their homes, discovering what was lost and what was spared. Whenever they came across another villager, they would softly trade information on who had been seen and who hadn't. No one knew if the missing were still in hiding or among the captives. They rejoiced when a loved one was spotted.

As the Blato villagers weighed their losses and their grief, seven Hercegovian barks sailed peacefully out of Grščica Bay, a share of the loot and captives secured in the center of each bark. A single tall man watched them from the pebbled beach, passing a small sack of coins from hand to hand.

Rats from a ship

Now, almost three weeks later, life had moved onward and Damir was bringing his olive oil into Korčula as his family did each year. Dusk had fallen by the time he reached the small arched portal that formed the southern entrance to the walled town. Revelin Tower was a limestone monolith reaching many times a man's height. A cannon's barrel peeked over its parapet, flanked idly by sentries. The tower's face was largely unadorned, except for the winged lion local stone masons had carved just above the portal, leaving no doubt that Korčula was part of the vast Venetian empire. The Doge in Venice named the town's rector. He collected taxes and kept track of the merchant ships coming and going. He granted land and rights to nobles. He even had his own name for Korčula. To the Venetians and perhaps the rest of the world, the town and island were *Curzola*.

When in town, Damir strained to remember to say *Curzola* whenever he spoke, fearing he would sound like an ignorant peasant otherwise. He still liked Korčula better, though. Its sharp tones sounded more rugged, more fitting for a land edged by jagged karsts. Father Anton at Saint Mark's Cathedral once told Damir that the Greeks and Romans called the island *Corcyra Nigra* because it reminded the ancients of the rocky Greek island of Corfu, only thick pine forests made Korčula darker and more sinister. So many things in Damir's world had different names, different titles, different identities. Almost all the islands around him had two names. It was only a year earlier that Damir found out that the Doge of Venice and "His Serenity" were actually the same person. The Ottomans were the Turks. And the royal seat of the Hapsburgs? Wien, Vienna, or Beč, depending on who was talking. Damir was quite pleased that he was only one thing, "Damir," son of Marija and Stefano Grgić.

By the time Damir passed through the gates of Korčula, the other cartmen and farmers from villages across the island had already arrived. Their goods were already stored in the warehouses owned by the church or the noble families. They would have claimed the best spots in the stables, where they would sleep with their livestock, using rucksacks as pillows and cloaks as blankets. As his donkey dragged the cart full of olive oil over the drawbridge, Damir wasn't worried about finding a place to sleep, as long as it was in Korčula.

"Dado! Dado!"

Damir looked up and saw a priest waving at him from the wall next to the gate tower. His dark cassock rendered the priest almost invisible in the fading twilight, but, in the light from the torches, his round, jovial face shone like a harvest moon. "I thought you would never come! Did you bring the olive oil? Of course, you did, lad. Where's your father? I hope he's OK! Wait! Wait! I'm coming down!"

All this before Damir had a chance to wave back.

The priest was bounding down the wooden steps leading from the wall when Damir pulled the cart to a stop just inside the gate. The young man jumped from the cart's hard bench and embraced the portly fellow.

"Father Anton! It's so good to see you!"

"And you, too, Dado. And you, too." The priest looked into the cart. "Just five casks this year? That will barely last us until Michaelmas! You're starving us, boy! Starving us! But where's your father? I hope he wasn't hurt during the raid at Blato. Nasty business that. Is he well?"

Father Anton and Damir walked the cart along the landward side of the eastern wall.

"The raid was terrible. Four people were killed, and forty or fifty were taken. But tata and I were in the groves when it happened. We only got to Blato later," Damir said. "No, tata cut his leg on a rake as we were loading oil onto the cart. He kept saying he could still make the trip. 'Why do I need both legs when I'll be riding in a cart?' But the bleeding was really bad, and in the end, mamma put him to bed with a flask of wine and told me to go. That's why I'm late."

The two continued to talk as they wound their way along the wall. Damir told the priest everything he knew about the attack on Blato. Father Anton insisted on all the details, numbers, the names of people hurt and taken, what was destroyed. Occasionally, the chat was interrupted as the priest greeted one of the townsfolk, then it started again where it left off. When Damir exhausted his information on the attack, he told the priest every detail of the uneventful trip across the island. Each bump in the road or noise in the brush all the more dangerous and thrilling because Damir was travelling alone.

The two had an easy relationship. Damir met Father Anton on his first trip to Korčula. His father was unloading the cart, six casks that year, and the priest was quizzing Damir on the saints. The twelve-year-old boy failed badly. After that, Damir stalked Father Anton through Korčula for the rest of the week, begging the priest to tell him the stories of the saints. Many, of course, he had heard of in church, but Father Anton told them as though he and Saint John were fishing mates, as though he and Saint Liborius had shared a campfire. Damir wasn't especially pious, but he enjoyed the stories. Soon, the priest and the olive grower were nearly inseparable during the few days Damir spent in Korčula each year around the Feast of the Assumption. Father Anton even came to Blato once for a special mass at the Church of All Saints after one of the lords had died.

Before long the pair arrived at one of the church warehouses, and Damir unloaded the casks of olive oil, except for one cask with a cracked stave, which meant the oil had probably gone bad. Father Anton waited until the casks were put away and Damir found a place for his donkey and cart in the church stable next door.

"Let us talk some more. The stable boy will watch your things." Father Anton glanced at an older boy who limped slightly among the horses and carts and lodgers. The boy nodded in understanding.

The pair walked silently until they reached the town's northern edge. They climbed a staircase to the parapet, a waist-high wall that traveled the length of the fortifications, and stood for a moment under a fresco of stars. The waves lapped pleasantly at the stone foundations beneath them.

"It's so good to be able to talk with someone who is not caught in the hysteria we've witnessed in Curzola these past few weeks," Father Anton began. "The rector is gone. Can you believe that? He bribed some Perastan pirates to take him back to Venice and left two days ago. I tried to convince him to stay, but failed. The best I could do was to stop him from sneaking out like some mangy rat from a sinking galley. He actually broke a hole in the southern wall near his palace, where he and his men were planning to slip out during the night.

"We told the townspeople he was leaving to get more guards. 'Only the weight of the rector's office will convince our allies to lend us some fighting men,' we lied, just before he left ceremoniously through the sea gate. I don't think very many people believed us. The rector is new to the post and doesn't have much loyalty to Curzola. Also, a few people knew about the hole in the wall."

Father Anton watched the sea and the stars for a moment. Defensive towers rose on each side of the two men, two of the twelve towers that punched high from the town's thick walls. On one tower, a sentry sang softly as he paced along the fortifications. Damir could not see anyone on the other.

"Dado, you cannot imagine the senseless fear that has gripped this town over the past few weeks. Ever since Nicosia in Cyprus fell to the Turks last year, every rumor has been treated as the Lord's truth. Every log that floats past becomes a fleet of Ottoman galleys. No one questions even the worst stories that you hear. Our island has been attacked by raiders before, of course – and mercy on those who were killed and maimed – but the attack on Blato was bigger than most. With all the other rumors, the raid sparked a new level of panic here. Most of the noble families and richer craftsmen have fled, either to Italy or islands further north. The Dominicans and Franciscans, too. Gone. They brought their most valuable relics and treasures from their monasteries here for safekeeping and left. Some of the poorer families have simply fled into the hills and woods.

" 'Where are you going?' I've pleaded. 'If all your rumors are true, we're surrounded on all sides by demons. The Ottomans to the south and east, and pirates – Hercegovians, Naretines and others – everywhere else. Would you not be safer inside our town's sturdy stone walls?' I failed here, too, and may the Lord forgive me for not being more persuasive.

"Since man left Eden, Dado, man has been at war with man. God has many ways to make us pay for our sins before taking us into His kingdom. You cannot escape His judgment by crawling through a hole in a wall or sailing away with pirates. But I believe we are safe here on our wooded island and inside these walls. The Venetians are gathering a massive fleet, I'm told, and they've joined with Pope Pius V and the Spaniards. I do not believe the Turks would dare to venture further north than Kotor. They are still occupied in Cyprus. With all the talk of a great war, why would any of these powers take time for our small island of farmers, shipwrights, and stonecutters?"

Damir listened as Father Anton told him about arranging extra masses to distract the town from its fears. The priest spoke of faith and confidence and of just punishment for man's imperfection. He talked military strategy with the assurance of a spectator. He seemed calm and certain in his views, but Damir was too young to fathom how deep Father Anton's confidence really ran.

The priest looked over the seas, and then back toward the town. "Well, Dado, I've kept you much too long. You must be exhausted from your trip. And I still have preparations to make for the celebration tomorrow. Until the morning, then." Father Anton hurried down the staircase to the street, leaving Damir alone on the wall.

The North Star was nearly touching the mountains of Pelješac as Damir turned back to the stables. Time had passed quickly as the two traded the most recent news. He wanted to find Iskra, but knew it was too late now. That pleasure – or perhaps disappointment, he reminded himself – would have to wait until the morning.

Sails to the east

The sounds of other people stirring in the stable woke Damir from a deep sleep. Men coughing. Men talking gently to their draft animals as they fed the beasts. Stable hands milling about, raking dung, and cleaning around the stalls. It was early Sunday, and Damir kept still for a moment, resting on the hay that made his bed. He thought about looking for Iskra immediately, but with so many people in town for the mass and the feast, she would probably be busy at her family's inn. And Damir wasn't entirely sure her father would welcome a village boy coming to see their daughter or, indeed, whether the daughter would welcome him. Or worse, maybe she had been married off over the year, to a stonecutter or fisherman. Damir decided it would be best to wait for later when everyone would be preoccupied with the feast and he could find her quietly.

The teen rose, stretched, put some hay down for his donkey, and walked outside. The sunlight was spreading leisurely from behind the Palješac hills, and the air was crisp and clear. Damir strolled up a narrow, steep street toward the cathedral, passing the workshops of jewelers, metal smiths, and other artisans. Stopping a moment, he looked back across the channel. The morning light was magical, and Damir felt he could simply reach out and touch the rugged hills rising up from the sea. He imagined he could see monks at work in a monastery, a white box on the hillside across the calm waters. Our Lady of Angels, Father Anton told him once, where the priests prayed for the men at sea.

Father Anton, already in his archdeacon vestments, was in the square in front of the cathedral when Damir reached the summit. His flowing white cope, embroidered in blue thread with scenes from Eden, hung nearly to the ground and was fastened across his chest with a silver chain. Behind him rose the arched portal to the nave, flanked by consoles that featured strange squatting figures of Adam and Eve and, above them, lions clutching lambs in their claws. Square above the doorway, a statuette of Saint Mark, the cathedral's namesake, welcomed worshippers and above the Evangelist a large rosette dominated the flat limestone wall. Damir was again amazed that man could build anything so majestic, and much of it carved by local stonecutters.

Despite the early hour, a small crowd of townsfolk and visitors was already gathering in the square for the day's ceremonies. Men in the white robes of the All Saints Brotherhood stood in one corner, eying the growing throng suspiciously. Other locals came together in small constellations of relations and friends throughout the square, waiting for the bells to call them in to mass. Many of the townswomen wore long, dark skirts with light-colored blouses decorated with fine embroidery of many colors, while their husbands wore somber waistcoats and close-fitting hats poked with feathers or cloth tassels. Like Damir, most of those from outside town wore simple pantaloons and course shirts ... plain, but clean. There were fewer people on the square this year than before, the young man thought. He looked unsuccessfully for any sign of Iskra.

"Dado! Beautiful morning!" the priest yelled when he spotted his friend coming through a narrow opening between buildings. He pointed upward. "Look! I've sent two men up the church tower to ring the bells by hand. Two this year! What a great way to start the Feast of the Assumption. When he comes back, the bishop will be pleased hear of this! It's almost time to start. Everyone will be here soon!"

The priest kept his gaze on the high bell tower, a bulky square structure rising to the left of the church. The tower was topped with an ornately carved stone canopy, more work from local craftsmen, and a platform with low stone walls. The crowd milled around the square as men struck the bells with their metal mallets. One strike. Two strikes. Then a pause.

Father Anton and others on the square craned their necks to see why the bells had stopped.

"Hey, gentlemen, what's wrong?'' the priest shouted toward the heavens. "Gentlemen!"

A gaunt face popped over the parapet. The man was yelling something, but Father Anton couldn't make it out above the general din.

"What?"

"Galleys! We see galleys!"

The few people on the square who heard the man's call fell quiet and turned to look upward. Then, like a ripple passing over a bay, more pale faces turned up to look at the bell tower.

"What did you say?" Father Anton shouted.

"We see galleys! Just beyond Badija. There must be fifty of them! Under full sail and oar!"

"Ships?"

"Yes! Fifty! They're coming this way!"

"Do you see any flags?"

The man on the bell tower shouted and pointed east wildly, but his words were lost in the din that rose suddenly from the square. No Venetian fleet was expected at Korčula, and, fed on a steady stream of rumors, the men and women on the square assumed the worst. They soon drained from the cathedral square, rushing downhill in every direction like water cascading toward the sea. One man knocked Damir into a wall, as he pushed his wife and son ahead of him. "We must leave!" he howled. "The hills will be safe!"

News of the approaching ships – "Fifty ships! Heading this way!" – raced quickly through the town. And almost everyone seemed of the same mind: Flee! Townspeople gathered a few valued possessions in bundles and ran toward the south gate, hoping to reach the wilderness beyond before the ships and soldiers arrived. The cartmen and farmers who had come for the festival were also gathering their gear to leave, only succeeding in adding to the congestion on the streets. When the mass reached the gate, it was already barred.

Father Anton and some others ran through the streets pleading with the people to stay and defend their homes. They were met largely by jeers, insults, and curses. The townspeople knew that the rector, most noble families, and many of the richer merchants were already gone. As the panicked wave reached Revelin Tower, it crashed against the locked gates. The rush created a tidal pool of frantic people that splashed against the closed portal.

"Open the gate! Open the gate!" the mob begged. "Open the gate, or we'll all die!"

People began climbing through cannon slits in the walls to escape. Some jumped to the sea from low parapets in a frenzied effort to get out of the closed town. Near the southern gate, a small group of young men pulled stones from the hole the rector had made near his palace and rushed through toward Varos. A man at the top of the tower was shouting.

"Everyone, come back!" he screamed, throwing stones down at the fleeing townspeople. "The enemy would kill you if they catch you! Come back, now! You're safer within the town walls. They're landing! They're landing! Come back!"

The few who heard him paid him no heed. There were as yet no signs of ships in the bay, and the trickle of townspeople who got beyond the walls continued across the short strip of land that led to Saint Blaise Hill and the safety of the remote pine forests beyond. The man in the tower stared at them and threw more stones in frustration.

Damir stayed close to Father Anton, and soon they returned to the square in front of the cathedral. The limestone terrace was nearly empty. Only a few townsmen remained, along with three altar boys. They looked around helplessly, unsure whether to fight or flee.

"What should we do," Damir asked the priest. "Should we run, too?"

"No," Father Anton replied. "Someone needs to defend the town and its churches. It might be too late to get away, anyway." He took a breath and glanced around the nearly deserted square.

"Damir, go to All Saints and see if you can help there. People might be panicking for nothing, who knows, but if these ships mean trouble, we'll find out first at All Saints."

"Right," Damir said, and then hesitated. "What's All Saints?"

"The southern tower by the eastern bay. You might have heard it called Rampada. Next to Varos. Now run, boy!"

Damir ran east, down a steep street lined with shuttered trade shops and overarched by passages between buildings. He was slowed by a small group blocking the tight passageway, but pushed through.

"You, men, go to the towers, too, and find a way to be useful,"

27

Father Anton shouted before whispering a quick prayer and disappearing into the dark nave. Once inside the cathedral, the priest removed his elaborate cope, kissed it, and locked it into a chest. He then ran up the wooden spiral steps to the bell tower, the silver cross around his neck swinging wildly. The two bellmen were still there gripping their mallets and staring toward the east.

Once on the platform, the priest edged against the low stone parapet and stared east as well. The galleys were nearer now. They had rounded the tip of Badija Island, and wind and oar were driving them closer to Korčula. The banners fluttering from the tallest masts – crescents of various designs – showed the galleys were definitely Turkish. One banner, a turbaned head in a field of red, seemed more common among the horde of red, green, blue, and white ensigns. Each ship was flanked by scores of oars, and already sails were being furled in preparation for battle. Cannon poked from forecastles at the galley's bows, and astern uniformed commanders watched from beneath canvas canopies emblazoned with more crescents and stars. Father Anton counted only twenty or so Ottoman galleys, not the fifty shouted by the men. But filled with cannon and fighting men, the galleys would be more than enough to overrun the town and its meager defensives. So far, the warships remained out of cannon range, but that wouldn't last much longer.

On the ground, Damir sprinted toward Rampada Tower. A large, circular edifice next to the Church of the All Saints Brotherhood, Rampada dominated the southeast corner of the walled town and commanded a clear view of the sea toward Badija Island. The shipbuilding village, Varos, rested in its shadows just outside the town walls. Damir's progress was hampered at every bend by knots of townspeople frozen in place by fear and uncertainty. As he neared the tower, he caught sight of a familiar face. Karlo, a bulky young laborer from Blato, was trying to push through the crowd clogging a passageway just ahead.

"Karlo!" Damir shouted. "Come with me! I'm going to the Rampada Tower."

The large man looked back and saw Damir, but continued jostling forward with the crowd. "I'm going to the land gate," he yelled over his shoulder. "They need help there, too!" Karlo turned the corner toward the main gate. Damir paused at the foot of

Rampada where the street bent toward Revelin. He watched the man melt into the throng that had grown around the gate.

Damir called to Karlo one last time before ducking under the low stone doorway leading into the tower. As his eyes adjusted to the darkness, he saw about a dozen men, women, and children standing before a sturdy wooden door with a large iron lock. A few appeared to be town guards, but most were dressed as workers or artisans ready for church. A wooden stairway hugged the inner wall, leading to the upper platforms. Damir asked a boy in the back of the crowd why everyone was inside the tower and not manning the cannon.

"The cannon are useless," the dark-haired boy said. "That there is the explosives room, and the gunpowder, balls, and the stuff we need are in it. Behind that locked door. The rector has the keys, but he's gone and no one knows if he took them or left them. Some people have gone looking. Nothing we can do but wait."

Damir wasn't good at waiting. He left the group and climbed the stairs to the firing platforms. On the first platform, two cannon sat idle and alone. Damir rushed past these to the higher platform. There, under a clear sky, three cannon sat mutely next to barrels of water, small pyramids of four balls, and some iron tools. The biggest gun was the one the townspeople called the Pope's Cannon, a thirty-pounder, and the others were new twenty-pounders, part of a recent shipment from Venice. Two men and a woman were on the platform watching across the ramparts. Outside, the waters just east of the town were already crowded with galleys.

Damir stood spellbound for a moment. He had never seen anything remotely like the seascape before him. The fleet had slowed on the far side of the bay and myriad banners of red, green, white, and blue fluttered from the tall masts. Cannon glared from the prows, while for the moment rowers kept the ships a safe distance from the town's defenses. It seemed someone was shouting to shore from the upper deck of the one of the galleys, but even in the strange serenity that had settled over the morning scene, Damir doubted anyone on land could hear what was being yelled.

Minutes passed with little movement among the ships. Then, oars began pulling the massive ships slowly toward Korčula. Before long, the galleys and the city would be within firing range

29

of each other, and only one side had gunpowder at hand.

Damir darted down the staircase to shout a warning to those below and was surprised to see Father Anton at the arsenal door with a massive hammer. In the center of a semicircle of people, the archdeacon faced the stout door with the anger of the righteous and raised the sledge. The iron peen crashed against the door and lock, sending off a shower of sparks, but causing little damage. Again, the high priest raised the hammer, and again it crashed against the door.

"Open, by all the saints," he cried as he brought the hammer up again. The small splinters around the lock mocked him. Another swing with little effect.

"Open, you infernal door! Open!" And with a final swing, the wood around the lock buckled and the door swung free.

"Gunners, take your pouches and get to your cannon. We're short of people, so grab someone to help you and teach them quickly," the archdeacon ordered and looked up to Damir. "You, boy, come down here and help us get these charges and wads up to the cannon. We have no time to waste!"

Damir ran down, jumping the last few feet to make room on the stairs for the cannon handlers who were rushing upward. He took an armful of charges – cylindrical bundles of cloth packed with powder – and returned up the winding stairs to the tower's upper levels. He dropped them near the crews and went back for more. Inside, Damir found that the priest had already organized some children, many not even in their teens, into a relay to carry charges, wads, balls, and other supplies to the firing crews up and down the walls.

Minutes passed, and then the cathedral's bells started ringing. Damir was carrying another load of charges to the upper deck when heard the noise. On signal, cannon from towers all along the eastern wall thundered into action. The clap echoed through the tower's interior. Moments later, the galleys in the bay answered the town's explosive bellow with their own low roar. Two beasts of war calling to each other in the same language. The teenager raced faster to the highest platform to see what was happening. Two guardsmen were shouting orders to townspeople working the cannon on the open deck.

"That must have been at least a sixty-pounder," the elder guard yelled, as he rammed a wet sponge into the bore of the Pope's Cannon. "Those will just bounce off these beautiful old walls, just like they did with Aragon. Stay calm, and Saint Barbara help us! Don't rush or you'll blow us all up! There's plenty of time to get off another volley!"

He pulled the sponge out and glanced at the other crews. One cannon was being manned by three women he knew, wives of stonecutters. Fast, but not hurried, he thought. Good work.

"You there," pointing at another crew, "make sure you dry out the barrel after you damp out the sparks. The charge will never go off if it's too wet. Here, boy, clean out this bore for me. Just jam it in there, and give it a shake."

The guard handed Damir a long rod with a cluster of spiraling metal tentacles at the end. Damir glanced at what others were doing, then took the rod and shoved it into the bore as the older guard moved over to help the neighboring crew. He pushed it as far in as it would go, and rammed it in and out for two or three strokes. By the time he pulled the rod out, the guard was back with a charge.

"Good work, boy," he said and without pausing slid the charge into the bore. "Watch closely!" The charge was followed by a ropey wad that fit snugly into the chamber and finally a cannon ball. The guard rammed another tool into the bore to pack everything tightly together and wrestled the cannon closer to the parapet, taking aim at one of the nearest galleys.

"Stand back!"

The guard poked a long needle through a hole in the back of the barrel and splashed it with a trickle of gunpowder from his pouch. He straightened and stepped away.

"OK, now!"

A boy who had been standing well behind the cannon came up to the gunner's side. He had a long stick with a smoldering wick at one end. He touched the red wick to the primed firing hole, setting off a shower of sparks. An eternity later, the cannon flashed with a loud blast. It bucked backwards as a flume of fiery smoke spat from the bore and a ball arced through the air.

It was a dance of fire and iron repeated among scores of cannon crew along the walls and on the ships. The thunder ebbed and flowed as the two sides exchanged volley after volley into the midmorning. Smoke from the cannon lingered in the bay, giving the Ottoman fleet a spectral appearance. Some of the foreign galleys were damaged in the early salvos, but the captains had switched tactics quickly. Now the ships were rowed into cannon range, fired, and briskly rowed away. Synchronized, loud, and bulky dancers on the waters.

"Watch that one," the old gunner told Damir, pointing to a galley moving into firing range. As the oars dug into the water bringing the big ship to an abrupt halt, all the crew on deck except for the gunners raced to the stern. Then the four bow cannon fired, a quartet of heat, smoke and metal, and the oars began pulling the ship away again. "That gives them a little extra range, boy, but Saint Babs knows all their tricks."

In town, plaster and masonry were flying as balls overshot the parapets. Others crashed into the thick stone walls, which held firm. The galleys fired along the perimeter searching for weaknesses. Meanwhile, the defenders hurried along the walls to deliver supplies, skirts and cloaks billowing as they raced along the platforms and up ladders and staircases.

The battle seemed a stalemate to Damir until late morning when it took a dangerous turn. Hundreds of Turkish footmen began landing on the far side of the east bay, at the shipyard beyond Varos. They assembled for a march toward the town's land gate.

Bura

Near a rocky outcrop a few hundred yards from Rampada Tower, several Ottoman galleys maneuvered up to the docks at a shipyard. Turkish janissaries in brightly colored kit and armed with muskets, bows, and swords leapt from the bowsprits. Small disassembled cannon were also lowered. The janissaries, captives trained their whole lives for war, slowly formed into disciplined units and began marching around the cove toward the thin spit of land that connected Korčula to the rest of the island.

The sea battle to the north continued loudly with neither side gaining a noticeable edge. Some of the galleys were damaged and one had to be towed back beyond the range of the town's cannon. Plenty of others stayed in the fray, moving into bay or around the walls, unleashing a volley from their bow cannon, and then pulling away again. The town wasn't spared the effect of their cannon. So far, however, the damage was limited to crumpled walls and collapsed roofs. The few injuries came from falling masonry or town cannon that misfired from inept handling. The walls held, and the town's gunners and their makeshift crews fired as opportunities arose.

The elder gunner atop Rampada Tower paused before giving another order to fire. He watched as the soldiers landed on the opposite side of the bay.

"They are going to need some help at the land gate," he shouted, as the boy with the glowing linstock stood ready to touch off the cannon again. The gunner pointed at Damir and a young townsman in a leather jerkin helping at another gun. "You and you, run over to Revelin. If you see any stragglers in the streets, get them to go with you. Teach them what I showed you, and may the blessed martyr help us."

33

He poked his needle into the small vent at the base of the cannon and splashed on some powder from his pouch. "Fire!" The cannon belched smoke and fire, and another ball sailed toward the Ottoman fleet.

The two young men, both barely out of boyhood, leapt down the tower stairs. They picked up a third companion on the lower platform, and the trio darted toward the land gate. The scene on the streets was unsettling. The pavement was littered with chunks of stone and plaster. Dust covered everything, giving the townscape a deathly pall. But most unnatural, there was not a soul in sight. Korčula's streets, normally bustling with activity day and night, were empty as a graveyard.

It was only when they reached the foot of Revelin that the small group met with a handful of others – four in all – coming down the main street from the cathedral. Now seven, the gang of ragtag defenders scaled the stairs to Revelin's top platform.

As Damir poked his head through the narrow hatchway, he found a group of people listening to orders from a guardsman whose red and gold tunic seemed a touch too big for his narrow shoulders. His helmet wobbled awkwardly.

"...the other side of Varos. We don't know how many there are, but they'll be heading this way. We don't have much time." The voice was hoarse, but calm, loud, and carried authority. Damir thought he recognized it. "Here's Jolanda and Marko now. Wonderful. They have blouses and helmets from the barracks. Everyone put them on. We don't want the Turks to know we're just a bunch of loafers and women."

The leader turned to see who was coming up through the hatchway.

"Iskra?" Damir was dumbfounded. Under the teetering helmet was the women with dark eyes and dark hair who had captured so much of his brief time a year earlier. A smile shone momentarily through a face smudged with soot and sweat.

"Damir?" If Iskra was surprised or pleased, she didn't show it. But the boy took note that she remembered his name. "Good that you're here ... and with friends. We need more hands. You and friends grab some tunics. Then, you go and help my brother with that cannon." She gestured toward a tall, thin man with jet black hair and brooding brows standing over a smaller cannon. Before

Damir could respond, she went back to organizing the others on the platform. "Jolanda, you and Marko go back to All Saints and see if you can get some more powder and balls. I think we need the twelve-pounders, but ask if anyone knows. And hurry. Sasha, find some help and roll wagons against the gate, any you can find."

Damir sprinted to the man by the cannon – Iskra's bother, it seemed – and noticed Karlo from Blato at the edge of the group. He was holding an old pike uneasily.

"Hey, we could use your help on the cannon," Damir said as he reached his friend. "I've been at the other tower, and I can show you what to do."

Karlo hesitated and looked around, first at the Turks gathering in formation in the distance and then toward the bell tower rising high above the cathedral. Someone had raised a large red and green banner from the cupola. "Look!" he said, pointing to the bell tower with his pike. "They might need help at the church! Let me go check!"

Before anyone could answer, Karlo ran down the stairs. Moments later, Damir and the other defenders saw him rushing up the main street toward Saint Mark's, passing a few men and women rushing in the other direction to help with the defense.

Iskra's brother, Nikola, was pushing the cannon toward the edge of the tower as Damir and another man joined him. Across the isthmus at the edge of a cypress grove, the Turkish troops were forming three ranks with cannon setting up in the gaps between the formations. They were holding position and waiting.

About forty people were scattered on the tower and along the southern walls. Most wore the red-and-gold tunics and steel helmets Iskra had passed around, and a few even had badly fitting breast plates. Two cannon pointed south from Revelin Tower's high platform toward the waiting Turks, and three others were ready at the Rector's Tower at the western corner of the fortifications. Along the walls, men and women – from teenagers to seniors – arrayed themselves at intervals, armed with bows, crossbows, and arquebuses.

"How far can this shoot?" Damir asked, leaning the sponge and other tools against the wall within easy reach.

"Not that far, I don't think. That has to be five hundred yards. Maybe more." Nikola said, "But I'm not really sure."

"Well, Niko?"

The two exchanged a glance and looked to see where Iskra was. She was on the wall west of the tower talking to a group of people with muskets and pointing toward the Ottoman troops. Damir and Nikola lost no time. Damir cleaned out the bore. There were no cartridges for these cannon, so, as the old gunner told him, he used a scoop to load a measure of gunpowder into the barrel, followed by a wad, and finally a ball. He rammed it all down tight into the cannon.

They pushed the cannon against the parapet, marked the troops at the tree line, and guessed at an angle.

"Ready! Go!" Nikola ordered. A third man, who had been standing back with the lighted linstock, lowered the glowing tip to the vent hole, and the three braced themselves.

Nothing.

"By the saints," Damir yelled. "We didn't set the charge!"

Nikola stepped back to the cannon and wiped debris from around the vent hole. He poked it with a needle, poured a dollop of gunpowder over the hole, and stepped back again.

"Ready! Try again! Go!"

The linstock came down to the vent again. This time, it triggered a cascade of sparks. A moment passed, and a loud report sent smoke, fire, and cannon ball blasting from the bore. The three men watched as the ball soared gracefully toward the enemy ranks. It reached the zenith of its arc and seemed to gather speed and strength as it careened toward the earth.

With a muted thud, the ball dug deep into the soft ground, barely half the distance to the enemy lines. Nikola turned to Damir and grinned, "Not bad for a baker, huh?"

"What are you doing, you halfwits!" Iskra had covered the distance from the wall to the tower platform with demonic speed, her face deep red as she breeched the top of the stairs. "This isn't a game, you imbeciles. We can't waste powder and shot so you can make things go, 'Boom!' What were you thinking?"

Before Nikola or Damir dared to answer, the Turkish troops replied instead. A rumble of shouts erupted from the tree line, rolled across the isthmus, and gave the defenders shivers. In front of the troops, some officers were giving orders, and the army began its practiced march toward the walls. The infantry stopped after two hundred yards or so, just short of where Nikola's cannon ball rested meekly. The ranks fanned out slightly as cannon crew moved their war machines ahead of the mass.

"Be ready," Iskra yelled. "And, Niko, get that blessed cannon loaded again!"

As others in the tower and along the wall stood frozen, Damir and Nikola busied themselves around the cannon, sponging out embers, drying, reloading. A few minutes later, they, too, were watching the Turkish formations. A half dozen cannon and their trained crew were arrayed a few hundred yards away, favoring the western edge of the isthmus. Behind them, armored troops stood ready, maybe a thousand or more in total.

The defenders saw flashes and puffs of smoke a half breath before they heard the cannon roar. The balls arced almost in unison toward Korčula, but fell with little effect, bouncing off the walls around the gate or soaring onto buildings beyond the wall. The Turkish crews expertly began to reload.

"What are you waiting for, you loafers! Bows, cannon, now!"

On Iskra's order the two cannon in Revelin Tower replied to their Turkish peers. Bows and crossbow from the walls joined the battle, along with the cannon on the neighboring Rector's Tower. Balls, bolts, and arrows sailed across the meager length of land that separated the two enemies. A second volley from the foreign cannons soon followed, and quickly the landside exchanges mirrored those at sea. A corner of the Rector's Palace next to Revelin Tower was shattered, but otherwise, there was little damage to the wall or gate.

A thin blanket of dull powder smoke settled low upon the land until a sudden puff of wind from the north scattered it into nothingness. Glancing up from his cycle of tasks at the cannon, Damir saw that a wheel had been torn off one of the Turkish cannon, making it useless, but the others were still firing with vicious efficiency. And worse, one rank of soldiers had started to advance across the strait of land. He stole a glance at Iskra in her cockeyed helmet.

"Watch the soldiers!" Iskra commanded. "Wait for them to get closer, and then focus everything you've got on them! Get those muskets ready! Drums!" From the courtyard behind the land gate, a strong steady tapping began as a group of children, also organized by the innkeeper's daughter, began beating on guards' drums. It was a simple rat-a-tat-tat, but loud.

The Turkish soldiers moved quickly toward the gate. A group of bowmen stopped just past the cannon and fired in high arcs toward the defenders on the wall. The rest continued forward, muskets at the ready and swords hanging from their belts. When they reached about 200 yards from the walls, they stopped to fire, and the defenders seized the chance to unleash their own weapons.

"Now, my friends!" Nikola shouted, and the linstock came down once again onto the powder spread around the vent. Damir and Niko's cannon and the others in the two towers fired against the approaching troops. Men and women along the walls let loose their arquebuses as well, pulling trigger levers and waiting a heartbeat as the powder in the pan triggered the main charge and sent a small lead shot hurling toward the troops.

With a thunderous report that dwarfed that of the other cannon, a ball careened into the Turkish troops from the Damir's left. He looked over to Rampada Tower and saw Father Anton waving. The priest had ordered the Pope's Cannon to shift away from the sea and train its sights in the advancing troops. Damir returned the wave with an excited and much-too-boyish yelp and again reloaded his cannon. While Turkish musket balls and cannon balls largely passed over the heads of the cannon crews in the tower, their arrows were more dangerous. Shot with a higher arc, they seemed to fall randomly from the sky onto the tower platform and the walkways along the walls. As Damir patted another load into the cannon's bore, one missile sailed downward, piercing the shoulder of the man handling the linstock. The blow sent the man to the ground with fresh blood spreading rapidly over his tunic and sleeve. Despite the wound, the man insisted on continuing and Nikola helped him to his feet. As soon as he was standing, though, he swooned and was on the ground again.

"Islić, we need some help," Nikola called over the inward edge of the tower platform, and an instant later his sister was on the landing. Together they lowered the man to the middle platform, which was more protected from the ongoing attack, and Nikola returned to the cannon. "No concerns, Dado, we can do this by ourselves. I'll take over lighting this beautiful thing." Nikola leaned the rod with the smoldering wick against the far wall, and he and Damir improvised a new drill, with Nikola setting the powder pouch down to the side before taking the linstock to fire the cannon.

The battle at the south wall thundered for nearly half an hour before the troops outside the gate retreated a safe distance, bringing their dead and wounded with them. A few more cannon shots were released from each side just ahead of a sudden calm. Firing from the naval battle continued over the bay, but on the isthmus both sides assessed their success and damage.

Iskra climbed up on the platform and surveyed the scene. The defenders on the tower and along the wall were drenched in sweat and soot, but except for the man pierced by the arrow, no one was seriously hurt. Outside the walls, scattered islets of abandoned weapons and armor littered the field beyond the shallow ditch, and the ground around many was stained scarlet with blood. But however many the Ottoman casualties numbered, it was small compared with the host of troops preparing for the next assault. On the bay, the sea battle continued in its own rhythm. The Turks would row within range of the walls, fire, and try to row away before the town's cannon caught them.

"How's everyone up here?" The women and men handling the guns made vague, reassuring noises. "Well, Niko – the other Niko – isn't going to breaking stone anytime soon, but we have him wrapped up, and I think he'll be fine. He took a nasty arrow, and now he has a story to tell his grandkids."

Iskra took off her helmet and looked across the narrow stretch of land that separated the town from the Ottoman guns and cannon. A gust of wind from behind her blew her black hair into her face, and she casually brushed it aside with a hand that still held an arquebus. It was a gesture Damir was sure he would remember the rest of his life, however short that might be. Still, Iskra didn't seem to notice him any more than anyone else on the wall.

"The wall took some hits from the cannon. It's weakening around the hole that the mouse-livered rector made. Some men are bracing it with timber though," Iskra said to no one in particular. "The gate's a problem, too. The wood's starting to buckle a little and splinter. It's holding for now, but maybe next time it won't."

"We need to be ready, then" Damir said, consciously lowering his voice to a shaky baritone. "We can use more powder and balls."

"Everyone can," Iskra said, stepping away from the wall. She looked at the people along the walls in their borrowed tunics and helmets and took a long breath. "The balls should be no problem. I think the whole town's running low on powder. We'll see what Jolanda and Marko can get. No more wasted shots, you two."

Iskra's gaze fell over Damir, and she might have smiled before heading down the stairs again.

Father Anton stood next to the Pope's Cannon on Rampada Tower and wasn't sure what to do next. The tower wasn't designed to protect the southern wall, and it took at least ten minutes to swing the gun's sites from the isthmus to the bay. Then ten minutes to swing it back again, if needed. Now that the land troops were in retreat, should he train the gun again on the ships, which hadn't stopped their cat-and-mouse attacks on the walls? Or was it better to be ready when the massive land formation began a new attack? These were questions for a man of the sword, not a man of the cloth.

It was barely noon, and a long day lay ahead. Some clouds were forming on the northern horizon – unusual for this time of year – but the sun was still beating down in the battlefields on sea and on land. The priest imagined the galleys' oarsmen must be exhausted from constantly bringing the ships in an out of cannon range. The ships' guns had also been working tirelessly. While a few ships seemed damaged beyond fighting – far too few – there were still sixteen or seventeen arced around the town's eastern and northern walls. If the trained Turkish troops and seamen were exhausted, the town's defenders must be near collapse.

Father Anton looked at the people along the walls and on the towers. They were courageous and strong, but not indefatigable. They and their weapons needed a rest. He turned to the man next to him.

"Go along the walls, and tell everyone to stop firing until I give the order," he said. "Stay low and out danger for a few minutes. Everyone should catch their breath. The sun sets late, and this battle could go on for many more hours."

The priest and the others on top of the tower sat on the platform floor, their backs against the parapet. The only exception was the elder gunner. He cooled the cannons carefully with clothes soaked in water and checked the equipment, balls, and charges. The gunner started down the stairs, but stopped before he had fully vanished.

"I'm going to check the lower guns. I think one could be out, but the blessed Barbara might be on our side," he said. "I'll check how much powder and shot we have left, too." And he disappeared.

Firing from the town gradually stopped as word of the priest's order spread, and soon the only sounds were the shots from the Turkish ships. Balls stretched over the walls, struck buildings and courtyards, and damaged stonework. Behind Rampada Tower, the entire wall of a tailor's workshop collapsed, exposing colorful bolts of cloth and finished finery to the gray dust and debris of war. Most of the balls continued to strike Korčula's thick sea walls, which began to show small chips here and there. As yet, there was no clear breach and the stalemate continued. Father Anton knew, however, that if stamina became the deciding factor, the town would fall.

The respite lasted maybe twenty minutes, maybe thirty, before the landed Turkish cannon signaled its end. The old gunner had long since returned to the tower platform with a disappointing, but expected report: the stores were running low. The inexperienced cannoneers were firing wildly and going through the power and shot much too quickly. Supplies would last until sunset, perhaps longer, but they would run out fast in a siege. With some quick repair, both cannon on the lower platform were ready, he said.

Father Anton rose and inspected the situation. The enemy cannon on the isthmus had begun a new barrage, focusing on the wall near the rector's palace, and wisely the town's cannon were not yet returning fire. They must also be worried about supplies, the priest thought. A rank of Turkish troops was again advancing toward Revelin Tower, and the defenders were waiting for them to come into closer range.

"By Saint Mark and all the other saints, here we go again," he sighed, not loud enough for anyone else to hear. The priest waved a red strip of cloth, and soon the seaward cannon were back in action. Minutes later, they were joined by the guns in the southern walls and towers. The Turkish janissaries had advanced almost to the ditch and the raised drawbridge.

Gray-blue smoke again obscured the land and sea battles as cannon and musket from both sides erupted into a new chapter of the battle. Father Anton found it difficult to judge whether the greater danger came from the galleys or the infantry, but he decided to keep the large cannon on his tower trained toward the land troops. Clean-load-fire. Each of the defenders' guns followed the same cycle even as they moved at different rhythms. Were the shots from Revelin Tower slower now? Maybe missing a beat? The priest couldn't tell. The faces around him showed growing worry and fear.

"They haven't beaten us!" Father Anton shouted, waving the red cloth. "Don't despair!"

Suddenly, clouds poured over the Pelješac mountains and a northern wind streamed into the bay. Within minutes, the sea was beset with white-capped waves. The squall caught the Ottoman captains by surprise and pushed the galleys closer to the rocks and town walls. The galleys' cannon fell silent as oarsmen strained against the powerful gusts and waves.

The sea change came quickly, and the Ottoman crews were caught unawares.

"Bura! Bura!" people shouted from the seaside walls. "Bura!"

"Fire with all you have!" Father Anton ordered, racing down from the tower to relay the command himself all along the walls. "It's a miracle! Fire! Fire!"

Townspeople and villagers all knew the Bura, a savage northern wind that could erupt suddenly from the mainland. Bura was a frequent visitor in the winter, but it occasionally dropped by the island in the summer as well, sending fishing boats dashing into safe bays. On this Feast Day, the Bura was sending the foreign ships within easy reach of the town's cannon, while the choppy sea made it near impossible for marine gunners to fire effectively.

Re-energized, the town's defenders fired volley after volley on the frenzied galleys. The tight formations the ships had held throughout the day were broken as the warships struggled against the Bura. Galleys brushed against one another as they pulled out of range. Oars split, and rigging tangled. Slowly all the Turkish vessels managed to move out of range. They lingered in a misshapen formation amid the high sea crests, their guns silent. Before long, the galleys began rowing toward a protected bay near the Dominican monastery. Some had to be towed, their oars no longer up to the effort.

42

From Revelin Tower, the change in the sea battle was also immediately apparent. The views east and west were clear enough for Damir and his mates, as well as the Turkish troops on the ground, to watch the beleaguered galleys fighting against the sudden fierce wind and limp toward shelter. Cannon on both sides fell silent for a moment as everyone followed the progress of the galleys. The Bura charging in from behind the Revelin defenders blew life into the banners and flags on the parapets before crossing over the Turkish troops and on through the forest beyond. The stillness was broken when the Ottomans sounded retreat and raced back to the tree line, carrying and dragging their fallen with them.

"Fire before the vermin get away!" Iskra shouted, and the Korčula cannon spat a few more times, their shot enjoying a tailwind. "That's good. Stop! Stop!"

The Spaniard

From his post beside the twelve-pound cannon, Damir could see three Turkish officers conferring at the tree line behind rows of their troops. The battlefield had been quiet for about half an hour, and the leaders in their colorful uniforms stood overlooking formations of relaxed troops. They gesticulated in all directions. The eastern bay, toward Badija Island, was now empty, while the Turkish galleys congregated in the western bay, lingering on the far side near the Dominican monastery where the town's cannon couldn't reach. A few were noticeably damaged, with fallen masts and spars. The quiet was unnatural.

"What are they talking about?" Nikola asked, sitting casually on the parapet. "Do you think they're going to attack again?"

"I don't know. It's still early. Maybe they'll wait out the winds and try again later or in the morning. It's going to be a long day and a long night. I don't think they're just going to give up." Damir stood next to his new friend, leaning on the cast iron worm he'd been using all afternoon to clear the cannon's bore. On the wall between Revelin and Rampada towers, he watched Iskra as she talked with Father Anton. Briefly, she seemed to fall against the priest, standing only with his support. But the moment passed, and soon she and Father Anton were conferring again. They, too, were pointing and waving, first at the loitering troops near forest and then at the restless galleys across the bay. Damir straightened up slightly and looked away when Iskra turned in his direction. The worst of the Bura had died down almost as quickly as it arrived, but a strong breeze blowing from the north remained, enough to make it difficult for the galleys to resume their attack immediately, but not impossible.

Damir self-consciously peered across the western bay and

across the channel toward Pelješac.

"Do you see that?" he asked Nikola, pointing toward the distant shore.

Iskra's brother turned away from the Turkish troops and looked across the waters, still churning from the Bura. From their vantage point on top of the tower they could see over Korčula's walls to the peninsula. Just offshore from an empty stretch of land, five or six small boats lingered in the choppy water. They were much smaller than the mighty galleys and flew no banners that Damir or Nikola could see.

"Fishermen?" the village boy asked.

Nikola laughed.

"Great time to fish, huh? Scavengers, more likely. I heard stories about them at the inn."

Damir was embarrassed by his ignorance in front of Iskra's brother, but was curious. "What are they doing?"

"They say raiders or pirates will sometimes follow big fleets. They stay away from any battle, but they row around at night looking for anything valuable left floating in the water. A ship's carpenter from Mljet once told me they even dive to sunken wrecks, pulling up what they can. Sometimes they even find someone in the water they can ransom."

"And the Turks just let them follow them?"

"I guess they're probably from the mainland. Who knows how long they've been following the galleys. They certainly aren't Venetian, and the Ragusans try hard to stay away from any fighting. They do all their battles in the counting houses."

The two watched the boats in the distance and surveyed the wide vista before them. The violent battles in sea and land had been transformed into still lifes. The recent din replaced by silence. To their right, the Ottoman galleys had merged into a single, bobbing entity, some ships latched together. Directly in front of the Korčulans, the land army was also resting. While the soldiers remained in rough formation, many were sitting or prone on the ground without their helmets. The officers continued to confer in the background. The bay on the left was deserted.

The hot midday sun was quickly drying the sweat from Damir and Nikola's clothes.

"You're Iskra's brother? I didn't know she had a brother."

"Yeah. Well, there are three of us. I'm the oldest, but don't tell Islić that. It's best she doesn't find out," Nikola smiled and slid down from the parapet. "And, you're the village boy she met last year? You're a bit smaller than I imagined, but you were a master with that cannon." Even for an islander, Nikola was tall. He stood almost a full head above Damir.

"Well, I'm a fast learner." Although Damir wanted to ask more about what Iskra had said about the "village boy," he strained to focus on the cannon. "I was over at the other tower – Rampada or maybe you call it All Saints – I was with one of the old cannon handlers before they sent me here when the Turks landed. If you don't blow yourself up, it's all pretty straightforward. I'm knackered, though. So, um, Iskra...."

Nikola interrupted, "Look! They're moving!"

Across the isthmus, the Ottoman troops rallied. On command, they were all on their feet again and adjusting their armor. The officers had broken their council and were moving among the ranks of men, stopping occasionally to give orders. The janissaries and other troops soon resumed their disciplined formations.

"Be ready!" Nikola called, as he took the smoldering linstock. Damir, back at his station next to the cannon, noticed Iskra hurrying along the wall back toward the tower.

But Nikola's warning wasn't necessary. As the two defenders and others along the walls and on the towers watched, the tight enemy formations dissolved into more casual assemblies of uniformed men. The majority of the troops and the cannon crews began drifting westward along the bayside, while a smaller group – still more than a hundred – trooped toward Varos. Well out of cannon and bow range, the Turks plundered what they could from the homes, shops, warehouses, and churches in the village and along the quayside. As they retreated, small fires erupted in their wake. The flames engulfed much of Varos and moved along the western bay, filling the void left by the departing Turkish troops, until finally the monastery itself was in flames.

"We can relax. It looks like those sons of jackals are done for the day." Iskra had appeared beside them. With the urgency ebbing, even she wasn't spared exhaustion. Her voice trembled slightly, and her eyes, almost hidden behind her fallen hair, were red and sunken. She pushed dark locks from her face with a heavy sigh and looked over at the growing flames. "Not much we can do for the village. It's too risky to send anyone outside the walls. Let's hope the boat makers took their best goodies with them when they ran away."

Over the next few hours, Damir, Iskra, and Nikola rested with others in the cool interior of Revelin Tower. Someone was always watching the Ottoman through the narrow slits in the tower's walls. The flames outside Korčula gamboled without restraint, villainous inmates freed from a madhouse, as the Turkish troops returned to their ships.

There was little talk within the tower beyond quiet murmurings. Iskra especially seemed lost in her thoughts as she sat leaning against an inner wall. Nikola sat beside her, his arm around her shoulder. They occasionally exchanged quiet words. Damir watched the siblings from across the platform, wondering whether he should move closer, but not daring to. The distance seemed too great. He looked for a sign of welcome and found none. As the afternoon passed, he felt alone in the crowd of townspeople.

Finally, as the day faded toward evening, Damir and some of the others moved back to the top platform. Silhouetted against a sinking sun, the Turkish warships were moving again. Under oar, the ones furthest away were heading northwest toward Pelješac. Others were cuing to join them, some on towlines. The shore was deserted.

Iskra and Nikola joined those on the tower.

"It looks like it's over for the night. The toads could be back in the morning, though," she said softly without her usual energy. She watched the fleet drift away, and then turned to Damir for the first time in hours. "Dado, go over and talk to Old Tony to see what you need to do with this cannon to settle it in for the night. He'll still be on top of All Saints."

Unexpectedly, she grabbed Damir's hand. "Wait. I'll go with you so you don't get lost. I need to tell the archdeacon what's happening."

Just before they turned to leave together, an orange glow began to spread across one of the last Ottoman ships in the bay. Iskra let go of Damir's hand as the two turned back toward the parapet to watch with the others. A half-dozen small fires dotted the galley's deck then joined into a single blaze.

"That's well out into the bay," Iskra said, her voice once again controlled and sharp. "There's no chance that that's an accident. They must be scuttling it. That's one for Korčula, anyway."

As the group watched, flames crawled up the ship's remaining mast. There were no explosions, just the slow combustion of wood and tar. The crew must have transferred gun powder, cannon, and anything else they could before the order was given to sink the galley. Other ships gave it wide berth as they moved out of the bay and across the channel.

In the fading light, the mighty galley's death was agonizingly slow, as though it stubbornly refused to leave its home on the water's surface. As the inferno grew, the hull offered a clear outline of a once strong fighting ship against a backdrop of fire and brimstone. Each porthole and cannon hatch screamed brightly. Fiery rigging fell to the water like demonic spider webs disturbed by the winds. Finally, just as the last Turkish galley rowed out of the bay, the burning ship collapsed onto itself and eased beneath the waves, leaving flaming flotsam to mark its passage.

"Don't shoot! I'm a Christian! Don't shoot!"

Immediately, two shots rang from the southern walls near the Rector's Palace, and the shadowy figure that had been approaching the town from the bay side fell hard onto the ground.

"Don't shoot!" the muffled cry came.

"Stop firing!" Iskra ordered. "Someone get Father Anton!"

The fading sun and the embers from the village cast ever-changing shades of orange across the mud flat in front of the south gate. The remnants of battle – swords, helmets and other discarded equipment – dotted the field and reflected the dying flames beyond. Amid this foul wasteland, a single prone figure near the quay moved slightly.

"Stand up!" Iskra shouted from platform atop the land gate, her voice again masterful. "Let us see you!"

"Don't shoot! I'm a Christian," the man responded in a foreign accent as he cautiously rose to his feet with his hands spread wide to his sides. "Don't shoot."

The man was drenched. His long, dark hair hung limply down his back, and his pantaloons clung desperately to his thighs. He was shirtless, showing a strong muscular torso and massive arms. He had no weapon and no armor.

Within minutes, Father Anton, his brother Vicko, and some other men climbed the stairs to join Iskra, Damir, and those who had defended the gate. Damir noticed the priest's blouse was stained with blood and still wet with sweat.

"Stay still, man. Who are you?" the priest called.

"I am Franco, long since of Granada," the dark figure answered. "I have been a slave of the vile Turks for many, many years, but now I have fled thanks to the brave deeds of you and your men. I only ask that you grant a fellow Christian refuge lest they return and find me. They would surely kill me as I am an escaped galley slave. I am hungry, but harmless!"

"How do we know you're not a Turkish spy?" Vicko demanded and fired his arquebus before his brother could stop him. The pellet dug into the ground close enough to the figure to make him jump back.

"Don't shoot, I pray you!" the man repeated. Then, there was silence. Finally, in a gruff, bass voice, he began to sing.

"A la puerta del cielo venden zapatos."

And he hummed loudly for a moment.

"Duermete, niño. Duermete, niño. A la puerta del cielo…"

And more humming.

The people in the tower were taken aback and unsure what to do next. They stood motionless and listened as the man struggled through the quiet melody, his voice hoarse from exhaustion. The words were repeated between guttural humming. The man who called himself Franco seems to get more nervous with each cycle.

"What is that?" Father Anton asked quietly on the tower. "Does anyone know?"

"It's Spanish," Iskra said. "I think it's a baby's song, a lullaby. Something about the gates of heaven … and shoes?"

The priest looked around at the others on the tower as they listened for a few more minutes.

"Stop, Franco of Granada," Father Anton called. "You can approach the wall, but come slowly."

The Spaniard walked carefully toward the wall and stopped at

49

the rim of the ditch. Father Anton looked again around at his colleagues. Vicko kept his long gun at the ready, but no one seemed to object.

"Vicko, Iskra, Damir, come with me," the priest said. "Niko, stay on the tower and keep watch. Let me know if anything changes out there." Father Anton led the small group off the tower and onto the town wall next to the Rector's Palace. "Throw down a rope."

As soon as the line dropped from the parapet, Franco clambered across the shallow ditch. Like any man of the sea, he made short work of the rope and was soon standing among the town's defenders on the wall's platform. As he looked around, his gaze stopped on Iskra a moment longer than on the others. Everyone stayed quiet as they weighed the situation.

"Tie the man's hands, Damir."

Iskra and Vicko stood guard with their long guns as the Spaniard held out his hands and let Damir tie them together. Damir was inwardly happy that the man didn't struggle. His arms looked stronger than any the village boy had ever seen, as though coiled stays were wrapped tightly around his bone. If the strange man didn't cooperate, it would take more than Vicko to hold him back. Franco's dark body was covered with scars, long-healed whelps. His face, free of scars, was instead crowded with thick-lined tattoos. The largest – fish bones or, perhaps, a tree – covered his left cheek, while seemingly random dots were etched on the right. Five irregular diamonds hovered above his heavy black eye brows. Franco noticed Damir gaping at the scars and tattoos. He grinned broadly, but said nothing.

Once the Spaniard was secure, Father Anton led the group off the wall and into a large, empty stable that abutted the Rector's Palace. The stable had high narrow windows for ventilation and a heavy pine door that could be easily bolted from the outside. Four stalls lined one wall. The rest of the space was open. The archdeacon sat the escaped slave on some hay bales at the far corner of the stable and considered the situation. The others, including a few curious townspeople who had followed them, waited in anticipation.

Finally, it seemed the priest came to a decision. He spoke quietly to one of the townswomen, who promptly left the stable, and turned back to the man sitting with his hands bound in the shadowy corner.

"Franco of Granada," he began, "you've arrived at a time that we're quite suspicious of strangers. But, if you are a Christian, as you say, the Scripture bids us to show you hospitality and charity. Indeed, even if you are not. I've ordered that water, fish, and bread be brought for you. And a blouse. We'll unbind your hands when they arrive, but after you've eaten and drunk you'll be bound again. For the moment, you'll understand if we lean to the side of caution."

The priest paused to see if there was any reaction. There was none.

"While we wait, can you tell us how you found yourself at our walls?"

Word had already spread through Korčula of the strange man, and more people began edging into the stable, including, Damir noticed, Karlo from Blato, who hadn't been seen since he left Revelin Tower to help defend the cathedral.

"Monseñor, I sincerely thank you for rescuing me and offering me refuge. You indeed have a true Christian heart. My story is tragic, but it is little different from the story of many others just like me. It is also sad and will move even the heaviest of hearts. As a child, just barely ten years old, I was taken from my mother's warm embrace by cutthroat Barbary raiders who had landed on the Spanish coast near my village. As they carried me off, I saw my beloved Lobres in flames and heard the screams of my people. I struggled, but I was a child and these were servants of the devil. The sight of the burning village would be my last memory of my beloved Spain."

Franco's deep-voiced, accented story captivated everyone within earshot. Lanterns were brought in as the Spaniard continued.

"The Berbers sold me as soon as we reached North Africa, and for more than twenty years now, I have been a galley slave on one Turkish ship or another. The devils forced me to convert to Islam on pain of torture or death and marked me with the tattoos that you see, but in my heart, I remained silently true to my mother's faith. I tried to escape many times, at first, and each time the lashing that followed brought me closer to death. I soon accepted my fate and believed I had indeed been forsaken, never again to walk the soft ground of Lobres or even to learn what destiny awaited my dear parents and family.

"But then, and may the saints be praised, that same fate brought me to the waters outside the famed town of Curzola. I was a wretched oarsman in one of the pasha's galleys that laid siege to your fair town. By a miracle, a cannon shot breached a hole in the hull just in front of me. In the confusion and chaos, I was able to leap through the shattered hull and swim for shore. I waited in the water among the debris until the ships and troops retreated. And then, knowing I risked instant death if I were caught, I raced toward your walls. I had faith that I would find succor among the brave defenders."

As Franco told his story, two women arrived with a bucket of fresh water, a platter of small salted fish, and a small loaf of bread. On a nod from Father Anton, Damir untied the Spaniard's hands. The foreigner drank deeply from a ladle and ate greedily. The crowd edged closer to watch, as though they had never before seen a man eating fish and bread or drinking water. The escaped slave eyed the crowd as he ate, but didn't pause until the platter was empty. He cleaned the final streaks of grease from it with a lump of bread. As he took another deep draft from the bucket, Father Anton handed him a coarse shirt.

Damir approached him with the rope.

"Is this really necessary, monseñor?" the man asked, as he swung the shirt over his head.

"I'm afraid, for now, it is, Franco of Granada," the priest replied.

The Spaniard pulled the shirt down. It was a tight fit. He looked around keenly and held his hands out again for Damir to bind them.

"But, tell us," Father Anton continued, "you say you were a galley slave, yet you have no irons, no chains."

The Spaniard adjusted himself on the hay bale and smiled. "A good question," he began. "Unlike the European custom, the Ottoman practice is to remove the shackles from their rowers before a battle begins. I wish I could tell you this was from a spark of charity, but that would not be the truth. The Turks enter every battle with the expectation of winning, and they would rather fish slaves from the water then have them sink with their ships, requiring further expenditures for replacements."

"A curious practice, but I have heard that the Ottoman is tight with his gold," Father Anton commented. Others standing in the darkness nodded knowingly. "And why is this fleet so far north? We've seen mainland raiders in this area before, of course, but rarely such a large fleet. Who is the captain? Why target our little town of Curzola with so much force?"

"You do not know?" the tattooed man seemed genuinely surprised. "My dear monseñor, you have had the great honor of trading cannon fire with the famed Uluj Ali, viceroy of all of Algiers and Tunis, corsair of the great Sultan Selim, successor of the famed Turgut Reis, admiral among the Ottomans, and, until today, my master. Did you not notice his ensign flying from the Algerian galleys? A corsair's head against a crimson field?"

"I have heard the name," Father Anton responded, "but why Curzola? We have very little here that would attract such a personage."

"That, I cannot answer with confidence, but I do overhear the officers and crew speak and galley slaves have little more to do than gossip when we're not at our oars." Franco shifted uncomfortably on his hay bale and took another draught of water with his bound hands. "We left Tripoli with great haste and were sailing east with the new pasha of Tripoli, Mehmed Mustafa, and his three sons. Some said we were destined for Koroni, where other Ottoman ships were gathering, but others said the great Uluj Ali had been called by Sultan Selim himself to attend him in Istanbul, which you know as Constantinople. Whatever our destination, it seemed to change as we sailed. We were met at sea near Marsa ibn Ghazi in Libya by a small group of galiots, and the viceroy ordered an immediate course change. We now sailed due north.

"I heard the sailors talk of seeking Venetian galleys, but if that were our purpose, we failed. We joined another Ottoman fleet laying siege to a town south of Ragusa, but when the town surrendered without a fight, we separated and sailed northward again. After several days under the burning Adriatic sun, the pasha brought us to your courageous island. Whether by design or accident I cannot say. We paused overnight, and then entered battle formations at the break of dawn. I believe the captains were astonished by the resistance given by your defenders. Orders were changed frequently, and there was much swearing. I was with Uluj Ali and the doomed Turgut Reis at Malta many years ago, and they displayed vast patience and cunning in that battle. But today? There was no patience. As soon as the gales erupted, we were told to row the galleys away from the battle. In the confusion, I managed to flee."

Onlookers drifted in and out of the stable as Father Anton questioned the Spaniard further, asking details about the number and strength of the galleys, their armament, and how many crewmen, infantry, and slaves they carried. But the core question remained a mystery: What did Uluj Ali want with Korčula? After more than an hour, the priest ordered everyone to leave the stable and left Franco with fresh water and a replenished plate of fish and figs. He had the doors barred and a guard posted before they left.

As Father Anton and others lingered in the courtyard, Nikola reported that some of the people who had fled were starting to return and were asking to be let back into town. The priest nodded his approval and gestured for Iskra and Damir to walk with him. They climbed to the wall at Revelin Tower, skirted the rector's tower, and walked along the western wall. Night had fallen, and along the bay, stretching from Varos to the Dominican monastery, the flames set by the retreating Turkish troops had mostly died. Orange embers reflected in the now quiet waters.

In the distance, across channel near the village of Viganj, the lanterns of the Turkish galleys were visible in the growing darkness. Most of the Pelješac peninsula toward the sea was a barren Ragusan outpost, a thin, porous border between Ottoman territory across the channel on the mainland and Venetian islands at seas. The loyalties of villagers constantly shifted as they focused on survival against raiders from both sides of a line they could not see. The Turkish commanders could barter for – or more likely demand – fresh supplies from the Ragusan villagers and find strong bodies to help repair their vessels.

"We were lucky," Father Anton said, breaking the silence. "The Blessed Mother sent the Bura to save us. It was a miracle. The Ottoman might still be back, though."

There was a long pause as the trio watched the flickering ship lights across the channel. Occasionally, someone would come to ask instructions from the priest then quickly depart.

"Eight people were killed here, most when buildings and walls collapsed. Many others were hurt, and more might still die." The priest cupped his silver cross in his hands and mouthed a quiet prayer. "I don't know how much we can trust the Spaniard. He might be everything he says he is, but they say Uluj Ali also started his ascension among the Ottoman as a galley slave, captured off Italy. We cannot risk that Franco tells the fleet of how weak our defenses really are. Our only hope is that they stay unsure and move onward, away from Curzola. We'll keep him comfortable, but under guard, at least until the rector returns."

"Do you think they'll try again?" Iskra asked.

"We'll know in the morning. But, why attack us in the first place? A Turkish fleet is not a raiding party, and there are easier places along the sea to restock on supplies. Surely, they had no desire to conquer and take control of Curzola. She would be difficult to hold against a Venetian assault, especially with an unfriendly populous. Perhaps they were indeed just hoping to catch Venetian galleys here by surprise and weaken the doge's fleet. For whatever reason, it's very usual for such a force to sail this far north."

Father Anton turned away from the sea and faced his companions, the reflective tone gone from his voice.

"Dado, take one of the church horses in the morning and ride to Blato. Our horse will be faster than your old donkey. We'll keep your cart and donkey safe. Tell those in Blato and other villages along the way what has happened here. Tell them if they see any more landings or galley movements they should send someone to Curzola immediately to let me know. Iskra, after you've had a chance to eat, meet me at the cathedral. We need to take measure of what supplies and arms remain in case the enemy returns. In the meantime, I'll set guards and make sure the injured are being attended properly."

The four barks

Frustrated, Damir left Korčula soon after dawn the next morning. On the night after the battle, the town was hectic with activity and agitation. When Father Anton wasn't sending him on a job, he kept close to Iskra, helping where he could. He tried to get her alone, just to talk, even for a moment, but she seemed to crave crowds and the busyness of that night. She applied herself to everything – conducting an inventory of the armory stores, making sure the wounded had fresh water and food, checking on the impromptu guards posted along the walls – everything except stepping away from the throng of people who seemed to gravitate toward her. Damir wondered if she was frustrated, too. Sometimes he thought she was and sometimes wasn't. They parted late with barely a good-night.

Now, after a quick breakfast of bread and olive oil, Damir saddled the church horse and led it toward Revelin Tower, where someone would be waiting to let him through. He didn't dare drop by Iskra's inn so early. Besides, the watch said the Ottoman fleet was still anchored off Pelješac, so he couldn't waste any time before setting off. As he approached Rampada Tower, the old gunner was at the doorway scrapping off the iron worms and other tools and leaning them neatly against the tower wall. They waved wordlessly to one another as Damir passed.

His spirits lifted when he turned the corner and saw Iskra waiting for him at the gate.

"There you are, lazy plavica," she smiled, waving. Iskra was wearing a simple blue dress and an apron and holding a small package. "Here. Mamma cut you some beard with smoked ham for the trip. It's Niko's bread."

"I like smoked ham," Damir said, taking the package and

feeling immediately foolish.

"Do you?" Iskra laughed. "I'll tell mamma. Be safe."

Damir's mind stalled on the idea that Iskra's mother knew about him, as Nikola did, and words formed slowly. In the vacuum, Iskra threw her arms around him for a quick hug and pushed him away. "Now get going, cannon man."

Damir was on the horse and through the gate before he had a chance to say more than "Goodbye." He looked back. Iskra waved once more and turned away as the massive wooden door closed between them.

"Goodbye, Dado!" Father Anton was standing in the wall in his black frock, just where he had been Saturday night as Damir rolled his cart into town. A day and a half, and so much had changed.

Damir pointed the horse westward. Already in the early morning, a few scavengers were combing the grounds in front of the walls for anything of value left behind by the retreating Turks. Damir, too, saw a sword half-buried at the edge of the defensive ditch and picked it up. For most of its length, the curved blade was shiny, but near the guard it was stained with blood. The grip, with its bulbous base, was also deep red. Damir swung the blade in front of him inexpertly before hiding it in his bag before anyone saw him. Moving onward, he passed scattered foragers, as well as townspeople returning from the surrounding forests, many carrying bundles of belongings and followed by children.

At the waterfront, Damir moved along warehouses and homes that had been pillaged and set afire by the retreating troops. Blackened stone walls still stood, but roofs and flooring from upper levels were destroyed. Wooden sheds, stables, and other outbuildings were piles of ash. Where once there was a two-story home, a family – mother, father, and son – was digging through the ruins and separating anything that could be saved. A baby slept in a basket nearby. Like most everyone else outside Korčula's walls, the family had fled long before the ground troops landed. They and the others lost much of their belongings, but not their lives.

Further down the bay, Saint Nicholas Monastery was also severely damaged, but as with the other buildings its stone walls held. The monks had no yet returned to sift through the destruction, and wisps of smoke continued to escape from the blackened woodwork. As Damir rounded the corner along the edge of the monastery grounds, he found a large pile of discarded goods heaped against the wall. Plundered items, he assumed, that on closer examination showed weren't worth bringing onto the galleys. Clothes, crude tools and weapons, empty chests … all too insignificant or heavy to take away. He urged the horse into a trot.

The teenager's trip brought him to Žrnovo, where terraced homes, sheds, and stables hugged a cypress-covered hillside at the edge of broad fields and a stone quarry, and Pupnat, a smaller village that rimmed a modest valley quilted with patches of onions, cabbages, carrots, and other produce, as well as smaller hamlets that might not have even had names. The locals in these villages had heard of the attack and were eager for details, but Damir paused only briefly if at all. At Pupnat, a younger boy, Mate, joined him on the journey west. About halfway across the island, the boy was tasked with alerting Čara and Smokvica, two relatively prosperous villages along the winding main road, while Damir a shortcut to Blato that serpentined along the spine of the island.

The trail Damir followed danced around the mountain peaks of Korčula. As it moved higher, the dirt path meandered out of the pine forests and into expanses of maquis. Even though the low-lying scrub offered better views of the surroundings, the rolling mountains obscured the vista north to the sea until Damir reached the pass he loved, the one that offered twin seascapes to the north and south.

He turned off the trail and climbed the mountainside to see more. To the south, the island of Lastovo reclined in the azure waters, only a mountainous head and the hint of two broad shoulders visible above a calm Adriatic. Northward was Hvar, long and rocky. Damir had already passed the western tip of the Pelješac Peninsula, and the narrow channel had widened to a ten-mile stretch of sea between the islands. An expanse big enough to hide a fleet ten times, a hundred times the size of the one that attacked Korčula.

Damir stopped on a rocky outcrop to rest the horse, which he had begun calling, Vilko, and to eat the ham Iskra's mother had packed. The waters on both sides were mostly flat and still like the steel along the length of a sword. Occasional ruffles betrayed currents below the restful surface. The sky and sea formed a tapestry of uncounted shades of blue, interrupted only by the rugged outlines of the islands north and south.

Alone, the teen pulled the sword out of his carry sack. The blade was maybe a yard long and curved with a slight S shape. A small indentation followed its length, making the blade lighter and faster. The hilt was thick and wrapped with leather strips, and it had a round end that reminded Damir of a garlic bulb. Dried blood discolored the blade near the guard and the hilt itself. Damir wanted to play with the sword, swish it around a bit, but the scarlet stain made him hesitate.

Like any villager, Damir was no stranger to blood. He had helped his family slaughter animals for almost as long as he could remember. This blood was different, though, and Damir gazed at it like a soothsayer staring into a crystal ball. Since it was on the grip, Damir thought, it was likely the blood of the Ottoman soldier who carried it. But what happened to the soldier? Was he shot by an arrow? Hit by a cannon ball? Had he survived? Maybe he had just dropped the sword as he dragged a fallen comrade to safety?

With an effort of will, Damir pushed these thoughts away and grabbed the sword by the hilt, forcing himself to forget about the blood. He swung the twice-curved blade through the air a few times. The sword moved lithely, even in the olive picker's inexperienced hands. Damir carved Xes into the clear mountain air until he stopped suddenly. For a moment, he saw himself as a spectator and saw a boy playing a man's game. In an uncomfortable instant, he returned the sword to his carry bag and took out the smoked ham and bread.

"Vilko, this is great ham," Damir said after a few minutes. He scanned seascapes on either side of the ridge for any movement and let his thoughts drift back to Korčula. "What do you think Iskra told her mother and her brother about me? Probably nothing, right? She barely talked to me last night after it was all over. She seemed upset. Maybe I did something wrong? But Nikola said she's like that. Once she takes on a duty, is convinced of something, she just barrels ahead. She hugged me this morning, though, and that was nice. But why couldn't she make time for me last night? I mean, except for the battle and everything. But I'll get to see her again when I bring you back. Do you think Father Anton planned that?

Probably not. He's a priest."

Vilko listened patiently as the monologue lasted almost an hour. Occasionally the pony neighed an understanding response. Otherwise, he let Damir do the talking. All the while, the teenager watched the waters north and south. He saw no ships. A stray thought eventually interrupted his musings over Iskra: Could the galleys have already passed before he reached this lookout? With a flash of panic, thinking he should have continued to Blato with haste rather than watch for the Turkish fleet amid daydreams, Damir scrambled down the slope with Vilko, met the small trail, and pushed forward.

By late afternoon, Damir arrived at Blato, finding it safe and secure from raiders and eager to hear of the battle at Korčula. He sat on the steps of All Saints Church as villagers brought bread, cheese, and wine and quizzed him on every detail. Klaro's mother was especially relieved to learn her son was uninjured. Ivan the cartman, less mobile in his later years, pressed Damir for every detail he could remember about the galleys and the troops, their banners and weapons.

With Blato's curiosity sated, Damir rushed to Bradat to see his own family. As soon as Damir emerged from the forest and came into view, his mother ran down the path and almost pulled him from Vilko in her eagerness to reach him. Her hugs would have broken the bones of a smaller man. At home, his father smiled widely from a chair on the ground floor. The wound in his leg wasn't healing well and had begun to turn an evil color. Everyone in the village came to their house to hear Damir retell the story of Korčula, the younger children suitably in awe at Damir's cannon skills and the souvenir sword.

It was late by the time the villagers left and Damir and his family lay down for the night. But first, Damir pounded nails into the wall above his bed and hung the Turkish blade he took from the field. With this, he thought, no one will doubt his stories. The peacefulness that settled over Bradat was a sharp contrast to the excitement Damir had left in Korčula. As he drifted to sleep, the only sounds were the crackling of the dying fire downstairs and the lonely unanswered "Chuke" of a small owl somewhere among the nearest trees.

By sunrise, the hero of Korčula had become just another olive grower to everyone but a few local children. The attack, of course, was still the talk of the village, but there were trees to prune and terraces to clear. With his father laid up in bed, Damir had to work extra hours to make sure the family didn't fall behind. Damir couldn't remember his dad ever staying home when there was work to be done in the groves. His mother assured him that the wound would heal with time, but her voice lacked its usual cheerfulness. She stayed near the house, tending the vegetable patches and goat, while Damir headed north where he and his father had started clearing land for a new hillside grove and building the dry stone walls that kept the soil from washing away from the terraces. Next spring, they would begin planting a new arm of the Nikoničić fields, and the trees would be ready to bear dark, juicy olives in a few years. As he carried his tools and lunch up the hillside, some of the younger boys tagged behind him, asking endless questions about the galleys and the cannon and the Turks.

Olives were sturdy trees that grew readily on the rocky hillsides that marked this end of the Korčula. But islanders had learned long ago that they grew best in terraced groves, with low, stone walls, held together by nothing but their own weight, keeping the soil from washing away in the rain and slowing the water from running off. Building the terraces was a laborious job that – as Damir's father repeated so often it was a family joke – didn't get any easier by waiting. With hammer, shovel, and pick, Damir broke the stone along the hillside, piling the flat pieces onto walls about as wide as a forearm and as high as a man's knees. He filled in gaps behind the wall with ground he dug out while leveling the next terrace down. The young boys from Bradat helped, in their way, placing smaller stones among the heavier ones that Damir stacked.

The work was tedious and time passed slowly without his father's jokes and company. Damir and his sapling crew stopped to eat and rest in mid-afternoon, when the sun was hottest, and then continued one rock at a time. The sea teased them from below. Far down the hillside, the cool, blue waters reached from shores of Korčula across to Hvar, interrupted only by Šćedro, a bump in the water with a small Dominican monastery. As the boys wandered off to play, Damir sat on the half-built wall and struggled with the temptation to race down the hillside himself and answer the gentle waves that were calling him. The water twinkled in the sun, the waves whispered, and Damir stared almost blankly until a movement drew his attention.

From the east, in the direction of Pelješac, four barks – much smaller than the Turkish galleys – were hugging the coastline. They showed no flags or other markings, and Damir thought these could be the boats he saw near the Turkish fleet in Korčula. They were too far away for him to be certain. Under sail in a light wind and in haphazard formation, the ships moved slowly westward. At the mouth of a small unused bay, first one, then the others lowered their sails and rocked to a stop. Damir watched with unease as the ships anchored near a bend of land. The crew showed no sign of leaving their barks.

Damir called the boys back from their frolicking and pointed out the ships. He sent them back to the village to tell their parents what they saw. He told them to make sure someone went to Blato with the news in case another raid was coming. Then, Damir sat on the unfinished wall and watched until the light faded and his bones ached from the cold stone. There was no movement from the ships and no lantern lights beyond their hulls. The crew appeared to have settled in for the night. The last sliver of a waning moon was high among the stars when the young man finally started back to Bradat.

When Damir returned to the hillside just after sunrise the next morning, the barks were gone. He searched for them, following the dirt trails that skirted the coast line toward the western tip of Korčula. The landscape often obscured the view to the sea, but each time he broke from the forest or mounted a ridge he scanned the sea for the four barks. Nothing. The path rounded the tip of the island, where a spirited channel separated Korčula from a small, barren island, then back toward Gradina Bay, where an even smaller islet held Saint John's Church and a bachelor farmer who tended the surrounding crops. Damir waited for low tide and waded across a narrow lick of sea to the islet. He found the farmer tending a tired grove of fig trees struggling on a shallow slope. The farmer told Damir he had seen nothing and invited him to stay for a modest repast. The two sat in the shade of the rounded fig leaves, and as they ate from a basket of late fruit, the farmer pressed Damir for news about the island and the battle in Korčula. He was eager for company, keeping Damir until late afternoon with his questions. All the while, Damir kept his eyes on the sea.

The tide was higher as he crossed from the tiny island back to Korčula proper. Damir had to strip to swim across, holding his simple clothes and carry sack high above the water. He reached the shore and paused. Even this late in the afternoon, the hot August sun beat down on him. Damir had already abandoned the day's work to hunt for the mysterious barks and the sea was again waving to him, an old friend begging for some fun. Damir dropped his bundle under some bushes and surrendered. The Adriatic waters were wonderfully cool, and when Damir dove he could see schools of colorful bream darting through the clear water, always just out of reach. Sea urchins assembled on the rocks that peppered the bottom. Korčula children learned early to avoid them, warned again and again by mammas and bakas with stories of the girl who never walked again after urchin spines drilled deep into her tender sole.

Damir swam and dove as the sun settled toward the horizon. He floated face down on the gentle waves and scanned the sea floor, moving just enough to keep his breath. After several minutes, he found what he was hunting. A squid extended its tentacles furtively from its hiding place beneath a rock. First with one long, sinuous arm, then with another, the squid seemed to pull itself along the floor toward shallower water. Damir floated above, following its progress and moving as little as possible. If he attacked too soon, while the water was still too deep, he would lose his prey. He had to be patient. With water still a few feet deep, the squid disappeared among a cluster of rocks. Damir waited. Again, one tentacle after another emerged, pulling a bulbous head behind them. When the squid reached a stretch of large pebbles beneath shallow water, Damir stabbed his hand toward it and grabbed blindly. He missed, and the squid swam wildly away from the attack and further toward the land. Damir splashed after it, found it nearly beached, and eventually scooped it onto dry land. He caught it while it was still stunned and, with a quick flick, killed it. His mother could fry it with some olive oil and herbs for dinner with when he got home.

Days were long in August on Korčula, and Damir sat on a rock to dry himself in the sun before putting his clothes back on and heading home. The hour before sunset was peaceful on his small, protected bay. Damir listened to the yellow birds in the surrounding woods and the hush of the sea lapping against the shore. In a flat field behind him, large bumble bees hummed among a thick patch of lavender. On the horizon, the silhouettes of Vis and its small cousin, Biševo, became more pronounced as the sky drifted from blue to shades of red and orange. Damir watched the tableau and imagined one day showing Iskra *his* side of the island, *his* bay.

The thought of Iskra took the young man out of his reverie. What was happening in Korčula town? Had the Turks returned? There was little chance that his parents would let him go back to the town immediately, but maybe Karlo had returned to Blato with news. Damir was immediately worried and anxious. Ashamed that he had wasted time, he dressed quickly to tramp home.

As though summoned by these dark thoughts, a single bark emerged from around the northern point and rowed into the bay. Even in the dimming light, Damir recognized it as one of the group he had seen the night before. The bark pulled toward the far shore, and about a dozen men jumped into the shallow water. They were armed with swords and long daggers. One had a musket. They split into groups of two and three and spread out along the sea line. Damir scurried up the hills that circled the bay as one party approached his end of the bay. The men were shouting in a foreign language as they peered into the woods and tromped among the low-lying scrub brush. Raiders, of course, but they didn't seem interested in venturing far inland. Damir stayed still as the men probed along the edge of the trees. He remembered the dead squid on the beach and wondered whether finding it would be enough to send the raiders pushing further into the hills and forest.

A sharp whistle came from the bark, and, after a final glance into the pine woods, the raiders nearest Damir trotted back around the bay. Damir watched quietly as they joined the others and the bark pulled away, toward the colors of the dying sun. He waited until they were out of sight, and then he ran along the bay to the trail that would take him back to Bradat. The sun had fallen below the horizon, but the sky cast enough light for him to find his way. Once on the trail, he could get home almost by instinct, as long as he didn't run into any night animals.

At a slight clearing at the crest of the hill, Damir turned to look back at the bay and see if the bark was still in sight. He saw no lights, not even around Saint John's Church. Perhaps the farmer had seen the raiders, too, and had kept himself hidden. As he strained to see any movement on the waters, he heard scraping near the trail. Damir let out a loud shout and expected to hear an animal scampering away. But there was nothing. Damir shouted again, and again nothing. Jackals and boar wouldn't usually attack a man unless they were frightened. They usually just run away at the slightest noise. Damir took out his knife and listened.

Faintly, he heard whimpering among the low bushes next to the trail. Damir tightened the grip on his knife and inched toward the sound. As Damir neared the bushes, the whimpering – if it was whimpering – stopped. Damir pushed some branches away, ready to attack. He found a boy in strange clothes huddled on the ground. Even in the fading light, the boy seemed exhausted and frightened.

The sodden boy

The boy looked to be no more than fourteen years old. His pantaloons – blue, baggy, and shiny – were soggy and clung to his legs. His white shirt, which hung far below his knees, was also dirty and damp, but still a sharp contrast to his dark skin. His bare feet scraped against the ground as he tried to scoot further away from Damir, and his large eyes stared, unblinking. Cowering against the thicket, he gasped for breath.

For a moment, the scene was frozen: the boy on the ground, backed as far against the maquis as possible, and Damir standing over him holding his knife. Seconds, maybe even a minute, passed.

Then the boy began to sob noiselessly. He tried not to. With all his strength he tried not to, but as Damir watched, the boy's body began to tremble, his eyes became puffy and watery, and tears slid down his cheeks, creating trails in the dirt. Through the tears, he still stared defiantly, silently at Damir.

Damir stepped toward the boy, who flinched impulsively. It was only then that Damir realized he was still holding the small knife. He sheathed it.

"Who are you?" Damir demanded in an overly brazen voice.

The boy sat motionless on the ground.

"Where are you from?"

Still no response.

"Were you with those men? Were they looking for you?"

Damir took a step toward the boy, and the boy seized the chance to dart past the islander. Caught unawares, Damir was knocked into a thorny bush as the boy rushed by him. The boy was already a few yards up the trail before Damir regained his footing and ran after him. The chase was no contest, however. Damir was rested and knew the terrain, while the boy was scared, exhausted, and lost. Damir overtook the boy after just a few paces and tackled him to the ground, pushing his face into a bed of pine needles.

"Stop! I don't want to hurt you," Damir said, pinning the boy down. "Just stop."

The boy struggled weakly, but was soon still again.

"Stop." Damir shifted his weight and, holding tightly to the boy's arm, let his captive sit up. "Who are you?" he repeated and was again answered with silence.

All the light of dusk had drained as the two boys, one almost a man and the other just barely out of childhood, sat uncertain on the hillside trail. Above them, stars began emerging in the clear moonless sky, forming patterns familiar to both. The strange boy stopped struggling, but could disappear quickly into the darkness if he freed himself from Damir's grip.

For his part, Damir wasn't sure what to do next. For a moment, he just sat there holding the strange boy. He obviously couldn't just let the boy go, he thought. He could be one of the raiders who got lost and was left behind. But what if he wasn't? If only he weren't so stubborn and answered Damir's questions.

"There's not much we can do tonight," Damir said with finality. He stood up and pulled at the boy's arm. "Come with me."

The boy didn't move.

"Come on!" Damir jerked the boy's arm harder and dragged him a few feet along the trail before stopping. He sighed. "We can't stay out here tonight."

The boy sat on the trail, as helpful as a sack of unripe olives.

Then, Damir reached into his carry bag with his free hand and pulled out two figs. He put one in the boy's free hand. The boy squeezed the fig tentatively and smelled it. He looked up for a moment, and then stuffed the fig into his mouth whole. He devoured it.

Damir held out the other fig, but pulled it away when the boy reached for it.

"Come on," he said, this time tugging at the boy's arm a little more gently. A moment passed, and the boy stood up slowly. "That's right. Come on." Damir led the boy forward along the trail and gave him the second fig when he followed without resisting.

Damir had played along these trails almost since he could walk. Following them under the dim starlight was no problem. The boy, however, stumbled on roots and scraped against trees, slowing their progress. After about half an hour, they reached a deserted hamlet. The tiny village – at its height holding no more than three families – was abandoned after most of the people there died as a sickness ravaged the island when Damir's father was a boy. The wooden and thatch homes were in ruins, but a stone larder held its ground and most of its roof over the decades.

The storeroom was a round building, maybe four yards wide or so. The walls were made of flat stones, stacked about chest height to a man. It was covered by a slate roof that had collapsed slightly at one edge. A low doorway was the only entrance. As a young boy, Damir had spent many hours playing soldier in this fort. Now, he would play jailer.

"Get in."

The strange boy paused.

"Get in!" Damir pushed the boy to the ground and toward the doorway. Reluctantly, the boy crawled through and into darkness. Damir quickly gathered some dry pine needles and dead wood and followed him in. He took a flint he kept in his sack and made a small fire under the collapsed bit of the roof.

"OK, let's take a look at you," Damir said. The boy had crawled to the far side of the round walls, and Damir handed him a few more figs and some bread from his sack, along with a water skin. Damir sat blocking the entrance to the ruin with his body and watched the strange boy as he ate. From his clothes and skin, Damir guessed he was foreign. He guessed probably Turkish because of the fleet. But how did he get to this side of the island? His slight build showed as his sodden clothes stuck to his skin. He didn't seem strong enough for a galley slave, and besides he didn't have any tattoos like the Spaniard in Korčula.

"What's your name? Were you on one of the galleys? A cabin boy? A sailor?" Damir asked, making waving motions with his hands. "Are you hurt?"

Again, the boy gave no response.

"Where are you from?" More slowly. "How did you get here?"

Minutes passed as the two sat wordlessly, each eying the other intently. The only sound to break the silence was a forlorn and unanswered "Chuke!" from a young owl somewhere in the branches overhead. When the owlet cried a second time, Damir grinned widely.

"CHUKE!" the islander called and waited. The owl was as cooperative as the strange boy. It gave no reply.

"Chuke!" Damir called again.

"Chuke!" came the answer after a pause, whether in response or a coincidence was unclear and unimportant.

"Chuke!" – "Chuke!"

The ritual – one every kid on Korčula passes – continued with mixed participation from the owl until Damir and the strange boy were both laughing. As they caught their breaths, Damir took the opportunity to try again.

"What is your name?" he said, still grinning. "I am Damir. Damir!" And for emphasis, he pounded his chest with his fist. "Damir! You?" Damir pointed to the boy.

The boy looked back. His smile melted from his face as though he just remembered where he was. He returned to his sullen countenance and said nothing.

"Damir! Damir!" And Damir pounded his chest again.

Damir waited, adding a small log to the fire as the silence again expanded. When the boy shifted his weight, Damir looked over expectantly, but was disappointed.

"OK, I'll call you Ali," Damir proclaimed finally, drawing out the first Turkish name he could think of. "Damir." Damir again pounded his chest. "Ali." He pointed to the boy.

"So, what do we do now, *Ali*? Mamma and tata will be worried about me, but it's too late to go home now, especially if I have to drag you the whole way. You're not being too helpful, you know. I'm hungry, though, and I've given you all my figs." Damir shuffled through his bag. "There's some bread left." He ripped the last chunk of bread in half and gave a share to the boy he called Ali.

"You were on those galleys, weren't you? Why did you attack us? We didn't do anything to you. They even sometimes get Turkish traders from Dubrovnik in Korčula. No one seems to care. We're just a poor island here. Barely enough food to feed ourselves, especially when raiders come from the east and north." He looked at Ali, trying to see if he understood any of this. Even though Ali just looked back mutely, Damir felt some relief in talking about the attack. "You know, we don't really like the

Viennese that much, either. They just take taxes, some of our crop. They say our real king is in Austria. But most of us don't care about that. We just work the fields and make wine and olive oil."

Damir poked at the fire, and the sparks brightened the shed for a moment.

"It did give me a chance to show Iskra that I can be more than an olive picker, though. She's a girl in Korčula. She told her family about me. The fight, though, it was awful … and fun at the same time. Was it like that on the galley? How long have you been sailing? Weeks? Months? Was this your first battle? Were you firing a cannon, too? Boom!" Damir made an elaborate gesture with his hands that he thought anyone would recognize as a cannon firing, but Ali just watched, still sullen.

Damir paused his monologue and looked at the boy. In the dimming firelight, Ali could have been just another young kid from his village, dressed funny, maybe, and too quiet for a Bradater, but not that different.

"Did you see dead people?" the islander asked more quietly, pulling a finger across his throat as though that were a universal sign for "dead" among all the world's children. Ali winced. "Everyone just wants to hear about the exciting parts, you know? The cannons. The flags. It's not all exciting, though. There were dead soldiers outside the walls. They were taken away when the army retreated, and I didn't see them up close. Some looked young. I guess the cannon must have killed some of them, huh? I didn't really see. An arrow hit a man next to me. There was a lot of blood, but he didn't die. Others in town did. Did you see people die?"

The wind dropped from Damir's soliloquy, and the teen slumped against the doorway. The fire crackled as the last log settled. The boys faced each other across the derelict storeroom in the growing darkness.

"Oh, well," Damir sighed, finally interrupting the silence. "I guess I should bring you to Blato. The people there will know what to do with you. What will they do, though? Blato was raided a couple weeks ago, you know, and they're still furious. They paid a ransom for the people who were taken – some cows and sacks of grain, tata said – but some people died in the attack. They say the bandits were from Herzegovina. That's Turkish territory, right? Some people might hold that against you. Maybe they'd be right.

We're not going to be catching those bandits or the sultan anytime soon, are we? But we have you."

Damir weighed the events of the night for a moment, brushing the final bits of flaming wood into a mound and trying to see into the boy's thoughts. He exhaled tiredly as the tendrils of his ideas disappeared into nothingness.

"But, then, why were those men chasing you? And why were you hiding?" Damir looked at the boy, uncertain. "What do we do now, Ali? What would Father Anton do?"

And suddenly, as the flames dimmed into embers, Damir had a plan. He would take Ali to Korčula and hand him over to Father Anton. The idea calmed Damir, and he could feel his body and his mind relaxing. Father Anton would know what to do, of course, and Damir would have a reason to return to Korčula sooner rather than later.

"So, that's it, Ali. We'll go to Korčula. We'll leave tomorrow."

The boy called Ali listened to all the talking without any reaction. If he understood any of it, he didn't show it. When the silence lengthened and the embers slowly died, he lay down on the dirt floor. Damir watched, still leaning against the wall at the entrance way. The dim figure across the floor faded into the shadows, and the breeze hushing through the pine branches lulled them both to sleep.

The owlet outside called with a final, pensive, "Chuke."

Garlic and wine

Damir woke up the next morning half wishing that Ali had fled overnight, but as the islander opened his eyes, the strange boy was still in the shed, awake and watchful. Damir rubbed his eyes and stretched as best he could under the low roof. He took a closer look at the boy, now in the morning light.

He was wearing a long shirt and had pulled his knees up under it. The effect was a cone of grimy, off-white cloth with a head poking out the top. The boy had large, brown eyes that dominated his smooth face, and as Damir looked he realized that boy's skin was really not that much darker than his own after a summer under the sun. His black hair was cropped short. His arms were wrapped around his hidden knees, hands with long, slim fingers clasped together.

"What's that?"

At the edge of Ali's sleeve, Damir saw something around the boy's arm, a bracelet maybe. He reached across the shed and grabbed Ali's hand before he had a chance to pull it away. When Damir pushed away sleeve, he saw that it wasn't a bracelet, but a lighter patch of skin that discolored half the boy's left forearm. Ali wrenched his hand away in anger and tried to shuffle away. The storehouse was small, though, and there was no place for Ali to go.

"Sorry," Damir said. "I thought it was gold or something."

Damir scooted back to his place by the door, not sure whether looking for treasure on Ali's arm was an acceptable excuse for pawing at the boy. Would he have stolen the boy's bracelet, he wondered as the two returned to the places they manned all night. Damir protected the exit, and Ali held a position as far away as possible, pulling his loose sleeve well past his wrist.

"Time to go," Damir announced to the silent boy after a

moment. "First, we need to go home, though. I have to let mamma and tata know I'm OK. Then we'll leave for Korčula." Damir started to back out of the storeroom, and then added, "It might be best if no one saw us, Ali. Let's let Father Anton figure out what to do with you."

Damir crawled out of the shed into the fresh morning air and waited. He pushed his head back into the low entranceway. He boy hadn't moved.

"Ali, come on," he called. "I'm not going to hurt you. I'm trying to help you." He motioned with his hands, beckoning the boy forward. "Come on."

When Damir started to crawl back into the shed, Ali stiffened. A heavy sigh escaped Damir as he stopped, his legs still poking out from the door.

"We have to go," he said, slowly. "We can't stay here. We're not that far from the bay, and those men might be back now that it's daylight. They have all day to search and might start exploring the trails from the cove. Come on before they find us."

Ali looked at Damir and raised his fingers to his mouth.

"I don't have any more figs or bread. I wasn't expecting to be out all night. But there will be food at home. I promise. Let's go, now."

The two stared at each other for a moment. Neither moved. Then, Damir crawled back a few inches, paused, and gestured again for Ali to follow him. Nothing. He crawled another few inches back and, now half in and half out of the shed, gestured again adding a motion of his fingers to his mouth. This time, Ali moved tentatively toward Damir and the door.

"That's right," Damir smiled.

For the second time that morning, Damir crawled out of the shed into the fresh air. And, for the first time, Ali was close behind him.

As soon as Ali cleared of the door, he bolted again – past Damir, past the ruins, down the trail, and back toward the bay.

"Ali!" Damir called, quick on the chase. The island boy was bigger and knew the trails well. Within minutes he had tackled Ali, and the two were again struggling on the ground. Rested, Ali put up a better fight than the night before, but he was still outmatched and soon pinned to the dirt path.

"Stop it!" Damir yelled. "Where are you running to? This is an island. Where by all the saints do you think you're going?" Catching his breath, he added, "Maybe I should just bring you to Blato if you're going to keep running like this."

Damir got up, grabbed Ali by the scruff of his long white shirt. He pulled the boy to his feet.

"No more of that!" he shouted, pushing Ali forward. They marched in formation – Ali in front and Damir just behind, keeping a tight hold of the boy's collar. They followed a narrow dirt path for almost an hour, twisting through pine forests and cypress stands, climbing over hillocks, and stopping periodically to listen if anyone was nearby. They slowed before reaching Bradat and veered away from the trail and through a stand of trees.

Damir motioned Ali to stay quiet – a pointless gesture since the boy had barely made a sound since Damir found him – and they circled along the tree line behind the village. Bradat was a small place. Most of the villagers devoted their time to tending the olive groves that spread from it across rolling hills. Nine families lived there, all working for the Nikoničić family. Low stone houses lined the two lanes that made up the village. The biggest building was a warehouse and barn next to the main trail to Blato. Damir pulled Ali to a stop and pointed to a crude stone house with a goat penned behind it, a neat stack of oil casks, and a vegetable patch.

"That's my house," he whispered and abruptly pulled Ali to the ground, needlessly shushing him.

Some sounds drifted over from the trees to their left. The noise wasn't close and sounded like footsteps on dry leaves ... and someone humming. Definitely not an animal. Damir pulled Ali a little further into the underbrush. He wasn't quite sure why he felt he had to hide the boy. It was likely that Father Anton would simply turn Ali over to the rector when he returns anyway, and he'd be held as a prisoner. Wouldn't the people in his village or in Blato do the same? Damir was vaguely worried that people here would treat Ali roughly, maybe even cruelly, especially after the raid and the attack. He was one of the enemy, after all. But if Damir paraded into the village with Ali, Damir would be a hero twice over: defender of Korčula and victor over ... over a little boy.

If Ali was going to be a prisoner, Damir decided definitively, it would be best if Father Anton took charge of him. Maybe someone could negotiate a ransom, and in the meantime the priest would probably make sure he was treated well. That was all less likely in Blato. For a moment, Damir imagined it could also go badly for Ali even in Korčula – he was a Turk who bombarded the town – but he chased that idea away as best he could.

To their left, about fifty yards away, a young man stepped from the trees, swinging an ax idly. It was Mislav, a villager a couple of years older than Damir and known for shirking his chores whenever he could. Mislav would sometimes disappear for days at a time, especially during harvest season, but he never seemed to get into trouble for it. Damir and his friends said this was because his parents were in charge of the warehouse, keeping inventory and doling out equipment, and no one wanted to upset them. It seemed very unfair, though, since Damir's parents punished him whenever he slacked off, usually with extra chores.

Mislav stopped at the edge of village, knocking some stones from the path with the butt of his axe. He stood restlessly for ten or fifteen minutes, staying at the edge of the woods. Then, a young woman appeared from the far end of the village. The two hurried together into the woods, but not before Mislav cast a last furtive glance along the buildings at the western edge of Bradat.

Damir waited for the sounds of footsteps to fade away and grabbed Ali's arm.

"Let's go"

The two scrambled over a low fence made of woven saplings, past the goat, and through the back door of a weathered stone house into a large open room. Once inside, Damir called out, "Mamma! Tata!"

The family's beds were on the upper floor, under a low slate roof. Damir and Ali heard some rustling above them, then a voice familiar to sons and daughters everywhere.

"Damir Grgić!" his mother shouted. "Where have you been? If you ever disappear like this again, I'll kill you with my own hands and feed you to the jackals! What have you been…"

His mother's broadside stopped midsentence as she descended a rough set of steps and found Damir standing in the open room with Ali by his side. For a moment, the goat bleating outside offered the only sound.

Damir's mother, a hardy woman in a coarse dress and

headscarf, came down the last few steps slowly. She circled the two boys slightly, coming closer to her son, but never letting her stare leave the strange boy.

"Mamma, I found him over near Gradina Bay," Damir began.

He explained how he was swimming when the men sailed in on a bark and searched the shoreline. How he found Ali after they left and he was coming home. How the night came quickly, so he decided they should stay at the old ghost village.

"He hasn't said a word since I found him, not even his name," Damir concluded the story of his adventures. Then he smiled, "I call him Ali."

"Ali, huh?" By then, Damir's mother was sitting on a wooden bench next to a large table in a kitchen that took up almost half the ground floor. She rose to take a closer look at the boy, holding his face softly in her rough hands. She, too, tried to get him to talk, to get his name, but was also met with silence.

"*Ali,*" she mused, drawing out the name almost lyrically. "Well, the first thing we need to do is clean you up and get you some food. You are a sight. Damir, go upstairs and let your tata know you're all right, and tell him what's happened. He was worried. His leg is getting worse, and he can't get around too well right now. I'll take care of … *Ali.*"

"But what if he tries to run again?" Damir asked, hesitating.

"Well, he's not going to get too far naked," his mother said and began pulling the long shirt off Ali. "You just go see your tata."

Damir found his father lying on his bed, the wound in his leg a troublesome color and festering slightly. His father's face was pale, and he looked weak, but he insisted that he was feeling better and would be up and around soon enough. After Damir told his father his tale, a more embellished, longer version than he offered his mother, his father insisted on going downstairs and seeing this foreign boy. The older man limped painfully as he got out of his straw bed, and Damir half carried him as they made their way down the wooden steps to the open room below.

They found Ali sparkling clean. He was sitting on the bench, a course cloth wrapped around him like a skirt. He looked thin and defeated, like a stray cat that had fallen into a well and needed rescuing. Now that he was scrubbed, the mark on his wrist stood in sharper contrast to the dark skin of the rest of his arm. A plate with the remnants of bread and smoked ham sat on the long table before him, next to a mug of goat's milk. They could see Damir's mother through the window, hanging Ali's freshly washed shirt and blue pantaloons to dry in the hot sun.

"Mamma!" Damir cried as he helped his father onto a chair. "We need to go. We can't stay here! Ali needs to get dressed!"

Damir's mother came casually through the back door carrying the empty laundry basket. "Well, let's talk about that."

The ground floor of Damir's home was typical for workers across the island. On one end was the kitchen, with a large fireplace and roughly hewn wooden cupboards. Vegetables and herbs – carrots, onions, garlic, kale, rosemary, lavender, peppers, and other local produce – were stored in one corner, near a slab of smoked ham, pršut, that hung from the rafters. Earthen jugs of wine rested on a small table near the food. Along with the fireplace, the broad table Ali sat at dominated that end of the room.

Most of the ground floor, however, was an open area covered with trampled straw. In bad weather, the family would bring the goat in for protection, but the area was used largely for making their famous olive oil. A massive olive press reigned in one corner, surrounded by its vassals: empty casks and olive bags waiting for the harvest to serve their lord and master. Tools and firewood were stacked along one wall.

"First of all, *Ali* is not going anywhere today," Damir's mother began, stressing the name almost comically as she sat beside him at the table. "The boy is exhausted and needs some rest. I think we can keep him here for a day, at least, while we decide what to do with him."

"I know what to do with him," Damir jumped in. "I'm going to take him to Korčula and let Father Anton take care of him."

"And what do you think Father Anton will do," mamma asked. "I don't know."

"I'll tell you what Father Anton will do," Damir's father said, speaking for the first time since he came downstairs. "He'll turn this boy over to the guard, and that's the same thing we should do. He's a foreigner, a Turk. His people just attacked Korčula, and, my Lord, they would have killed you, Damir, if they got into the city. Praise the saints that that didn't happen. We owe him nothing, and we should turn him over to the watch in Blato as soon as we can.

They'll take care of him. We don't need you going back to Korčula. We need you here. I'll get better, but right now I can't get around too well. There's work in the fields that can't wait. Mamma has her hands full around the house."

"Tata, I would just be gone a day or two. I have to bring the horse back, anyway."

Damir's mother shot her son a look that silenced him.

"Stefano, this is just a boy," his wife said, turning to her husband. "He wasn't about to storm Korčula and take Damir away."

"How do you know that, Marija? I've heard those Ottomans have really young boys in their armies. 'Janissaries' they're called. How do we know he's not one of them or a spy?" Stefano asked, gesturing toward Ali. "They tried to take Korčula once, and failed. God knows how. Maybe they're looking for another way in? Who would suspect a little boy, right?"

Damir's father rose absentmindedly to step closer to Ali, but the pain forced him back on his chair immediately. Marija and Damir both rushed over to help him. His wound was oozing again.

"Let's not get excited, Fanić," the woman said gently. "We have plenty of time to think about this. The boy isn't going anywhere until his clothes are dried. Then maybe we'll take him to Blato. Just sit down and keep the weight off that leg. We're not fighting a war in this house.

"Damir, get your father some wine, some red wine."

As Damir turned toward the kitchen area, he saw that Ali was also on his feet.

"Where are you going?" Damir demanded, moving to block the way to the door.

But Ali wasn't moving toward the door. Instead, still wrapped in the cloth, he moved awkwardly toward Damir's tata. Without uttering a sound, he knelt in front of the older man and looked carefully at the wound. It was just above the ankle and only a few inches long. Although it didn't seem especially deep, the gash refused to heal and a sickly color had started to spread up Stefano's calf. Ali touched the cut carefully, and the man recoiled in pain.

Wordlessly, the boy stood again and shuffled toward the kitchen as the family watched. Ali pointed to a small knife and looked at Marija. She nodded, but shifted protectively in front of her husband, while motioning for Damir to move away from the foreign boy. Ali looked through the produce hanging in the corner and cut off a bulb of garlic. He peeled and minced a few cloves into a wooden bowl. Next, he examined the jugs of wine and chose a fragrant red one. He poured a splash of the wine into the bowl and crushed it all together until he created a thin, purple paste.

Holding his makeshift skirt in one hand and the bowl in the other, Ali returned to the man sitting at the chair. He showed the bowl to Damir's parents and pointed to the wound on his father's leg.

"I think he wants to pour that onto the gash," Damir said.

"He wants to kill me! It's not going to happen."

"Why would he want to kill you, Fanić?" The woman took the bowl from Ali and looked at it very closely, smelling the mixture, and sloshing it around a bit. "It's just our wine and some garlic. Toss in some meat and vegetables, and I could make a nice stew. I don't think Ali was hiding any poisons. At least none that I found when I bathed him."

"I don't know," the man started, "it just seems strange and foreign. If this helps, why didn't the priest do it when he was here yesterday?"

"I think Father Pero came by more to see whether we had any more of last year's oil and less to see how your leg was. He barely looked at you," Damir's mother replied, still rolling the thin paste around inside the bowl. "Well, it might not help, but it's not going to kill you. I'm sure of that. Your leg hasn't been getting better, Fanić, and it could do some good. Who knows? I think we should try it. If demons start bubbling up from it, we'll wipe it off right away."

Stefano hesitated and argued a while longer, but in the end, he agreed, and Damir's mother handed the bowl back to Ali. She gripped a dish rag at the ready as she and Damir leaned close over Ali to watch. Ali turned to them, hovering just above him, and almost smiled.

Damir's father clinched his face as Ali opened the wound slightly and drained the puss. He kept his leg steady. Ali scooped his finger into the garlicky paste and dabbed it onto the cut. He worked slowly and gingerly until the wound was well slathered. Damir and his mother leaned in closer as Ali emptied the bowl.

Stefano's calf was a garish mosaic of colors when the boy finished: ruddy purple around the wound, surrounded by a halo of greenish flesh, and flanked by the earthy brown of the man's sunbaked skin.

"Well, no demons, so it looks like we're fine so far," Marija said, then in a kinder voice. "How does is feel, Fanić?"

"It feels foreign," the man said brusquely, and then conceded, "but it's not hurting any more than it has been."

After about half an hour, Ali wet a rag in a bucket of water and gently wiped the paste from around Stefano's wound. He rinsed the rag in the bucket and went back to sit at his place on the long table in his makeshift skirt. Throughout the entire performance, he hadn't uttered a sound.

'Death to them all'

Not long after Ali wiped the salve from Stefano's leg, a boy from Blato came to the Grgić house, knocking excitedly at the front door. Giovanni Depolo, the son of one of the island's largest landowners, was at his villa in the village, the boy told Marija and Damir when they opened the door. Other villagers who were in Korčula during the battle had now returned, and the young Depolo was having a feast for them all that night in Blato. Damir was invited as a guest of honor.

"Thank Gospodin Depolo for the invitation, and let him know you have delivered his message," Marija said as she started to close the door.

"And your answer?" the boy asked. "The lord insists that Damir attend!"

Marija looked at her son. With Ali in the house, she felt it would be best for everyone to stay put, but it would be nearly impossible to refuse the invitation. And how could she deny Damir his moment in the celebration with the nobility?

"Tell the lord that Damir's father has been injured," Marija started, then caught a flash of disappointment in her son's face. "But Damir will attend the feast if at all possible."

The boy, satisfied with the answer, turned to leave.

"Wait," Damir stopped him. "What's the news from Korčula?"

"The dogs sailed north without returning," the boy reported. "The people who fled into the woods have returned. Most of the nobles are still gone, though. Gospodin Depolo is only here because he was staying at his palace in Blato over the summer."

The family kept Ali hidden while the boy was at the door. As soon as he left, a heated discussion erupted. Stefano wanted Damir to take Ali into Blato that night and turn him over to Depolo and the village leaders. "We need Damir here, especially with my leg busted," he argued, his usual animation stifled by not being able to move around the room. "Damir can't be going to Korčula. He'll be gone for days again. Depolo is a good man. He'll treat Ali fine."

It was the first time Damir's father had said anything good about the Depolo family. Usually, when he talked about the Depoloes, the themes centered on taking an unfair share of their tenant's produce, drinking too much, lording over the villagers, and, especially, building a villa in the middle of Blato that was like "a fist in the eye." Stefano had never before attributed a single positive trait to a Depolo.

Damir started to challenge his father. "You always said the people in Blato were idiots who could barely put a cork back in a wine bottle. And now you want me to take Ali there? And to Little Lord Lush?"

Damir's mother let them both go on for a while before suggesting there was no hurry to make a decision. Ali was too exhausted and weak to go with Damir to Blato, she said, and there would be no harm in waiting another day or two if they decided that's what needed to be done. Besides, she continued, if he goes, this should be Damir's night, and with the feast the village would be too busy to figure out what to do with a stranger washed up on the island.

Ali sat quietly in a corner near the kitchen listening, and once his mother joined the argument, Damir felt sidelined, too. The discussion moved forward quickly, and in the end, his parents seemed to have agreed not to act hastily. If anyone asked, however, Damir would have been hard pressed to say exactly when his father came around to his mother's way of thinking.

Once that was settled, Marija contemplated ruses that might excuse Damir from the feast. In the end, however, the family couldn't disrespect the Depolo invitation. The plan became for Damir to take the horse Father Anton lent him and head to Blato later in the afternoon. He would explain that his mamma had to stay home to tend to his tata and he, too, would have to leave the feast early to help. Of course, Ali would stay put and no mention would be made of him. In the meantime, Damir should milk the goat and attend to his other chores.

By late afternoon, Damir was ready. Wearing a clean shirt his mother prepared him, he rode over familiar paths through woods teeming with small yellow-breasted birds and unseen animals. On horseback, the trip to the inland village took less than an hour. When Damir arrived, the hot day had already begun to cool, and the celebration was well under way. Villagers had arranged tables in the courtyard in front of All Saints Church, and two lambs were roasting on an open spit in the corner that, a month earlier, had served as a makeshift morgue.

The young Depolo was sitting at the head table with Karlo and about a dozen other men from Blato. Damir assumed they had all been at Korčula during the battle, but he only remembered seeing Karlo. He got to the town late, though, and didn't see very many people before the battle began. The wine at the head table had been flowing freely, it seemed, and everyone was in a jovial mood. One of the Blato men spotted Damir and brought him to the table, where Giovanni Depolo clasped him firmly and ordered a mug of local wine for the "valiant young olive boy." The young Depolo congratulated Damir on his heroism and motioned for him to sit with them. But the table was full to bursting. Instead, Damir took a place with some of the younger villagers at a table on one side of the open courtyard.

Even though Damir knew many of the villagers by sight, he didn't travel to Blato often and had no real friends there. Old Ivan the cartman, older than the days when he told stories around the campfire going to Korčula, was sitting next to the spit telling the men turning the lamb what they were doing wrong. The village head was busy moving from table to table, making sure everything was to the young Depolo's satisfaction. A group of musicians with chitarras and pipes were playing folk songs in the corner opposite the roast, while children danced improvised jigs around them. The men and women sitting with Damir were mostly a few years older than him and insisted that he tell his stories from Korčula again, refilling his mug whenever it was empty.

Damir was retelling the story of his and Nikola's first shot at the Turkish army when a commotion rose from the corner with the musicians.

"Božidar! Božidar!" people started yelling and the chant spread across the tables, even reaching the rowdy young lord, who joined in heartily. The lead musician waved his stringed chitarra in

the air above his head, and the ruckus settled down as the crowd
waited for the ballad to begin. First some spirited chords from the
chitarras, then the pipes joined in, and finally the singer burst out,

Božidar kissed his mamma one day.
Told his tata he's going away.
Grabbed his sack.
Threw it over his back.
Tripped on a pig tryin' to make him stay.

The crowd swayed to the old tune, jumping in for the chorus,
and clapping or banging their mugs at the end of each line.

No, no, Bozo, don't you go! (Clap!)
There's seed in the warehouse you gotta sow! (Clap!)
No, no, Bozo, don't you go! (Clap!)
The fields around Blato need your hoe! (Clap! Clap! Clap!)

Some continued to sing into the next verse, while others
formed a chain and skipped around the tables. One of the girls from
Blato grabbed Damir's hand and forced him into the chain.

Božidar walked to Korčula's gate.
Told himself it was gonna to be great.
Went to an inn.
Had a drink or ten.
Lost all his money to a girl named Kate!

The dancing chain collapsed as everyone released their hands
to clap for the chorus. Damir took the opportunity to dart back to
his table, taking a chair the dancers couldn't pass.

Božidar took a ride on a boat.
Got to 'Brovnik by selling his coat.
Looked for a job.
Was beat by a mob.
Slept in the gutter with a cat and a goat.

No, no, Bozo, don't you go! (Clap!)...

Karlo and some of his friends were standing on top of the head table, stomping to the chorus and waving their mugs wildly. They pulled the young noble, wine in hand, up with them just as the final verse began.

Božidar begged for a ride back west.
Got on a galley; you know the rest.
Tata killed a beast
Mamma cooked a feast
Blato's the place that we all love best!

No, no, Bozo, don't you go! (Clap!)
There's seed in the warehouse you gotta sow! (Clap!)
No, no, Bozo, don't you go! (Clap!)
The fields around Blato need your hoe! (Clap! Clap! Clap!)

By the final refrain, most of the dancers had fallen back into their seats, sweaty and tipsy. A few soldiered on, though, and tried unsuccessfully to get the chorus going once again. In the end, the musicians were rewarded with scattered applause as they took a final bow. When the music stopped, the young Depolo stood to speak, and the guests fell silent, except for a baby near Damir who continued to insist on something unknowable.

"Farmers and workers of Blato," the young nobleman began, "Ere but a few days, our beautiful island of Curzola was under attack by the vile Ottoman who had sailed forth with a massive fleet and legions of footmen to pillage what is ours. Gathered around my table this summer's evening..."

Depolo paused and swayed slightly. He motioned vaguely with his mug and looked around at the scores people surrounding him. He took a swig and continued.

"Gathered around my table, I heard many stories of valor and bravery committed by some of our village's most upstanding members. Hear me! They have all brought glory to your dusty hamlet by their deeds against the evil invader from the east. How I wish I had been there with them, shoulder to shoulder to fight off those foreigners, facing certain death to protect our palaces, churches, shops, and homes. Alas, I had been forced away to attend to family matters here at our palace. But I was there in spirit, my friends, and it is with pleasure that I welcome the heroes of Blato to my generous table."

Wine sloshed from his cup as he gestured across the table.

"While the story of each of these valiant men deserves lavish praise, Karlo's gallantry and courage will hold a special place in the chronicles of this village. Karlo, a mere laborer – indeed, I was not aware of him until tonight – held the south wall against the advancing hoard while others cowered. If I were to recite his tale, it would be but a pale reflection of his daring deeds.

"Karlo, tell us all of your feats!" Depolo ordered, raising his mug, bringing it to his mouth, and finding it empty.

Karlo stood, unaccustomed to the attention. He saluted Depolo before beginning a tale that left Damir dumbstruck. In it, Karlo, armed with a borrowed arquebus, fended off almost single-handedly the advancing Turkish infantry and artillery as they neared the southern gate. He started a bit timidly, glancing occasionally at Damir, and quickly found his stride.

At one point, it seemed, Karlo repelled the army with just a strong stare as the janissaries, hungry for blood, were about to breach the wall.

"I must have killed or 10 or 15 of the filthy Turks as they crossed the ditch coming to Revelin Tower," Karlo recounted, his voice loud and true. "Sure, there were others on the wall with me, but I didn't see any of them. That's how it is in battle. All I saw was the wild-eyed vermin charging toward me. 'Death to them all,' I shouted and fired as quickly as I could load. By the end, the cowardly Turks were in retreat, and my musket was so hot it burned my hands. I had to dip it in water to keep it from bursting."

Karlo paused, and someone refilled his mug.

"Death to them all!" he shouted, as people around the courtyard cheered and raised their own drinks.

Then, someone at Damir's table yelled, "Damir, you were there at the south wall, too. What did you see?"

Everyone turned to Damir, but the only person Damir noticed was Karlo, who glared at him challengingly. Amid the crowd in the courtyard, Damir felt eerily alone. His breathing stuttered, and he felt each heart beat pounding through his body. He tried to ignore the question, but it was soon taken up by others at the tables.

"Yes, Damir, tell us."

"What was it like at Revelin Tower?"

Damir gathered his nerve, and stood up, laughing nervously.

"Everybody already knows my story," Damir said softly, only to be stopped by cries of, "Louder!"

"I'm not as good a storyteller as Karlo. Everyone already knows what happened with me," he began again, almost shouting. "I was high up on the Revelin Tower, helping with a cannon. I could barely see over the parapets, and I couldn't see most of the people defending from the walls. As Karlo said, you stop seeing everything around you as soon as the fighting begins. There was a lot of shooting and a lot of death. In the end, we won."

Karlo smiled at Damir, one conspirator to another, and raised his mug before any more questions were asked.

"Death to them all," he repeated, raising his wine high, still looking hard at Damir.

Damir obliged, responding with the others, "Death to them all!" Then he sat back on his bench, neglecting the others at the table while slabs of lamb dripping in its own juices, trays of local vegetables, and more wine were brought around. As those around him dug into their food, Damir was surprised how quickly the conversation turned to the routine, even mundane, events of village life. A huge sow had gotten loose and dug through a neighbor's garden, ruining the crops. The owner was horrified and promised a piglet from the next litter to make up for the damage. A new baby was crying all night long, and his parents should do something about it so people could get some sleep.

At the head table, Gospodar Depolo was laughing madly with his guests, and Karlo, at his side, made extravagant motions with his hands. Damir noticed vaguely that Mislav from Bradat had also come for the feast and was sitting on a wine keg behind Karlo, roaring with the others. Life just isn't fair, Damir thought as he watched them. He should be there sitting next to the young nobleman, getting drunk on his wine, and telling real stories of what happened in Korčula. Instead, there's Karlo, who hid in the cathedral cellars while the Turks surrounded the town, and his buddy Mislav, who's never done his share of work. They're laughing and toasting, while Damir sits listening to stories about escaped pigs and crying babies.

Damir looked deeply into his mug of wine, swirling it a little. Maybe he should get Ali right now, he thought as the wine formed ripples that crashed around the brim. If he brought Ali, the young Depolo would see who the real hero was. Imagine that. A real Turk right here in the middle of Blato. No one would question Damir's courage and bravery, and they'd all be shouting "Živjeli!" to him. Tata would be proud, and they wouldn't have to worry any more about what to do with Ali. Damir drained his mug, and the girl across from him, the one who had pulled him into the dance, immediately filled it again. Good riddance, he thought, he's an enemy.

"Death to them all," Damir mouthed the words and glowered at Depolo and Karlo.

The old cartman

Even though the sun lingers stubbornly during the summer on Korčula, the first stars were already poking through the eastern sky by the time Damir had eaten his fill and stood to leave the feast. He looked at the head table and considered taking his leave formerly. Giovanni Depolo was quite drunk, as were most of the men there, and Damir decided no one would notice one way or the other. He moved through the shadows at the edge of the courtyard toward where he left Vilko, steadying himself occasionally against a wall.

"Are you all right there, young man?"

Damir turned and found Old Ivan still sitting at his perch near the empty spit and its dying embers.

"Sit down and have some water," Ivan offered. "It's a long way back to Bradat, and you should catch your breath before starting out. I don't think that old pony of yours will find its way on its own. It's the church's horse, right?"

It had been years since Damir last met Ivan on the road to Korčula, and the cartman looked much older than Damir remembered. In Damir's mind, Ivan's face was always crisscrossed with deep wrinkles. Now, it seemed thin and shrunken, too. Thin rivulets of white hair cascaded onto his shoulders. The old man ladled some clear water into a mug and handed it to Damir, along with a chunk of bread.

"Um, the horse? Yeah." Damir absentmindedly sat on the bench with Ivan. He looked back at the head table, thinking he should be ending the feast there and not with this old man.

"I wish I had been in Korčula for the battle," Ivan said in a voice that hadn't lost any of its vigor. "Then I would have had my own stories to tell the grandkids, not just passing on the ones that my deda told me. But my legs aren't what they used to be, and I don't travel that well anymore." Ivan tapped a rough cane resting near him. "It's been a while since I've been out of Blato. I hid in an empty barn during that raid, behind a stack of hay."

The two sat quietly for a moment, and then Damir looked up at Ivan. "Well, don't believe the stories Karlo is telling."

"Karlo?" Ivan snorted? "I don't think anyone expect drunken Gianni believes a word he's saying. They say when the raiders came a few weeks ago, Karlo ran out of his house so fast he knocked over his own grandmamma as he pushed past her in the doorway. Ha! They're just happy Gianni has an excuse to break out some wine barrels and slaughter two of his lambs. Those Depoloes love a feast, but the village is rarely invited, except as servers and cooks, of course. So, živjeli!"

Ivan raised his own mug of water in a mock toast with Damir.

He glared at the mug. "It's also been years since my daughter-in-law would let me have more than a drop or two of wine. She says I'm insufferable for days afterward and one day I'm going to fall and break something," Ivan lamented. "It's a shame, really. We make some excellent red wine here…. Have some more bread."

Damir nibbled on the bread. From nowhere, he asked, "Do you hate the Turks?"

Ivan looked closely at Damir before he answered.

"Of course, I hate the Turks," the cartman eventually responded, "just like my deda hated the Spanish Aragons and some ancestor before him hated the Genoese. His Serenity in Venice tells me to hate the Turks because they interfere with his trade ships in the Adriatic, so I hate the Turks. Next year, maybe he'll have made peace with the Turks and tell me to hate the Hapsburgs because they support those raiders in Senj. And then I'll hate the Hapsburgs. That'll be a little harder, though, because you know we gave them the Crown of Croatia a while back. A lot of good it did us."

He paused and held Damir's eyes in a hard stare.

"Young man, for hundreds of years, knights from Europe sailed over to Ottoman lands – invading, burning, conquering – just because a pope or a king told them to. And now, the Turks are over here because a sultan told them to – invading, burning, conquering. I'll tell you something, we'd all get along just fine if the kings and sultans just fought among themselves and left the rest of us alone.

"So, yeah, 'Death to them all!'" Ivan raised his water again, this time with a slight grin that made Damir wonder who Ivan meant by *all*. Ivan stirred the embers with his cane, raising a fountain of sparks in the darkening night. The two watched as the shower played out.

"Do you think there's someone in some Ottoman village somewhere drinking his wine with friends and shouting 'death to them all,' too?" Damir asked.

"I don't know," Ivan replied, looking absently around at the other tables. "They tell me Muslims aren't supposed to drink wine or anything else strong. So maybe there's a Karlo sitting around a campfire outside Tripoli or Tirana or somewhere with a flask of cool water shouting, 'Death to them all!' If so, I hope they at least have some nice meat on the fire for the others who have to listen to such cow dung. At least we got some pretty good lamb out of it. And zucchini and peppers.

"What do you care what's going on in some Ottoman village anyway?"

Damir felt himself flush. He had agreed with his parents – his mother anyway – not to mention Ali to anyone. Damir hoped his blush was hidden by the ember's dying glow. Anyway, Ivan wasn't even looking at him. The old man was watching as the crowd thinned from the courtyard.

"I guess just seeing the Turks at Korčula got me thinking." He waited for Ivan to say something, and when Ivan didn't, Damir rushed to fill the silence. "During the battle, they were the enemy, and I don't think anyone thought twice about firing the cannon and shooting their muskets. They charged; we fired. Simple. And people died. Then, as I was riding home, I started thinking that I could have died, too, and it struck me how sad mamma and tata would have been."

Damir paused before continuing, looking at the ancient cartman as he decided what to say next. Ivan had turned back to Damir and was listening intently.

"Well, I don't know, they all looked so young. I started thinking that those dead Turks had mammas and tatas, too, or maybe children. But they're the enemy, right? They came here to kill us."

"Most of them," Ivan started slowly, "probably came here because someone told them to. Maybe for the loot, too, I guess, or maybe because they were forced from their own villages to work the oars or be soldiers. It's the same on both sides. Just a few months ago, the Venetians came through Blato looking for volunteers for their ships. They made it pretty clear that there was no option not to volunteer, at least not until they got the number of young men they wanted. Everyone who joined was promised a share of booty, but most would rather have stayed by their warm fires and their mamma's cooking.

"No, the only ones who really want to go somewhere and kill someone are the kings and doges and the sultans and the viceroys. They look at a map and see a piece of land that used to be theirs or could be theirs or, worse still, should be theirs, and they send their ships and troops over and hope for the best. Most everybody else is just trying to get back home with most of their limbs."

Ivan leaned in to Damir and almost whispered, "So, yeah, death to them all, and let the rest of us pick olives and take them to market or whatever else it is that we would rather be doing wherever we are." Then louder, "By all the saints, what I would give for another taste of good red wine."

Damir noticed how dark it had become and suddenly rose from the table.

"Mamma's gonna kill me!"

He hastily said goodbye to the cartman, asking him to pass his greetings to the rest of the family, and rushed out of the courtyard to where he had left Vilko. Just as he was mounting the church horse, Karlo and Mislav came around the corner of a house. Karlo was steadier and more controlled than Damir would have guessed.

"Leaving so soon?" Karlo asked. "There's still a lot more drinking to do. The generous Giovanni Depolo, heir to this estate, has promised to bring out a cask of anise rakija, the finest anisette on the island, he says. All for the heroes of Korčula who stay and give him a reason to keep drinking. You won't want to miss that."

Even though he had been drinking all night, Karlo seemed keen and watchful. Mislav teetered noticeably behind him. Damir didn't know for certain whether the meeting was a coincidence or something more sinister.

"Mamma wants me home early. They have chores for me in the morning."

"A hero of Korčula has chores? That cannot be so! I'll have a word with Gianni, if he has any sense left in him he'll send a messenger to your mamma. Surely she wouldn't defy such a noble man."

"No, no. I really have to go. Give the young Depolo my regrets."

"Ha! He doesn't want your regrets. He wants more people to drink with. If everyone leaves, he'll just stumble to bed and lock his storerooms behind him. What's so important about your chores tomorrow, anyway? Your mamma's a fine woman. She can handle weeding and fetching water without you for a morning."

"Actually, well, I have get this horse back to Father Anton. He said he needed it before Sunday. I don't want him angry at me. You know how priests are," Damir said as he nudged the horse forward.

"That old archdeacon has plenty of horses, but if you want to play his footman, I guess no one's stopping you." Karlo grabbed the bridle so Damir couldn't leave quite yet. "You were smart back there during the feast when they asked about the fight. It wouldn't be smart to suddenly get dumb."

"I was just firing the cannon. That's all."

"Then off you go, smart boy," Karlo let go of the bridle and gave Damir a jaunty wave. "To mamma!" Karlo and Mislav turned back around the corner and strolled out of sight humming the tune to Božidar.

The emerging moon – a thin crescent like the grin with a secret – gave Damir enough light to find his way home over familiar paths. But still, progress was slow and he didn't arrive until late. There were only a few windows in Bradat lit with firelight and lantern. Most of the people in the village slept early and woke early, getting as much work in between dawn and dusk as possible.

Damir's mother met him at the door and brought him inside. Ali was sitting in the shadows on the kitchen side of the room, back in his clothes, now clean. Damir's father was still in his chair.

Damir told everyone about the feast, the food and the drink, what Giovanni Depolo said, and what everyone wore. He told them about Karlo's boasting, and his mother agreed that it was best to let drunken men have their moment. He assured his mother that he didn't drink too much. While recounting the events, he skipped over the encounter later with Karlo and the entire conversation with the cartman. He wasn't certain why he kept these as his secrets, but it was late and he was tired. The important point was that he told no one about Ali.

Marija and Stefano Grgić were proud of their son, a hero of Korčula who had been feted by the Depolo family. And they had news of their own.

"Your tata's leg looks like it is getting better," Marija said, her voice brighter than it was that morning. "Look!"

It was hard to see in the firelight, but the wound looked drier than it had been earlier, and Damir's father insisted it hurt less.

"We put some more garlic and wine on it a while ago," Damir's mother said. "Tata still can't stand well, but, praise the saints, it does look like it's finally started to heal. Ali keeps holding up two fingers, so I think we're supposed to do this twice a day. Well, we'll see. I'm going to have to dig up some more garlic bulbs."

Damir noticed his mother had stopped stressing "Ali" so comically. He turned to where Ali was sitting near the herb cabinet and held up two fingers. Ali responded, holding up two fingers and smiling slightly.

"What happens to Ali now?" Damir asked as he turned back to his parents. "The people in Blato are all worked up, especially after listening to Karlo all night. They were all getting drunk, but you should have heard them. 'Death to them all! Death to them all!' Maybe…"

"We're not going to take Ali to Blato," Stefano interrupted firmly. "They're just a bunch of island dullards there, not a good mussel among them. OK. Maybe with a couple of exceptions. Those hotheads would probably hand Ali over to that Depolo boy, and nothing good would come of that. He'd parade Ali around like some war trophy. As I always said, we need to get Ali to Korčula and Father Anton. He's a smart man, knows the world. He'd do the right thing."

"But I thought you said you needed me here," Damir asked.

"We'll get by. My leg's getting better, and there really won't be much work until it's time to gather the olives. You better be ready and rested by then, young man."

"Now, Fanić, it's still going to be days at least before you're fit and on your feet again. I don't want you to overdo it and end up back in bed, leaving all the work for Dado and me. If you promise to rest and let me take care of that wound of yours, though, I think you're right. Dado should take Ali to Korčula as soon as possible."

"He should leave in the morning. I don't know how long we can hide Ali here. You can't break an egg in Bradat without everyone coming by for a piece of cake."

And without any more discussion, it was decided. Damir would leave with Ali just after sunrise. They'd take the main road for most of the way across the island. There shouldn't be many others traveling this time of year, but they would take smaller paths around the villages and try to avoid people. If anyone saw them and asked, Damir would say Ali was a houseboy being taken back to Korčula. With both of them on the horse, they should get there easily by the end of the day.

With a plan settled, everyone headed upstairs to get some sleep. There were only two beds, and Damir would have to reluctantly share his with Ali. Marija led the way with a lantern, and Damir helped his father up the wooden stairs. Ali followed.

As soon as Ali reached the top of the stairs, he saw the Turkish sword hanging from the nails above Damir's bed, glinting in the lamp light. His face changed immediately, moving in a moment from friendly to dour. He stood at the landing and looked at the suspended sword.

"It's, well, a memento, I guess, a reminder," Damir tried to explain to the unlistening Ali. "I picked it up as I came home. It doesn't mean anything, really. Um, it's late. Let's go to bed."

Damir tried to lead Ali to his bed, but the foreign boy pulled away. He withdrew to a corner away from the bed, where he lay down on the hard, pine floor. No amount of coaxing from Damir or his parents could entice him into the bed, and he only grudgingly accepted the blankets that Marija offered him.

Back to Korčula

Damir and Ali left Bradat at day break the next morning and were about two hours out of the village when they stopped to give Vilko a rest. They had just passed the eastern outskirts of Blato and, so far, had not seen anyone else on the road. Not a word had passed between them over the miles. Ali had let Damir's mother hug him before they left, but otherwise the boy was even quieter than before, if that were even possible. Damir took out some of his mother's bread, pulled off a chunk, and gave it to Ali.

"The sword," Damir said, making a vague slashing motion without enthusiasm, "I just picked it up, that's all. I didn't kill the guy or anything. Well, I don't think I did. You don't really know with a cannon, do you? I just picked it up."

Ali sat wordlessly, staring steadfastly away from Damir. He pecked at the bread and sipped from the flask of water they shared. Though it was early, the August sun was already starting to bake the island. No breeze brought relief, and the cloudless sky foretold that it would just keep getting hotter. The shade of the cypresses and pines that lined the trail brought only marginal respite when the winds were so calm.

"It's going to be hot today. We'll have to rest the horse often, and maybe walk with it for a while. I'm not sure how we're going to get water for Vilko if we don't go into a village. It hasn't rained for days, and there are no rivers or lakes on the island."

Damir's monologue was interrupted by sounds coming from down the trail in the direction of Blato. Whoever it was would be coming around the bend soon.

"Quick! Hide!" Damir whispered loudly. When Ali didn't react, Damir took him gruffly by the shoulder and pushed him into the bushes. "Hide!" Damir motioned downward with his hands, and Ali moved further off the trail and scrunched behind the foliage.

The noises grew louder – unhurried footsteps, an occasional cough – until a young man Damir didn't recognize came around an ancient fig tree and into view.

As he got closer, the man slowed, and the two exchanged greetings.

"The sun's burning down today," said the stranger, a workman, judging by his dress. The man was notably short, barely reaching Damir's shoulders, but he was stocky like a woodsman.

"That's true."

"Where are you going? I was visiting a cousin outside Blato, but heading back to Pupnat now. It'd be nice to have some company on the road. It makes the time pass faster, and you can almost forget about the god-forsaken heat."

As Damir hesitated, he noticed Ali's half-eaten bread lying next to the trail. He moved slightly to block the man's view of it.

"I'm not going nearly that far," Damir said, "just to a village a few more miles down the road."

"Even a few miles are better than nothing!"

"I don't want to hold you back. You have a long journey ahead of you, and I need to give this nag a chance to rest," Damir patted Vilko's snout to show which horse he meant. "This heat really gets to the old boy."

The man looked as though he was going persist, and then thought better of it.

"We all have our own rhythms. Have a safe journey." The stranger lingered a moment longer and, with a wave, continued eastward.

There was a rustling in the maquis, but Damir motioned for Ali to stay put. The sounds of the stranger slowly faded. Damir waited for several minutes before he called quietly to Ali. The boy crawled from among the low bushes, looking nervously down the trail.

"We'll have to walk with Vilko for a while, otherwise we're going to catch up with that man pretty quickly." Damir said, mostly to himself. "But we'll never get to Korčula by nightfall if we have to walk the whole way. Once we get close to Smokvica, we'll turn off the main trail and go through the mountains. It's shorter, but more rugged. With the horse, though, we should be able to get ahead of him. We want to avoid the villages anyway."

The two gathered their kit and walked in silence down the trail. After about half an hour, two men emerged from a trailside grove, blocking the path. One was Karlo from Blato. The other was much older and no one Damir recognized. Both had short swords hanging from their belts, a detail Damir couldn't miss. A moment later, two other men – Mislav and the stranger going to Pupnat – jumped onto the road behind Damir and Ali.

"Damir! I was hoping I would find you. I wanted you to meet my friends," Karlo cried jovially. "We were worried you would run into trouble taking that horse back to Korčula alone. But … it looks like you're not alone."

Karlo glanced at the older man next to him and stepped forward to get a closer look at Ali.

"See? I told you!" Mislav yelled from down the trail. "I told you I saw some strange clothes hanging behind little Dado's house! He's always up to something."

"Shut up," Karlo ordered, and turned back to Damir with a slight sneer in his voice. "These are strange clothes, and a strange little boy. Damir, who is this strange little boy?"

Damir stepped back slightly, pulling Ali with him.

"Him?" Damir answered, trying to keep his voice steady. "He's a servant from Saint Mark's. Father Anton sent him to tell me to bring the horse back. I told you yesterday Father Anton wanted it back. He's just a houseboy, I guess. Who knows where he's from."

"A houseboy, huh? I've seen a lot of servants, most of them from the mainland and the villages here. I don't remember seeing one quite so dark. Boy, what do you do for the archdeacon?"

Ali said nothing.

"Come on, boy. Answer me!"

"He doesn't talk."

"No?"

"No," Damir answered, adding after a pause, "Maybe he can't or maybe it's a religious vow or something. Father Anton says there are some monks who don't talk. I can't a get a word out of him."

"He doesn't look too religious to me. What do you think, fellows?" Karlo laughed, and the men blocking the trail in both directions joined him. He stopped when an idea struck him. "If he doesn't talk, how did he give you a message from Father Anton?"

"It was a written message."

"You can read?"

"Father Anton taught me how."

"Let's see it."

Damir made a show of looking through his carry sack, pulling out bread and wrapped cheese. Meanwhile, the men with Karlo had stepped closer, hemming in Damir and Ali further.

"I don't have it. I guess I left it at home. I'll show you when I'm back at Bradat."

"Yeah, show me when you get back home to your mamma and tata. What's his name?"

"I don't know. The note didn't say."

Karlo looked again at the man behind him. He was the best dressed of the four, with a leather jerkin and a finer sword.

"No matter," Karlo said to Damir, smiling. "We're just here to help you get that horse back to Korčula safely. These roads are dangerous, you know, and bandits can be waiting around any bend for a fine steed like this. We'll take the horse to town for you. You can run back home to your mamma's aprons. And, I'm sure there are olives that need picking. I'll personally make sure the nag gets to Father Anton."

Damir started to protest and was cut short when the man with Karlo interrupted.

"We'll bring the houseboy, too," he said, speaking for the first time. He had stepped level with Karlo. He spoke slowly, a deep rasp enveloping each word. "I'm sure the father will be anxious to get his fragile servant back. He must be missed greatly."

"Thanks, but I have to go to Korčula anyway to get something for the groves, some tools. Gospodar Nikoničić wants us to finish the terraces by winter, and our shovels are old."

"It's a long time before winter," the man said, edging closer to the Damir and Ali. "You should wait for a day when it's not so hot."

Damir tried to laugh. "Who knows when that will be, huh?" He suddenly grabbed Ali's hand and yelled, "Run!" Ali made no move, and Damir had to push him toward the bushes. As they turned, though, they found Mislav and the stranger just behind them. The men grabbed the boys before they had any chance of fleeing. Damir and Ali struggled briefly, but there was no hope of breaking free.

The older man came closer for a better look at Ali. He grabbed the boy's face and moved it from side to side, felt the texture of his shirt, and looked closely at his hands. The leader paid special attention to the birthmark on Ali's wrist.

"These aren't the hands of a houseboy," he said absently. "Who are you? What are you?" He stepped back to get a full view of the foreign boy. "This changes things, lads. We might end up with more than just a scrawny horse today."

The older man idly went through Damir's carry sack and stroked Vilko on the muzzle as he thought.

"Lads, we're going to Korčula," he announced. "If the rector's back, he might pay a price for this stranger. Mislav, you take the horse back to camp and wait for us. We'll be a couple of days. Mali, Karlo, we'll take this boy to Korčula with the boat. We don't want to meet anyone on the road. Too many questions."

"Boss, what do we do about Dado ... about Damir?" Karlo asked.

The man's brows furrowed as he inspected Damir.

"We could kill him, but that seems ... unnecessary," the boss answered eventually. "But we can't let him go right away, either. He might run and tell someone and ruin everything. That Father Anton could convince the rector we don't deserve any reward for our efforts."

After mulling the options for another moment, he continued, "We'll take him with us. When we're done, we'll let him go. He'll stick to the story we give him, just like he stuck to your wonderful story at the feast. Otherwise that could be, well, unfortunate. Right, *Dado*?"

Damir stared in reply.

"Good. I'm glad you agree. Who knows? Maybe after a few days with us, you'll want to join our little group. It's quite fun. Let's go!"

The six turned back toward Blato with Mislav leading Vilko. Soon – indeed, just after the point where Damir first met the stranger – they parted ways. Mislav and the horse continued down the road, while the rest turned onto an almost invisible path northward. Karlo led the way, followed by Damir and Ali, with the boss and the stranger called Mali in the rear. Occasionally, Mali would give one of the boys a shove to keep them moving.

The path twisted along the contours of the hills and mountains before dropping steeply toward the coast. As they descended, a small bay came into view. The cove was surrounded mostly by rugged, forested hillsides and opened to the sea through a narrow passage. The still water mirrored all the shades of green around it. Then the cove disappeared again as the trail ducked under the tall pines once more.

The next time the fivesome emerged from the woods, it was near the water's edge. They circled the cove until they came to a small boat grounded beneath some trees and secreted under loose branches. The shade from the trees made the cove somewhat cooler, but the humidity hung heavily in the unmoving air.

"Here we are, lads. Let's get this glorious vessel into the water. We'll catch a breeze once we're in the channel. We'll get to Korčula in no time." He wrapped an arm each around Damir and Ali and pulled them close. The boss looked up at the bright sun. "What a day to be on the water, right boys? Let's go sailing."

Pleased to meet you

The boat was much smaller than the barks Damir had seen in Gradina Bay. It had locks for four oars on each side and space for maybe a dozen men. The wood along the gunnels was chipped and splintered, while small, ominous pools of water sloshed among the bottom boards. A single mast near the bow was rigged with a modest triangular sail, discolored, torn, and sewn together awkwardly. Even once they left the bay, the sail hung limply as the air remained calm and useless.

The boss ordered his men and the captives to take the oars, while he took the tiller. At first, progress was slow. Damir and Ali kept locking oars with the others or skipping their blades across the surface of the water. After much shouting and threatening, they began coordinating their strokes better with those of Karlo and Mali, and the small craft moved furtively eastward. It was hot work under the bare sun.

The trip to Korčula was a sudden decision. No one had prepared provisions, and soon they had emptied their water flasks. Adding to the troubles, as the boat entered the Pelješac Channel, the current was against them and grew stronger. Four weary oarsmen in a boat built for eight fought water's flow, and at best they reached a stalemate.

"This is useless," Karlo complained.

"Shut up, you lazy pig, and row harder! All of you!" the boss bellowed in his gravelly voice. He scowled at a particular rock formation as they inched past it. The rocks, staring down from a jagged hillside, mocked their efforts and stayed stubbornly ahead of the boat. Suddenly the boss jerked the tiller into a starboard turn. "Spawn of Lazarus! We're not even halfway to Korčula!"

It took almost half an hour to maneuver the little craft into a small cut on the shoreline and anchor it off a rocky beach. The five waded onto land and sat exhausted in the narrow shadow of a stone crag on the western edge.

"You two, hurry up and get your wind. There's a fishing village east of here, I'm not sure how far. You should be able to fill the water flasks there. Smile, and be nice. On the way out, maybe you can palm some food if there's no one about. Don't raise an alarm, though. I'll stay here with the boys and make sure they don't go anywhere. Now, go."

Once they were alone, the boss sat next to Damir and Ali on a sun-bleached log.

"At least it's a little cooler here. It was hell on that boat," he said, trying for a tender tone that was just outside the reach of his rasp. He scooped up some small stones and tossed them one by one into the azure water. He offered one to Damir, who refused. The leader was a tall, gaunt man. His face, a skull covered with tight, sun-browned skin and framed on top by wavy black hair and on bottom by an equally dark beard.

"You boys don't need to worry. Everything is going to be just fine. We'll get this little fellow to Korčula, maybe get a small reward, a delivery fee of sorts, and then, Dado, we'll all sail back to Blato and celebrate over some ale."

Silence followed, except for the occasional ripple of a wave against the rocks and the splash of an idly tossed stone.

"It's going to be a long wait for the lads to come back. Especially if I'm just sitting here talking to myself," the man tried again. "Why don't you tell me who your friend really is? We can talk about that for a while."

Damir looked at the man and returned his gaze to the sea. He remained as mute as Ali.

"Hellfire, boy!" the boss stood up and took a step toward Damir and Ali. His hand dropped toward his sword's hilt, but shifted at the last moment and instead scratched his side. He began again, gently again, "If you help us out, Dado, you'll get a part of the reward – a big part, really, because you're the one who brought us this kid. Just tell me what you know about him."

Damir didn't dare move, afraid any reaction would cascade uncontrollably. He sat on the rocks next to Ali and studied the waters. Across the sea, about ten miles away, he could see the shimmering outline of Hvar. He wished he and Ali were there now, safely away from this man and his sword.

"No reward for you, I guess," the boss sat back down on his own stone, and the time dragged on in silence as they waited for the others to return. The crag's shadow had moved into the water by time the Karlo and Mali tramped into view from the eastern path.

"We have water and some food," Mali called as they rounded the small cove.

"It took you long enough."

"There were people all over the village fixing their nets," Karlo explained. "The water was easy enough. Who doesn't give water to a stranger? We did the best we could for food."

Karlo took two tired heads of cabbage from his sack and gave them to the leader.

"This was the best you could do?" He frowned at the limp leaves, clots of dirt still hanging from them, and back at Karlo. "It'll do for now. We'll get better in Korčula. Give us some water. I'm parched."

The boss tore off clumps of cabbage and gave them to the boys. He doled the rest out to himself and his men. They passed the water around as they ate in the shade.

"I was thinking," Karlo said after a moment.

The boss stopped chewing and looked over, doubtfully.

"We don't know anything about this boy except that he's foreign and definitely not a houseboy. Maybe he's worth more to someone else besides the rector?"

"That could be true," the boss said, "but we don't know anyone except the rector who would want him. Maybe Father Anton, if he really is a houseboy. We could say we caught him in the woods trying to escape. But I don't think he's a houseboy, and the church is never generous with its gold."

"There is someone else," Karlo said, uncertainly. "Remember I told you about the Spaniard, Franco or Frederico, who came to Korčula the evening of the battle? He might know someone who would pay good money for someone like this. Someone foreign. He's traveled. He might help us for a share of the money. If he's still in Korčula, that is."

The leader pondered the idea. "You might be right, Karlo," he said at last, a note of praise in his rough bass. "Let's wait to give the boy to the rector until we can talk with this Spaniard. You know where to find him?"

The three men became absorbed in their scheming and neglected Damir and Ali. Damir took the opportunity to tug on Ali's sleeve and perform an elaborate series of subtle gestures, all the while making sure the men remained distracted. He pointed between the two of them and pantomimed with his fingers someone running. He pulled at Ali's arm and pantomimed, pulled and pantomimed. When Ali rose suddenly, the motion drew the men out of their discussion and they all turned toward the boys. Ali mimed a stretch, and sat back down.

"Time to go," the boss declared.

The five were quickly on the boat again and rowing toward the channel, where a light breeze had arrived as the men rested and ate in the cove. Once clear of the land, the men stowed their oars and let the mottled, ochre sail carry them over the gentle waves. Their thirst slaked and the light, early evening wind doing the work, the men joked and made plans for the money that would weigh down their sacks. Even the boss' spirits seemed to rise as they tacked smoothly past the island landscapes.

"We might get to Korčula before they lock the gates after all," the older man laughed. "Karlo, you and I will go in and try to find this Spaniard of yours. Mali, that leaves you watching the boys."

After another hour or so of sailing, the meager crew lowered the canvass and broke out the oars again: Damir and Ali in front, and Karlo and the stranger further aft. They all had their backs to the bow, facing the boss at the tiller. As the leader guided the boat into an empty cove, they came within a dozen yards of a break in the hills with what looked like a path leading up from the small pebble beach.

Damir caught Ali's eye, then jerked his oar into his chest, crashing the blade into Karlo's in front of him.

"Run!" Damir shouted and pushed Ali toward the side of the boat. The boys dove into the water. When they broke the surface, Damir made sure that Ali was behind him – and could swim – and made his way toward the break in the hills.

"Hellfire! After them! Row!" the leader barked, steering the boat around. But with two oars dead in the water, the craft was slow to respond. Karlo and Mali pulled hard, but their rhythm was broken by constantly banging into boys' abandoned oars. By the time they turned and approached the shore, Damir and Ali were wading waist deep toward land.

"Mali, jump! Go after them!" the leader commanded. "If they separate, get the foreign kid. We'll take care of Dado later, if we need to. And believe me, we'll take care of him. Karlo and I will find you."

Mali was in the water at once, swimming strongly toward shore and eroding the boy's head start. Meanwhile, the boss dropped the rudder, slammed the abandoned oars back into the boat, and joined Karlo at an oar. There was nowhere near the pebbled opening to leave their boat, so the two rowed into a cove further east, pulling strong at the oars.

Once on land, Damir took Ali's hand and ran along the tree line until they found a narrow path up the hill. The two had barely started the steep ascent when Mali slogged out of the sea behind them. The climb was hard in their wet clothes and shoes. The path was little more than a natural break through the trees, and thorny creepers spread across the ground. The boys stumbled more than once, each time letting the stranger get a pace or two closer.

As the boys scrambled higher, Mali cursed and taunted them.

"You sea scum! You're not going to get far! You know that!" he shouted. "Yeah, boss and Karlo got you in front, and I got you in back. Just give up, damnation, and save us all the sweat." Damir looked through the trees and saw the stranger swing his sword wildly. He had already started up the path.

As the boys climbed, Damir shoved Ali ahead of him and started wedging fallen branches he found along the way between the trees behind him. The branches wouldn't stop the short stranger, but they might slow him down more than the time it took to push them into place. When opportunities arose, Damir threw stones blindly down the hillside, vaguely toward their pursuer.

"You just wait 'til I catch you," Mali called. As he climbed after the boys, he paused to grab his breath between each tirade. "You're going to feel the edge of my blade, you will, you bastards."

At the top of the hill, the boys broke upon a real path that ran east and west. Even though Mali was out of sight, they could hear him cursing his luck, the boys, and everything in general. He was tiring, they could tell. He gasped for breath between each volley of abuse.

Damir pushed Ali west along the trail and motioned him to run. Instead of following the foreign boy, though, Damir ducked behind a thick grove of cypress a few yards east of the junction. Ali darted down the path. When he looked back and didn't see Damir he froze. Ali looked up and down the trail desperately trying to spot the island boy.

But all he saw was Mali, panting and pushing out the woods. Ali was just a few yards down the path, and for an instant they stared motionless at each other.

"Dado left you, huh? Well, I'm still here," Mali shouted, "and you're mine now." He took another lungful of air and straightened up.

Just then, Damir rushed from behind the trees and crashed into the stranger with all his weight, his shoulder punching into Mali's stomach. The sword flew from the man's hand as the two tumbled into the trees beside the trail. They rolled in a heap for a few yards until hitting a tree stump. Mali took the brunt of the impact against the solid bark, and Damir swung madly with his fists as he tried to twist on top of him. Any advantage Damir had, however, faded quickly. The man grabbed Damir by the shoulders and flung him onto the ground, almost effortlessly. Mali began kicking the boy, and Damir blocked the blows with his arms and legs, all the while trying to crawl out of reach.

Mali shifted to attack Damir from a different angle and saw his sword lying among the bushes. As he reached for it, Damir tried to stand and run away, but was tripped by the undergrowth and slammed against the ground.

"You ain't joining the crew after all," the man chortled as he approached Damir. "We never saw you," he gasped, raising the sword. "Accidents happen on this island. Sometimes, bad accidents."

Damir edged backwards, away from the sharp blade, but there was nowhere to escape. His hand felt a thick branch on the ground. He grabbed it and held it up in defense, but the man only laughed. As Mali waved his sword above his head, ready to strike, he crumbled awkwardly to the ground. Behind where Mali had towered above Damir, Ali now stood, his eyes as wide as ever. He held in both hands a stone the size of a man's head covered in fresh blood.

Damir scrambled to his feet. Mali lay on a bed of pine needles, a pool of blood for a pillow. He and Ali stared for second in the sudden quiet before Damir took the rock from Ali's hands and tossed it aside.

"Come on!" he said.

The pair backed onto the main trail in time to hear voices coming from the east. Ali started west, but Damir grabbed his sleeve.

"No. This way."

He took Ali into the woods across where they had left the stranger. There was no trail, so they twisted between the trees, trying not to disturb the needles and forest debris carpeting the ground. When the voices grew near, they stopped and dropped to their knees, ducking under a bush. In unison, they each motioned the other to be quiet.

"...gone too far." The first voice they could make out was Karlo's. "We should go back. Mali will bring them to the bay, and we can finish this. We'll never find them just running around like this."

"Shut your trap, Karlo, and save your wind. I won't trust that worthless dog to catch a cold. I had no choice, though." The boss was fuming as the two trotted quickly along the path. "This is the only trail they could be on. If we didn't pass them, they must be heading west. When I get my hands on that friend of yours, he's going to wish he'd run off to Senj.

"Wait! Listen," the boss rasped. The two men stopped. "There's something in the bushes."

Damir and Ali couldn't see the trail from where they hid, but they could hear the men halt and draw their swords. Next, they heard twigs crack under heavy boots and branches rustle. The boys looked at one another. Damir pointed further into woods.

"Mali!" Karlo cried. The noises suggested a fury of activity.

"Hellfire, you wretched dog, what happened?" the boss barked. Damir strained to listen. The voices of the men were muffled and low, and he could only discern a random word here and there. It was clear, though, that Mali wasn't dead and that the boss wasn't pleased. Damir felt a surprising sense of relief knowing that Ali hadn't killed the man. He tried to convey the news with hand signals and was unsuccessful.

They heard movement again, this time on the trail. Despite an edge that remained in his voice, the boss sounder calmer.

"They didn't head east toward Korčula, that's certain," he said. "They know that's where we are, and, besides, we would have seen them. They had to have gone this way. They won't get far without food and water.

"Mali, you get back to the boat and tend to that hard head of yours. Keep an eye out, though, in case they are that stupid. We'll keep going west. We'll catch up with them or hit a village where someone must have seen them. Either way, you'll find us at the Rusted Anchor later. Now, get going."

Damir and Ali listened as footfalls left in opposite directions. Two pair rushed westward down the trail, while a third pair moved more slowly and less rhythmically eastward. Even when the sounds were gone, Damir and Ali dared not move from their hiding place immediately.

The tension eased with each passing minute, though, and once it was clear that the men weren't coming back, the boys started breathing normally again. Damir was scratched and bruised from the fight, but the wounds didn't seem serious. They sat wordlessly for hours as the early evening turned into night and the sky passed through untold shades of blue and pink and purple and red before settling into a canopy of black salted with bright stars and an emerging, grinning moon.

As the night progressed, Ali tugged on Damir's sleeve. Enough moonlight drifted down through the trees for the boys see each other plainly, although tinted with an eerie pale blueness.

Ali pointed at Damir.

"Damir," the foreign boy said softly, and then pointed to himself. "Orhan."

"Orhan?" Damir repeated, smiling at the boy. "Pleased to meet you, Orhan."

Cat and mouse

Damir and the newly named Orhan spent the night in the same spot in the woods. They tried to take turns sleeping, but any rest came in fits and starts. Every noise – an animal scampering through the brush, a pine cone falling in the breeze, a bird changing its perch – signaled that the men were returning. Each was a false alarm. Neither the men nor anyone else passed along the path that night, yet the boys were exhausted when the sun began lighting the eastern sky.

"We have to get to Father Anton," Damir said as the two rose and stretched their stiff limbs. "I don't know what else to do. Let's go, Orhan."

Orhan, who had returned to his quiet ways, reacted when he heard his name. He looked over to his companion, smiled, and waited.

"Come on." Damir led them carefully back to the trial, stopping every few paces to listen. All they heard were the normal background sounds of the island.

Reassured, they stepped onto the trail and started eastward toward town. They moved cautiously and quietly, stopping whenever a dry twig cracked under their feet or the breeze stirred branches along the path. Slowly they followed the twists and turns of the trail, reaching a high pass that overlooked a small cove. Orhan stopped abruptly and pointed to the far side. The boat that brought them was beached, partially hidden beneath low hanging branches. Mali was leaning against it, perhaps asleep. A bloody cloth was wrapped around his head. There was no sign of the boss or Karlo.

Damir pulled Orhan to the landward side of the trial, out of view of the cove, and they moved on, more slowly and quietly than before. Once, they hastily jumped away from the trail as a fisherman with his morning's catch lumbered westward. Otherwise, there were no incidents. The pair stayed on inland trails to avoid any coastal villages. Soon they reached the main road that led toward Saint Nicholas' monastery, the same road Damir had joyfully followed almost a week earlier as he anticipated seeing Iskra again. They glanced furtively in both directions and dashed across.

They climbed a hill that rose southwest of the town, and from its peak, they could see the walled town less than a mile away. Houses with burned out roofs were also visible along the western bay through breaks in the trees. Orhan's face darkened as he pointed to them.

"Turks. Ottoman," Damir said tersely. He led Orhan further along the curve of the hill until they found a small clearing on the eastern slope. "Wait here."

Orhan paused, and then followed Damir when he began retracing their steps toward the main road.

"*Wait here,*" Damir repeated, with a touch of frustration, and then sighed. He took Orhan to the edge of the clearing and nudged him to sit on the ground. He held his hands up, palms toward Orhan. "Wait," he said again. "I can't bring you into Korčula without someone seeing us. I'll have to bring Father Anton here."

Orhan looked at Damir blankly, but didn't move.

"Just wait here ... please," Damir said softly as he backed away, his hands still raised. When Orhan showed no sign of moving this time, Damir turned and walked away, glancing back once more to make sure the foreign boy understood.

Alone now, Damir headed around the hill back to the road most travelers take into Korčula. Without Orhan, he didn't have to worry about explaining a foreign boy's presence to any random passerby and his thoughts had a chance to meander. In the background of his mind, one question lingered quietly around all the others: How soon would be able to see Iskra? Once on the dirt thoroughfare, he strode quickly toward town, rounding the wall around the monastery, skirting the western bay, and crossing the flat that he last saw littered with discarded weapons and pools of blood.

The gutted, roofless buildings along the path were the only signs that remained of the battle. Families had returned to their homes and were beginning the task of rebuilding. For most, this meant stacking their charred possessions in a pile in their yards. A few had already stretched fragments of old sails as makeshift roofs. Along the way, some children were selling produce from baskets in front of blackened houses that their parents were still clearing.

As Damir approached the south gate, he noticed that, unusually, two watchmen were guarding the entrance, armed with pikes and dressed in full regalia. The boy tried to convince himself that their presence was just a late reaction to the battle with the Turks. In practice, they would have no real effect if there were a renewed attack, he thought. They were probably there to give a sense of security to townspeople and travelers. They were saying, "Korčula is safe. Now, let's get back to our business." Yet, in a corner of his mind, Damir worried that the boss and Karlo had told someone, possibly the rector, about Orhan, and the guards were waiting in case someone tried to sneak him into town.

Could they be looking for Damir, as well? How would they recognize him? Damir self-consciously looked down at his clothes. They were grubby, but nothing unusual for a peasant boy: plain white shirt and dark, coarse britches. His boots were muddy and dull. There was nothing to make him stand out, except maybe his height and blue eyes. Iskra had told him she had never seen eyes like his. Had the boss? Had he even noticed?

As his anxiety grew, it clouded his own self assurances, like weeds overtaking a carefully arranged garden. Damir paused by a young girl selling wild apples from a small wooden bowl. He feigned interest in her fruit and chatted with her until finally a party of tradesmen ambled down the path toward the gate. He fell in behind the three men, not so close as to get their attention, but – he hoped – close enough to seem part of their group. He hutched over a bit, kept his eyes low, and tried to walk loosely. He wasn't certain whether he was trying to look older or younger.

In the end, the precautions seemed unnecessary as all four passed under Revelin Tower with scant notice from the watchmen.

Once inside the gate, Damir slowed and let the three tradesmen continue ahead of him along the street that hugged the western wall. It was early morning, and the town's streets were already bustling with merchants and laborers, servants and visitors. Damir decided to risk taking the most direct route to the cathedral and

Father Anton. He started climbing up the town's center street. After just a few steps, he saw someone in the crowd who, from a distance, could be the boss. Damir changed his route and scurried down a side street. He dashed a few yards until he reached the road along the eastern wall and waited.

After a minute or so, the boss – and it was the boss – turned onto the same side street. The big man walked with an unhurried gait, and Damir couldn't tell whether he had been spotted. The boy ran along the wall and found an open workshop. He ducked inside. At the opposite end of the room, a gangly man with disproportionately large arms stood facing a roaring fire. The rhythmic clangs of metal on metal resounded through the room and showers of sparks added a dramatic aura to the man's silhouette.

The blacksmith's shop was long and narrow. A furnace dominated the far end of the chamber, while tables covered with freshly made stone chisels, hammers, saws, carpenters' axes, and other tools lined the walls as far as the doorway. Barrels with longer tools – boathooks of various designs and pitchforks – congregated near the entrance. Damir ducked under one of the heavy wooden tables next to the door and was partially hidden by a collection of anchors leaning on one end.

The crash of the door slamming open gave Damir a start.

"Good day, sir!" Although Damir could only see boots, the leader's rasp was unmistakable.

The blacksmith turned from his work, holding a glowing iron ingot by tongs in one hand and a massive hammer in the other. He squinted against the sunlight coming through the door. "Good day, sir. Have we business?"

"Perhaps, we might," the boss replied, staying near the doorway, barely an arm's length from where Damir hid under the table. "I've come to discuss my sword. Its edge is not what it should be. Would you be able to sharpen it? With all the excitement around Curzola, it would be good to have a keen blade. You never know when you'll need it to skewer a Turk – a Mohammed or an Abdul or an Ali … You know what I mean. I want to be ready."

"I'm afraid I can't help you, sir. My work is in tools, mostly. The blade smith is on the north end, near Berim Tower. That's his stock and trade."

The boss hesitated before thanking the blacksmith and turning back onto the street, leaving the door ajar. Damir wasn't certain whether it was a coincidence that the boss used "Ali." He couldn't remember using Orhan's name – his made-up name – around the boss at all. Maybe it was just a coincidence, too, that the boss happened into this shop. The avalanche of thoughts made the island boy anxious again, and he decided to stay put for a while. The blacksmith, meanwhile, returned to his forge, putting the cooled ingot again into the fire and pulling out a bright orange one.

The blacksmith had rotated bars of iron in and out of the furnace several times before Damir felt it was safe to leave. He chose the moment the blacksmith was putting an ingot back on the flames and pulling out the next to dash through the door. The blacksmith looked over at the sudden burst of sunlight, and, seeing no one, dismissed the disturbance as the wind.

It was past noon when Damir emerged from the shop. The streets were emptier as the people of Korčula retreated from the heat into their houses, workshops, hidden courtyards, and taverns. The boss was nowhere to be seen.

Damir followed the eastern wall for most of its circuit around the town, and then darted up a narrow street that rose straight to the cathedral. He stopped just short of the church square and peered around the corner of a nobleman's palace. Under the blazing sun, the square was mostly empty, and Damir hurried across and into Saint Mark's Cathedral. The nave was musty, dark, and cool. A dozen or so townspeople were scattered among the pews, as much to seek refuge from the heat as refuge for their souls. Damir joined them, sitting on a back bench as far away from the others as he could manage and watching for Father Anton.

Along with a sea of candles, light came into the nave from a single, narrow window above the altar. From the back of the cathedral, the grey walls of the nave towered above Damir. Fat arches held high by columns with ornate caps marched eternally forward, meeting at an altar shielded by a richly carved stone baldachin, more work from the local artisans. A painting of Saint Mark hung behind the stone canopy. Father Anton had said the painting came from Venice about the time Damir was born, and Damir studied it for inspiration. Instead of inspiration, he found only two lions at the feet of the cathedral's namesake. Venice never missed an opportunity to remind Korčula of its sovereign. Saint

Mark, aglow in mystic light, was flanked by Saint Bartholomew and Saint Jerome, each carrying a book. Perhaps, Damir thought as the painting held his attention a moment longer, the saints, too, were unsure what course was best.

Several priests busied themselves around the altar, but Father Anton was not among them. Damir waited more than an hour in the cool church as parishioners came and went, lighting candles, talking softly, praying. Eventually, a young boy limped in and Damir recognized him as one of the church's stable hands. The boy crossed himself, genuflected, and settled into a back pew across the aisle from Damir. The stable hand bowed his head and moved his lips silently.

After a few minutes, Damir slid onto the pew next to the boy, who looked up briefly before continuing his wordless entreaty. Damir waited beside the boy until his patience evaporated and he nudged the stable hand with his elbow.

"Hey," Damir whispered. "Are my horse and cart fine? I just got into town and haven't been able to get to the stables."

The stable hand turned to Damir, irritated by the interruption.

"Shhh," he hissed. "Yes, they are fine." He returned to his prayer.

Damir sat awkwardly before nudging the boy again.

"Have you seen Father Anton? I have news of his horse."

"Please!" the boy said in a voice just above a whisper. Some people in the nearer pews turned toward them, embarrassing the stable hand. Then, more quietly, "He's gone. He'll be back in a few days. Father Paulo is celebrating the mass while he's away. Now, please...."

The stable hand slid across the polished wooden pew, and Damir left him in peace. No one – not mamma, not tata, not Damir – had thought that Father Anton would be gone. Waiting a few days for the priest to return would be risky, but what were the other options? Damir sat quietly on the pew, as though in prayer, as he considered what to do next. In the end, he realized he had only one other trusted friend in Korčula, Iskra. His next logical move had to be to find her, a pleasing revelation. Maybe she knew a place he and Orhan could hide while waiting for Father Anton's return. She would certainly give them food, he thought.

115

A crisis of heart

Damir rose to leave the cathedral, moving along the edges of the chamber, passing beneath the crucifixes and the Madonnas with Child, rather than along the center aisle. He paused in a corner under a display of weapons captured a century earlier during the battle with the Aragonese. Spears and pikes were spread out like a fan on the stone wall. As he turned toward the exit, he thought he saw Karlo in the dim light near the cathedral entrance. He stopped dead still underneath the array of weapons until he realized it was actually another man with roughly the same build as Karlo.

The bright sun blinded Damir as he left the church. He paused to adjust to the change and headed straight for the inn run by Iskra's family. Iskra's grandfather was granted a license to run the inn decades earlier by the powerful Ismaeli family. The three-story building was a modest establishment resting near the western wall, not far from the sea gate. The location and unassuming tone made it a favorite of prudent merchants and ship's officers who came through the town. In addition, the ground floor, an open hall with tables and benches, was an asylum from heat and boredom for local tradesmen. Two private rooms and a larger dormitory made up the middle floor, and the family chambers were carved into the broiling half attic. The Ismaeli crest, two lions rearing against a fortified tower, was carved above the lintel at the entrance.

Iskra was in the back courtyard, ironing linen. Except when the sun was at its height, the courtyard was bathed in shadow and a swirling breeze, making the mundane tasks of running an inn more tolerable. The aroma of fresh bread from her brother's bakery, which also abutted the courtyard, added to Iskra's calm as she moved from the sheets for the private rooms to her and her mother's blouses.

The girl's ebony hair was tied back with a headscarf so only a few wisps gave a gossamer frame to her blissful face. Iskra appreciated the routine jobs that were needed to keep the inn running smoothly. Whether ironing or balancing the books or making sure there were sufficient supplies, she could lose herself in a world of precision and order. Of course, like her mother and father, she also spent time in the common room filling tankards and clearing plates. She had much less patience for those duties than her parents – handling dullards, rakes, and drunks – a clear disadvantage in her family's business. On the not quite rare occasions when her restraint failed, the collapse would lead to loud quarrels and upset guests. But among locals just looking for a cool quaff or a warm meal, Iskra's demeanor and no-nonsense approach projected an air of respectability on the inn that others around town – especially the Rusted Anchor in Varos – lacked.

"They said you were back here."

Iskra looked up from her work and was surprised to see Damir standing in the stone doorway. Her slight smile was in sharp contrast to her furrowed brow as she took in Damir filthy clothes.

"Bok, plavica. You're back." She put the iron down and walked toward him, taking in his muddy clothes and grimy face. Her smile never faded. "Maybe you should have cleaned up a little before seeing my parents? They say first impressions last forever."

Damir looked down at his clothes and arms. Baking in the hot sun, sloshing through the sea, climbing through the woods, fighting, and sleeping under the stars had taken their toll. Damir hadn't noticed, though, until Iskra mentioned it. He forgot, briefly, what he had come to say. Iskra, on the other hand, was impeccable. A pristine light blue apron covered a white blouse that was unbuttoned slightly in the heat, a detail that wasn't missed by Damir. Even the tiny beads of sweat on her forehead seemed clean and orderly, until Iskra mopped them off with a crisp handkerchief.

"Um, I don't think they saw me," he suggested.

"Oh, you're not as invisible as you think, country boy. They see everything that happens in the inn."

"Iskra, I need your help," Damir began, abruptly turning the conversation to a comfortable, practical subject.

The two sat on a long stone bench under some shade in the courtyard, and Damir quietly told Iskra of his adventures since

117

leaving Korčula. He spoke in conspiratorial tones, watching nervously to see if anyone was listening from the windows or doorways opening onto the courtyard. Iskra listened intently, and her easy smile vanished as Damir told his story. Damir was absorbed in the telling and didn't notice the change.

"So, we have to help Orhan, hide him until Father Anton comes back."

Damir finished and waited for Iskra's response. Instead of helping eagerly, as he expected, Iskra remained silent. She looked at the ground around the courtyard and up at the surrounding windows. Her hands lay on her lap, and if Damir had been more perceptive, he would have seen they were trembling slightly.

"Dado," she began slowly and softly. "He's a Turk. You should turn this boy over to the guard."

Damir was stunned. He had been positive that Iskra would understand and help.

"I can't turn him over to the guard," he said. "Who knows what they'll do to him?"

"I know you mean well, Damir, but he's the enemy. His people attacked our town."

"He's not the enemy. He's just a boy."

The trembling seized Iskra's whole body now, and even Damir noticed. He felt lost and confused. Tears pooled in Iskra's eyes. Damir moved closer to her and tentatively put an arm around her shoulder. Iskra remained stiff and continued to stare away from him. She seemed numb to the tears that were now wetting her cheeks.

Minutes passed before she spoke, still slow, soft, steady, outwardly still in control.

"Jolanda was killed in the attack," she began. "Maybe you saw her. She was bringing cannon balls and others supplies from Rampada."

"I'm so sorry," Damir said, filling the silence that followed.

Iskra fought to keep an even voice. "She and I were babies together. We played together all our lives. She knew all my secrets … even you."

In the ensuing quiet, Iskra leaned gently against Damir. Her shoulders lost their edge.

"I kept her off the walls to keep her safe. Had her run errands

118

between the towers where she would be away from the arrows and the musket balls. Little Jolić was coming back to Revelin when a Turkish cannon ball hit the granary and the wall collapsed on her. It must have been one of the last shots. It took us most of the day Monday to move the stone blocks and get to her. It was horrible. Father Anton said she must have died quickly. How does he know?"

"You didn't tell me."

"No." The curt response carried no explanation. Iskra took some deep breaths and stood without warning, breaking free of Damir's arm.

"But now, I am." Her voice was suddenly controlled and harsh. "And you want me to help you protect this Turk? This Turk who killed Jolanda?"

With each repetition of *Turk* her voice hardened. Iskra paced around the courtyard, her glare striking Damir each time she turned in his direction.

"He's just a boy, Iskra. He didn't do anything."

"How do you know that, Damir? Jolanda was just a girl, and I know for certain that she didn't do anything." Iskra stopped next to the washing and picked up the cold iron. She looked like she would throw it if she could find the right target. "We should turn this Turk over to the guard. They'll know what to do, and I'm sure he deserves anything they'll do to him."

"Listen to yourself," Damir snapped back, more abrasively than he intended. "You sound just like the folks in Blato. 'Death to them all! Death to them all!' This doesn't sound like you."

"You don't know me, Damir Grgić. You don't know what sounds like me. You don't know me at all."

"I know enough. I know you're smarter than almost anyone I know. I know you have a temper – you told me that yourself – but I've seen you calm and level-headed when everyone else around you was panicking and looking for someone to tell them what to do."

Iskra stood staring at Damir, clutching the iron, and said nothing.

"And I know you're hurt." Damir stood and took a step toward Iskra, but the girl who commanded the defense of the south wall wasn't ready to be consoled or flattered. She stood firm, a stone statue like the righteous saints that lined the cathedral walls, the iron her holy orb.

"Maybe you're right." Damir changed tact and walked away from Iskra. "Maybe I should just give the boy over to the guard and be rid of him. What do I know, really? But when I look at Orhan, I don't see a Turk. I just see a kid who's lost and maybe even scared. I'd be scared. It just doesn't seem right to turn him over to a mob of idiots. That's why I wanted to take him to Father Anton. He's not an idiot and would at least try to make sure the right thing was done."

Damir's pacing brought him full circuit around the courtyard, and now he found himself in front of Iskra again. The inn keeper's daughter spun slowly in her place as she followed Damir's progress over the cobblestones. She had put the iron back in its place.

"You forgot something," she said flatly, when it seemed like Damir was done.

"What do you mean?"

"You forgot to say that you would try to hide – *Orhan? –* Orhan whether I helped you or not." Iskra sat back on the bench. Even though Iskra's voice had lost its sharpness, Damir was unsure whether she was mocking him or simply pre-empting any further argument. She looked up at him, and started to speak, then stopped.

Iskra let out a long breath before finally turning again to Damir.

"So, where is your little Turkish buddy?"

Damir was uncertain and hesitated. He considered that Iskra might be trying to find out where Orhan was just so she could turn the boy over to the guard herself. She was smart enough to be clever. As he looked at Iskra, though, he knew that he had no choice but to trust her, but not because there were no other options. He could have left and kept Orhan hidden himself. Damir had no choice because not trusting Iskra was unimaginable.

"I left him in a clearing on Saint Blaise Hill."

"That's not good," Iskra replied immediately, matter-of-factly. "The children from Korčula play on that hill all the time. No one's leaving town right now, but it's only a matter of time."

They were silent for a few minutes as Iskra considered the situation and Damir yearned for the empty spot on the bench beside

120

her.

"We're not going to be able to bring your buddy into the town," she began. "Franco the Spaniard got loose last night, and the guard is on the alert. We were still keeping him in the rector's stables, but the watchmen got drunk and he slipped past them. You said Karlo suggested that this boss man should talk with Franco? His escape might not be just a coincidence. Anyway, with everyone on alert we couldn't bring Orhan in without someone noticing.

"Father Anton has gone to the monastery on Badija. The monks there say some of their treasures are missing. They brought them to Korčula for safekeeping before the attack. The archdeacon is trying to straighten it all out, and I don't know when he'll be back. It could be days.

"Everyone else is still reeling from the attack. I'm not sure who can help us."

After taking inventory of the situation, Iskra shifted on the bench, making room for Damir. When he sat down, she took his hands in hers.

"But you're right. We can't turn this boy over to the rector or the guard. He would never see home again, even if he did nothing wrong." Her grip on Damir's hand tightened briefly. "And punishing him won't help Jolanda."

Iskra closed her eyes and sighed deeply. She lost herself in thought, again, and Damir watched her, intensely aware of the warmth of her hands in his.

"This isn't our war. We just got caught between the Venetians and the Ottoman. How can a boy be responsible for that? He's just caught, too." Iskra looked at Damir, her face a portrait of assurance. "We have to take your little Turkish buddy to Ragusa, to Dubrovnik."

"What!" Iskra's pronouncement broke the spell that had captured Damir. "Dubrovnik? We can't go to Dubrovnik."

"Hush!" Iskra went to the doorway to the inn to see if anyone had noticed the outburst. She waved and smiled to someone inside and returned to the bench.

"What a village boy, you are," she said in a chiding voice. "Dubrovnik isn't much further than crossing the island twice. There's just water in between, not hills. If we can get a boat, we can get there and back before anyone has time to ask any questions. Those Ragusans have good relations with the Ottomans, and there should be a Turkish emissary there or someone. Orhan would be safe with him. Are you sure he wasn't a slave?"

"I don't think so, and neither did the man who was with Karlo, the boss. He said Orhan's hands were too smooth for him to have been a slave or any kind of worker. But maybe we should just wait for Father Anton to get back. Dubrovnik?"

"I don't know when he'll be back, and the longer we wait, the more chance your little Turkish buddy has of being discovered." She took Damir's hands again. "This is his best chance."

Damir thought through the possibilities, but in the end could do nothing but agree.

Indeed, Damir was quietly excited about the prospect of seeing Dubrovnik. While he once met a pair of Ragusan stone merchants in Korčula, no one he knew had ever travelled to the republic. To him, Dubrovnik was as much out of reach and almost as exotic as far-off Vienna or Constantinople. According to stories, almost twenty thousand people lived in Dubrovnik, a number Damir could scarcely imagine. In addition, hundreds of seamen and merchants from all over the world trod the city's marble streets every day. Yet, Iskra was confident they could get there and find the Turkish emissary amid this multitude, and her confidence was contagious.

"Dado, we need to get you out of sight while I try to make arrangements. You can use some rest anyway. And maybe some water and clothes."

Iskra took Damir up an open stone staircase to the middle floor of the inn. She led him into one of the private bedrooms, a small chamber with a bed, a chair, and a washbowl on a cabinet under a window looking onto the courtyard. She told Damir to stay out of sight and left. Before he could move, she was back with a pitcher of water, which she poured into the washbowl, and a coarse towel.

"Clean yourself up and rest, Dado. Latch the door. I'll be back soon." Iskra started to leave, but stopped at the door and turned. "Don't go under the sheets, I just changed them. In fact, don't get in the bed at all with those filthy clothes. Take them off if you must."

Damir looked at her with a surprised expression that would have stopped a jackal.

122

"*After* I'm gone, you bilge rat. I'll bring you some of Niko's old clothes. They should fit you. Wait."

And she left. A minute later the door opened slightly, and a hand tossed an old shirt and trousers into the room. And it disappeared.

Iskra was gone for more than an hour. When she returned, she found Damir in Niko's old clothes, all just a bit too big, sitting on the chair by the window. The bed was unmussed, she noticed.

"Good boy," she said playfully as she threw the muddy water in the basin out the window. She gave the washbowl a quick wipe with the towel.

"Are you ready to go, my clean plavica? I'm worried that we've left your little Turkish buddy alone too long already." Iskra distributed some water flasks and fruit into their carry sacks. "We need to go."

It was already early evening when the two left the apartment, again down the back staircase into the courtyard. The pair avoided the inn, and instead passed through a narrow storage area lined with barrels that brought them onto the western street. She told him the plan quietly as they walked. Iskra moved briskly with Damir at her side until they reached the small square at the foot of Revelin Tower. They hesitated, eyeing the crowd for any sign of the boss or Karlo, and then they walked together under the Venetian coat of arms and out of town.

Within minutes, they had rounded the Benedictine monastery and were climbing the hill behind it. When they reached the clearing on the western slope, it was empty.

"Are you sure this is where you left him?"

"Yes, I'm sure." Damir answered, irritably. "Orhan!"

"Quiet!" Iskra, hissed, "There could be others around looking for him, too."

The two looked around the edges of the clearing. They found no sign of the boy and no clue of where he might have gone. As the sun began dropping toward the west, the shadows in the woods deepened. If they didn't find Orhan soon, they might not until morning, if at all.

Damir was frantic, circling the clearing like a caged animal looking for a way out. Iskra was still, but no less nervous as she thought through all the nearby places that the boy might be. He wasn't in town, she was certain, or else she would have heard about it.

Then Damir stopped in his tracks and cupped his hands over his mouth.

"Chuke!" he hooted. "Chuke!"

Iskra looked at him puzzled. Damir held his hand up, signaling silence, and waited.

"Chuke!" he called again.

This time a reply came from down the hill: "Chuke!"

Damir looked at Iskra and grinned in the fading light.

"Chuke! Chuke!" he hooted again.

The response was more immediate this time. "Chuke! Chuke!"

Damir took Iskra's hand, and they rushed toward the sound, down the slope to the hillside facing away from town.

"Chuke!"

"Chuke!"

They were much closer now, and after a few more yards Damir and Iskra bolted past a cypress stand into another break in the woods. They found Orhan huddled under some low hanging boughs. He jumped up and beamed when he saw Damir enter the small clearing, and then froze as Iskra came out of the woods next to him. On the ground rested a basket, empty except for a couple of figs.

"Orhan, thank the saints," Damir sighed. "This is Iskra. Iskra, Orhan." Damir pointed back and forth between the two.

The foreign boy remained mute, as usual, and into the awkward silence Iskra added habitually, "Pleased to meet you."

The three sat down in the clearing and Damir and Iskra tried to explain their plan in pantomime and hand gestures. It wasn't clear how much Orhan understood, but his face brightened at the word 'Dubrovnik.'

"Dubrovnik is good?" Iskra tried. "Dubrovnik?"

Orhan only smiled in response, which was enough for Iskra and Damir. Iskra said it was time to leave, and they gathered the remaining figs from the basket – apparently the leftovers of a foraging mission – and led Orhan toward Korčula. They skirted the main road, which meant they were forced to push through a pathless pine grove. When they reached the wall surrounding the monastery, Iskra told Damir and Orhan to wait there as she scouted ahead. She soon returned.

"Come on! Quickly!"

When the trio turned the corner behind the monastery, they saw a small boat in the twilight with two men. As they got closer, Damir recognized one was Iskra's brother.

"Hurry up, Dado! Bring your friend!" Nikola called jovially in a hushed shout.

Damir, Iskra, and Orhan waded into the sea and reached the small fishing boat when the water was about waist high. A knotted rope hung from the side to help the three board, and Niko and his companion – a young fisherman named Tomas – pulled each over the gunnels as soon as they were within reach.

"Stay down," Tomas ordered. "Anyone who saw us leave, saw two people in the boat. Even the guard can count. This is a bad idea. We have some wind, but I don't know for how long. Did anyone see you? Niko, take an oar."

Tomas and Nicolas rowed the boat a few yards further away for shoreline before Tomas pulled the sail up the mast. The triangular canvas billowed uselessly for a moment before a slight pull on the boom filled it with wind. Tomas fastened the lines, jumped over his passengers to the tiller, and turned the craft out of the small bay, staying far from Korčula's walls. The growing moon cast enough light on the sea to make Tomas wince whenever it appeared from behind the scattered clouds.

Nevertheless, the fishing boat was soon well into the channel, playing amid gentle waves and a friendly breeze. Tomas gave the helm to Nikola and tacked the boat onto a more easterly course. As the five began to relax, Iskra explained that Tomas' family had supplied her inn with fish since before her father's time. They had known Tomas since the crib, and whenever Nikola could take a break from baking, which wasn't often, he would go to sea with Tomas, sometimes staying away for days surviving on grilled fish and stale beer.

"What's that?" Tomas asked suddenly, pointing behind them. The wind had picked up slightly, coming now from the open sea. They were well past Badija Island and quickly overtaking a small island group to the north, lights from Orebić on the peninsula flickering in the distance. To the west, a lateen sail briefly gleamed on the horizon. It disappeared quickly as the moon fled again behind a cloud bank.

"It's just another fishing boat, Tomić," Nikola laughed. "Not every fin in the water is a shark."

Tomas looked back once again. Seeing nothing on the darkened sea, he turned his attention again to the canvas, making minute adjustments to its angle as he gave orders to Nikola at the tiller. Damir moved closer to Iskra on a plank that stretched between the hulls and took her hand. She made no effort to resist and even closed hers around his slightly. Orhan seemed more relaxed than he had been since Damir found him. He watched the horizon ahead for signs of light, even though they were still miles from Dubrovnik.

The little fishing boat continued eastward in silence. The sea became choppier as they approached the channel between the mainland and Mljet, the last large island before they reached the outer rim of the Republic of Ragusa. Tomas assured everyone this was normal for these waters, yet he still slowed the boat as they began crashing through the waves. Although the stars above were still interrupted frequently by wispy clouds, there was no sign of rain or an approaching storm.

A bright flash to the south caught everyone's attention, and a burst of sound followed.

"Thunder?" Damir asked?

"No? Worse!" Tomas yelled, looking back. He quickly adjusted the sail to catch the full wind again, and the boat jerked forward across the rising waves. "Keep that tiller steady, Niko!"

The sudden speed caught everyone except Tomas off guard. When they regained their bearings, they saw behind them a boat somewhat larger than theirs under full sail. It was only two hundred yards or so away, and as they watched another bright explosion lit the sea followed by a sharp report. The muzzle flash lit the approaching boat for an instance, long enough to see about half a dozen men.

"Stay down," Tomas shouted. "Swing to starboard, Niko. To starboard! Right! Not too much!"

The fishing boat veered to the right, toward the approaching island. For a moment, the other boat was lost behind a wave.

"By Saint Andrew, I knew this was stupid," Tomas cursed as he swung the boom and readjusted the lines. "Larboard! Larboard!

Niko, if I lose this boat, my tata will kill me on the church square and sell tickets. And it'll be on your head!"

Nikola pulled the tiller, and the boat swung left, catching the growing wind from the south.

"Who are they?" Damir braved.

Salt water smashed across the bow as the fishing boat bounced from swell to swell.

"The town guard," Tomas shouted, as he held the sail. "They're probably looking for the escaped Spaniard. Niko, I told you this was stupid!"

Damir, Iskra, and Orhan huddled on the bottom boards, keeping low and trying to stay out of Tomas' way. As they crested one wave, the distinct boom of a small cannon erupted to their left and something splashed into the water behind them.

"That's one!" Tomas yelled, more cheerfully than anyone expected. "We might save the boat after all, Niko. That's one of the patrol boats. It only has one cannon, and they're not going to be able to reload it on this sea. Keep it steady now. We're racing to Pelješac, and even Father Tony could outrace a stinking patrol boat!"

Despite Tomas' confidence, the patrol boat was still close behind them and seemed to be closing the gap. Strong gusts began blowing from seaward, churning the water harder. Tomas took over the tiller from Nikola and sent him to work the sail lines.

"Keep the ropes tight, Niko, and hold tight! We need to be careful not to swamp the boat."

"Is this another Bura?" Damir shouted from the bottom boards, where he, Iskra, and Orhan were clinging to anything that gave them a handhold. Each roll on the waves tossed them hard against the hull and threatened to toss them into the water.

"Oh, no!" Tomas cackled. "This wind's from the south. We call it Jugo. But it's close enough. They've never had a good sailor in the guard."

At the helm, Tomas caressed the boat across the waves, striking a critical balance between rushing hard into the swells and taking on as little water as possible. He pulled and pushed the rudder with a hard grip, all the while shouting orders to Nikola at the sail lines.

"Look, they're foundering!" he shouted.

127

Close behind them, the patrol boat had dropped its sail and noticeably slowed. A final muzzle flash burst forth as the fishing boat crested a wave. The gunfire was drowned out by the roaring sea.

Water crushing over the bow caught Nikola off guard, throwing him over the gunnels. He held tight to the boom line and dangled over the angry waters. Orhan and Damir jumped to grab his legs before he fell over completely and was lost in the raging seas. Nikola held fast to the line, and soon they had him back in the boat.

"Niko's hurt!" Damir yelled above the waves.

Iskra leapt across the boat to her brother. Even in the pale moonlight she could see that the back of his shirt was darker, and not from the sea's wetness. The blood seeping into the fabric was warm to her touch.

"Get us somewhere safe, Tomić! Get us there now!" she cried. She cradled her brother's body against her own. "Niko! Niko! Can you hear me?"

"Yes, little sis, I can hear you," he said, looking at Iskra's eyes and breathing heavily. He smiled. "It's not bad, really. I'm just winded."

Escape by sea

Away from their pursuers, Tomas could focus on piloting the fishing boat through the heavy Jugo winds. Directing Damir at the sail, it took Tomas another twenty minutes to bring the boat into a safe cove on Pelješac. The boat careened slightly as its momentum brought it into shallow waters and onto a pebbled beach. He and Damir carried Nikola to land and sat him down as Iskra and Orhan secured the boat to a nearby tree.

They gathered around Nikola in the faint light.

Iskra carefully took off his bloody shirt. Nikola winced as the wet fabric was peeled away from his back. He held steady when his sister poured some of their drinking water over the wound to clear away the blood. A musket ball had torn into his back just below his right shoulder. Even though the wound was small, blood dribbled out steadily.

"How are you feeling, Niko" Iskra asked, trying to keep her voice calm and reassuring.

"It hurts, but not as much as that time I stepped on that nail in the shipyard," he said. "The excitement's made me a little dizzy, though. Tomić, maybe you were right about this whole thing."

Iskra rinsed the wound out again, and blood continued to trickle down Nikola's back.

Orhan stood behind the knot of islanders and watched. He tapped Damir on the back and made slashing motions with his hands.

"We're safe here, Orhan," Damir said. "No one's going to find us for a while."

But Orhan wasn't placated. He pushed on Damir's shoulder and kept making the motions with his hand, more aggressively now.

129

"Orhan, stop!"

Damir turned back to Nikola and joined Iskra in assuring him that he would be fine. He wondered if they really sounded more confident than he felt. The flow of blood seemed to be slowing. Perhaps not, though. It was hard to judge in the moonlight.

From nowhere, Orhan shoved Damir to his side and grabbed a knife from the scabbard at his waist. Damir jumped to his feet and joined Tomas, who had moved between Orhan and Nikola. Together they faced down the foreign boy. Tomas holding his own knife in his hand.

"Get out of here, then!" Damir shouted, pointing vaguely toward Dubrovnik. "We're not going to stop you! Good luck finding your own way home! Go!"

Instead of running, though, Orhan started slashing at his long shirt with the knife. He cut the cloth to his waist, and ripped it further into coarse cotton strips. He stepped toward Nikola, but Tomas and Damir blocked his way. When the foreign boy dropped the knife to the pebble beach, the two exchanged a glance and let him pass. Iskra was more reluctant.

"Maybe he can help," Damir suggested. "He helped my tata."

Iskra hesitated before moving aside. She stayed close to Orhan as he knelt beside her brother. She touched Orhan's shoulder gently and spoke softly. "Please."

Orhan looked at the wound and cleaned it once more with the sweet water. He folded one strip of cloth into a tight square and pressed it against the musket hole. He took Iskra's hand and showed her how to hold the cloth in place. As Iskra pushed the cotton square against her brother's back, Orhan tied the other strips he had made from his shirt into a long ribbon. He wound this around Nikola's back as best he could to keep the square firmly in place. The blood flowing down Nikola's back slowed, but didn't quite stop.

"Give me the knife!" Iskra called, her voice trembling. She took the knife from Damir and shredded the bottom of her own skirt. Together, she and Orhan wrapped these strips around Nikola's back and shoulders. His torso looked like the top half of a badly made rag doll, but the bleeding seemed to have stopped.

Iskra stared at her brother's back, daring the blood to start again. When it didn't, she threw her arms around Orhan. "Thank you. Thank you," she managed between sobs.

Orhan pushed her away roughly, his face showing no relief. He pointed to Nikola and then toward the sea, toward Korčula. The sadness in his face was clear as he stabbed his finger desperately in the direction of the walled town. Orhan looked deep into Iskra's eyes, trying to make her understand. He relaxed when Iskra mimicked his gesture.

"I see," Iskra said after a pause, regaining some of her usual calm. "We need to get Niko back to Korčula. Sometimes, it's not just the bleeding that will ... that's bad. Niko needs someone to look at this, to clean it better."

"Then let's go," Tomas said, standing and reaching to lift Nikola.

"We can't. The wind's too strong," Iskra said. "The bleeding could start up again the moment we hit those waves. We need a calmer sea."

"Can we wait?"

"I don't know, Tomić. If we wait... If we go on this rough sea... I don't know." It was rare for Iskra to be indecisive, and she felt helpless. She looked around the small bay as though there was an answer hidden there somewhere, under a rock or behind a tree. Maybe in the sound of the sea itself. Her gaze stopped on Orhan, who was standing near the fishing boat. "And we also need to get Orhan to Dubrovnik."

"I can take Orhan to Dubrovnik while you and Tomas bring Niko to Korčula," Damir offered. "It can't be more than a day's walk from here, if a day."

"Dado, I don't know whether you could find the emissary alone without getting into some trouble," Iskra answered. "You've barely touched the world outside your beloved Bradat."

"So, we'll wait here for a few days until you can return."

Iskra looked at Damir suspiciously and calculated all the possibilities. In her mind, she went through all the different paths for getting Nikola back to Korčula and Orhan to Dubrovnik. None seemed ideal. Each seemed to put either her brother or the foreign boy in greater danger to save the other. In her heart, she knew she would choose Nikola above Orhan, and she hated that it had to come down to a choice.

Then, she realized it didn't.

"Orhan doesn't have to go to Dubrovnik," she declared. "We can take him to Ston."

"Ston?"

"It's a Ragusan town, much closer." Iskra explained quickly. "It should be sympathetic to Turks as well. It belongs to Dubrovnik. We could hand Orhan over to the garrison at Ston and trust that they would take him safely to Dubrovnik.

"Tomić, when the sea calms, can you bring the boat and Niko back to Korčula by yourself?"

"I could bring them back now, if we didn't have to worry about the wound opening."

"And you can get some friends to help you bring him to the inn?"

"Of course."

"Then it's settled," Iskra declared, although no one else had had a chance to offer other opinions. "As soon as it's safe, we'll put Niko into the boat, and Tomić will take him home as fast as possible. Tell my folks what happened, and they'll know what to do. They'll kill me, but they'll take care of Niko first.

"In the meantime, Dado and I will bring Orhan to Ston. I'd rather take him to Dubrovnik, but this should be fine, and it's the best we can do at the moment. I'm sure he'll be fine. Once that's done, we'll head back to Orebić and find a boat there that will take us to Korčula. We should be back before another nightfall."

The five passed the time quietly waiting for the southern winds to settle. They kept Nikola still, and the bleeding never resumed. He was weak, but insisted that otherwise he felt fine and chided Iskra and Tomas for babying him so much. Damir and Orhan sat a small distance away and watched the stars tracing their arcs overhead. All the clouds had vanished from the sky, leaving a canopy of tiny lights and a nearly quarter moon.

Finally, the sea lost its edge. Tomas and Damir helped Nikola to his feet. Iskra and Orhan climbed into the fishing boat, which been lifted in the rising tide, and together the four struggled to get the big man into the boat. Those in the boat took Nikola's arms while he stepped onto Tomas and Damir's shoulders. They lifted him like the rising tide lifted the boat until he could make it over the hull. Nikola sat on a plank by the tiller as his sister examined his back. The blood had started to seep down his back again, although not as eagerly as earlier.

Iskra pushed down over the wound and insisted that they stay until the bleeding had stopped again. When it did, she kissed her brother's forehead, and announced it was time to leave.

"Keep the straps tight, little one," she whispered to her brother.

"Don't worry, Islić, in a couple of days this will just be a good story to tell the girls."

"Get him home, Tomić," she said as she gave the family friend an anxious hug. "Get him to mamma, and everything will be good."

The three staying behind took the sparse supplies from the boat – fresh water and bread Nikola had baked – and pushed the craft again toward the open sea. Tomas raised the sail and quickly caught the breeze that had shifted to the southeast. Damir, Iskra, and Orhan watched as the boat gained speed and rocked over the gentle swells out of the cove. Iskra stared at the horizon for minutes after the boat had disappeared behind a grove of trees at land's edge.

Damir stood beside her.

"We need to rest now," he told her as he put his arm around her shoulder and led her from the waterside. "At sunrise, we'll head to Ston. We'll go quickly. We'll be back to Korčula before dark."

"Do you think he'll be all right?"

Damir held her a little more tightly in response.

The town built of salt

Ston rose from salt. The small town grew at the fortuitous juncture of the Pelješac Peninsula and the Balkan mainland. The location had no particular strategic or military value. Ships and troops could easily avoid it on their way to more important destinations, and the peninsula itself offered nothing more promising than a handful of villages and rolling vineyards.

Ston's power and importance derived from the great salt pans that stretched along a deep-cut bay south of the town. Sea water that covered the shallow pans evaporated in the broiling Dalmatian summer, leaving mounds of salt that were shoveled into heaps and eventually delivered to Dubrovnik. Sales of the salt provided substantial revenues for the Ragusan treasury and gave the republic a reason to protect its interests on the peninsula.

Indeed, soon after claiming the peninsula as its own, the republic built a web of stone walls and fortifications connecting Ston and Mali Ston, a smaller settlement a short walk to the north. These battlements crisscrossed the mile-wide isthmus that joined Palješac to the mainland, and the heavy garrison that manned them protected the salt works and the towns from any raiders. Anyone traveling down the peninsula to Dubrovnik or anywhere further inland had to negotiate their way past these walls, towers, and soldiers.

Damir, Iskra, and Orhan made it to the foothills overlooking Ston by midmorning. No one slept well, and even though they left the cove at first light, their trek across the peninsula was slow. To avoid meeting any strangers, the trio kept to the smaller paths that hugged the ridge line along the southern rim of Pelješac. When they reached a clearing along the way, they could usually see the main trail cutting across a valley below them and once spotted an older woman with a donkey cart full of small barrels. Any suggestion that moving faster along the trail was worth the risk was dismissed by Iskra. She insisted that either way they'd be back to Orebić and then Korčula by that evening. It was better to stay safe, she argued.

Resting in the hillside at the western edge of the peninsula, misgivings about their plan crept into Iskra's thoughts. From where they sat, eating the last of their bread and sipping the remaining water, Ston looked hostile and foreboding. Across a small plain, a large square fortress with towers at each corner dominated the landscape. To the right, the bright salt pans glistened in the midday sun. Even in the distance, the constant movements of scores of workers were noticeable. To the left of the fortress rested the town, nestled within pentagon walls. And from there, parallel walls like tentacles on a squid rose and disappeared across a neighboring hillside, ultimately reaching the unseen Mali Ston.

"It's not going to be hard to find the garrison," Iskra said, pointing to a group of footmen marching in formation on the road to the fortress. She wasn't necessarily relieved. "I think there are some more on the walls, too."

The trio watched the distant movements of the soldiers, little more than dark spots drifting against a static background.

"Maybe giving Orhan to the garrison isn't a good idea," she continued, thinking out loud. "Some of the watchmen I know in Korčula are as dumb as mussels. A town that size, there must be a rector or a captain of the watch that would take responsibility for getting Orhan to Dubrovnik."

"We're not going to find the rector taking a stroll outside those walls," Damir noted, himself wavering on what to do next.

"No. No we're not, Dado." Iskra sighed and peered across the plateau to the fortified town. "What choice do we have, though? Even if we wanted to go to Dubrovnik, we'd still have get through those gates and past the guards. We'd still have to answer questions. Maybe I should talk to the garrison first and see if they're somewhat smarter than mussels."

"Then what, Iskra? You make a signal, and Orhan and I jump out of the bushes? And what if they aren't trustworthy? We either go in together or we don't go. Maybe we can find a boat, go across the bay, and avoid the walls altogether?"

"Neither of us can sail a boat. We'd be helpless without Tomas. Besides, I'm sure they have watches on the coast as well. I don't want to wait until night and lose a day before getting back to Korčula."

With that, Iskra stood and the others followed. They scrambled down the hillside to the main road and began a determined march toward Ston. As a group, they made a raggedy unit. Iskra and Orhan's clothes were tattered at the hems, and all three were dirty and sweaty. They slowed unconsciously as they neared the walls and fortress. The Ragusan flags boasting the image of Saint Blaise fluttered high from the battlements. To the right, an army of workers were shoveling and sifting on the vast salt pans, and, ahead, a squad of guardsmen in red and white livery was just noticing the approaching trio.

The six men, armed with pikes and swords, walked casually toward the three. One of the guardsmen, apparently the sergeant, took the lead.

"Good day, folks," the portly man called when they were close enough. "Welcome to Ston!"

"Good day, sir," Iskra answered.

"You're not from here. Who are you, and what is your business in Ston?" the sergeant asked pleasantly, but with authority. His men had stopped in a haphazard semicircle behind him. They were vaguely interested in the exchange, but had already decided these children posed no threat, even though one seemed quite foreign. The men were happy to leave it to the sergeant whether the group would pass freely or, perhaps, be charged an impromptu toll.

"We're here to see the rector, please," Iskra said. "We have news that might interest him."

"Young lady, I'm afraid we're not so elegant as to have a rector, but perhaps the magistrate can be of service? He more or less runs Ston and Mali Ston, under authority from Dubrovnik, of course. That would be appropriate, yes?"

"The magistrate, yes. We would like see the magistrate, please."

"Of course, I'm happy to see if that can be arranged," the sergeant said with a slight, over-courteous bow. "He will ask who you are and where you're from."

Iskra glanced at Damir and Orhan, but they had little help to offer.

"We are just peasants from the island of Korčula," Iskra answered after a pause. "Our names would have no meaning. But our news concerns the recent battle with Uluj Ali, viceroy of Algiers. The archdeacon, Father Antonio Rosanović, told us to bring it personally to Ston."

The guardsmen took notice at the mention of Uluj Ali and were looking at the three strangers now with increased interest. The sergeant looked at Iskra, taking in her tattered dress and soiled face, and he looked at her companions.

"And there were no, well, let's say, more official messengers that your archdeacon could send?"

Iskra looked again at her Korčulan delegation and realized they indeed looked quite raggedy.

"The archdeacon," she began, "wanted to keep all the men in Korčula in case there was more trouble. We were dropped off near Orebić, but missed the main trail and had to hike through the hills. Please, sir, we're all anxious to get home."

"Then, by all means," he smiled. "Let me make the arrangements."

The sergeant stepped back and talked quietly to one of his men, who frequently looked over at the children with new interest. The sudden attention made Damir nervous, and he was ready to run off with Orhan if Iskra gave a signal. Running would have been futile, however. During the talk with the sergeant, two guardsmen had circled around the trio, blocking any escape.

After a few minutes, the sergeant patted the guardsman he was talking with on the shoulder, and the guardsman left, trotting toward the city gates. The sergeant rejoined Iskra and her friends.

"My man has gone to inform the magistrate," he announced. "Now we must await his reply. Let's rest in the shadows of Kaštio, our fortress, where it's cooler. I'll have one of the women bring fresh water and food. I hope you like mussels."

Damir, Iskra, Orhan and the five guardsmen walked to a grassy stretch at the base of the massive fortress they had seen from the distance. While the subordinate guardsmen kept to themselves, the sergeant chatted warmly with the trio, asking about the attack and regaling them with stories of Ston's history. They watched as the salt workers took their midday break, escaping from the blazing sun in the nearby woods. It's a shame, the sergeant complained light-heartedly, that so much of the town's wealth goes to Dubrovnik, while the townspeople are left with barely enough to survive.

"I guess if we wanted the easy life, we should have been born to a noble house, yes?" he laughed, washing down some smoked mussels on bread with a hearty quaff of water. "Can't be drinking while in patrol!" he said, glaring into at the mug for a moment.

The workers were already returning to the salt pans by the time the sergeant's man returned. He seemed out of breath. The sergeant excused himself and went to talk privately with the guardsman. He soon returned to the group.

"The magistrate will see you," he told Iskra and the others, "but he is entertaining some important merchants from Dubrovnik at the moment. Probably drinking cool Pelješac wine with them in his palace, away from this blazing sun. The burdens of governing, yes? So, unfortunately, you must wait some more.

"I'll leave you with two of my men. They will see that you get anything you need, water or more food. Try to make yourself comfortable. My time is not my own, and I have some minor duties to attend. I will be back soon."

The three rested in the cool shadows with the guardsmen. The time passed in silence. Occasionally a peasant would arrive on foot or with a cart and pass unchallenged. Overall, it was hot and few people were on the road.

Another hour or so passed before the sergeant returned. He and one of his guardsmen were riding a horse, while the other two were driving a flatbed wagon.

"I hope my men have kept you comfortable," the sergeant called from atop his dabbled mount. "The magistrate will see you now, I'm told. He's in Mali Ston inspecting the warehouses with his visitors. Too far to walk, yes? He'll see you when the inspection is completed. Please."

The sergeant gestured toward the wagon, and one of the men opened the drop gate at the back. He helped Damir, Iskra, and Orhan climb in, and then he and another guardsman jumped in behind them.

"It's not a luxury carriage, but it's a short journey and our kind is accustomed to hard wood." The sergeant nudged the horse ahead

138

of the wagon. "Let's go," he called. The wagon's driver slapped the reins against a tired-looking horse's flank, and the wagon jerked into motion. The other guard on horseback followed a few yards behind them.

They wheeled around the walls of Kaštio Fortress and joined a straight road that ran along the eastern edge of Ston. The town was orderly with streets laid out in a perfect grid. They passed neat rows of stone buildings with red tile roofs, a testament to the prosperity of the town, before the road veered right following the contours of a wooded valley. As they turned, Iskra and Damir marveled at the walls that continued straight up the hillside before disappearing across the ridge.

After a few hundred meters, the procession came to a fork in the road, and, surprisingly, the sergeant led them onto the eastern leg, a lesser used trail that ascended onto a small hill.

"Isn't Mali Ston to the west?" Damir asked curiously from the wagon bed.

"Clever boy," the sergeant called over his shoulder, "and correct! Bravo! Mali Ston is just over the western hill. We call it the Wench because, well, you spend significant time on it in the guard. Ha! The main road, however, was washed out by flooding and wagons cannot pass easily. This trail is used mostly by loggers and is just a slight detour. It will take us to Mali Ston just as fast. Don't worry, young man."

But the trio did start worrying when the company pulled up to a neglected hut along the trail and stopped. The guardsmen surrounding them in the wagon were noticeably more alert, and the sergeant dismounted. A moment passed, and the hut's door creaked open.

"Let's finish this, yes?" the sergeant called.

Damir gasped as three men stepped out of the hut: Franco the Spaniard, the boss, and Karlo. "Stay still you three," the sergeant ordered when Iskra started to stand up. All the friendliness had vanished from his voice.

Franco stepped up to Orhan and grabbed his left arm roughly. He pulled the boy's sleeve up and looked at the birthmark, the white blotch that circled Orhan's wrist and travelled almost to his elbow. Franco laughed loudly as he turned back to the sergeant.

"Fortune has indeed smiled upon you, my dear friend," the

Spaniard announced lyrically. "This is the boy who was lost ... and his comrades, too. Whatever god you pray to must be exceptionally pleased with your devotion to have placed such a prize in your lap."

"If wine is a god, we'll certainly be praying to him tonight," the sergeant said. "So here's the boy. Where's the money?"

The boss pitched a small pouch to the sergeant. It jingled when he caught it.

"We'll need the wagon, too," he said. "If all goes well, you'll get it back soon."

"That wasn't in the deal," the sergeant protested, weighing the coins casually in one hand. He looked at his men and at the boss and his companions. "But it's an old horse and an older wagon, yes? No one will notice it missing for a few days. Perhaps you'll favor us with a round of ale when you pass through on your way home?"

"Yeah. Maybe," the boss said. "Karlo, take the wagon. I'm sure these men have somewhere to go."

A ride in a wagon

Franco held Orhan firmly by the arm as the Ston company trooped off, two on horseback and four on foot. Damir and Iskra stayed in the wagon, not wanting to run and leave the foreign boy at the mercy of these men. As soon at the Ston men disappeared around a bend, the boss drew his sword and started toward Damir.

"This is for Mali, you little bastard," he hissed, raising his sword as he walked.

Damir didn't have time to jump from the wagon before the boss was upon him. He cringed low against the wagon's walls and raised his hands to try to protect himself. Iskra instinctively leaned away.

"Wait, señor," Franco shouted. "There will be time to deal with this little peasant once we've finished the task at hand."

The boss paused, the sword raised above his shoulder ready for a backhanded slice. He looked over at the Spaniard.

"Señor," Franco continued, "I recognize this boy. He was there in Korčula when they locked me in the pig sty that you found me in and, praised be the saints, that you liberated me from. He even helped bind my hands after I finished the meager offering they considered hospitality worthy a returning brother. I, too, would like to see him pay for his arrogance. But may I suggest waiting until we are certain to have no more use for him? When the time comes, I will gladly hold the troublesome demon down for you."

The boss, his face red with rage, looked at the Spaniard and turned deliberately toward Damir.

"Hellfire," he shouted and brought the sword down slowly. With the flat of the tip of the blade under Damir's chin, the boss lifted the boys head to stare deeply at his face. The boss grunted savagely and turned away. "Let's get them inside. It's too late to start for Dubrovnik today. Karlo, take care of the horse."

The boss and Franco brought Damir, Iskra, and Orhan into the loggers' hut, a one-room shed with a hearth at one end. "Tie them up, Franco. Use one of those sailor's knots of yours. I don't want them going anywhere again."

The hut was little more than a work shed, a respite from the rain or sun for the Ston men sent to harvest timber from the forest. At the height of summer, when all able townspeople were needed at the salt pans, no one used the structure, at least according to the sergeant. Next to the fireplace was a heavy wooden table with seven chairs. Various saws, axes, and other tools, mostly old and rusted, leaned against the walls. A breeze drifting through the empty windows kept the shack cool.

Franco tied the captives' hands in front of them and sat them against a section of wall, careful to move the tools well out of their reach. Suddenly, he grinned broadly and stepped back.

"Ah, my little friends, this pleasant tableau appears very familiar, does it not?" he asked. "Last time, of course, our roles were somewhat reversed. It was I, Franco of Granada, a fellow Christian seeking succor, who was being tied, while you, young lad … and, I believe your pretty friend as well, were tying my hands. A very sloppy job, but it served its purpose.

"Forgive us for not offering you the same hospitality, I was offered, rotten fish and stale bread, but our resources are much more limited here in this desert. If you rest nicely and cause no problems, I will ask the señor if we can share our water with you, like good brothers of faith."

"We didn't know who you were," Damir responded. "Korčula had just been attacked. There's no need to tie us up. We have no place to go. We're just kids."

"Hush, hush, hush," Franco chided, "of course, I understand. I have traveled the world and seen many things. I understand much. These binds are not meant as offense, but – what was it that the monseñor said? – oh yes, we choose to lean on the side of caution."

"Cut the talking," the boss yelled, sitting next to the empty fireplace. "We need to make plans for tomorrow. I want to get this done quickly and get back to Korčula. Too many things I don't know about this country."

Karlo came in, slamming the door and slapping the dirt off his hands. "Horse is tied up, and I found some grass for it. I rolled the wagon behind the shack so no one from the trail can see it."

"Good job, Karlo. Lash the door so no one can get in or out without us knowing about it."

Karlo secured the door with some loose cord and crossed the room to join the other two men at the table. He exchanged glances with Damir as he passed.

At the table, the men, mostly the boss, spoke softly. Damir couldn't make out what they were saying beyond some grumbling about not having wine or ale. Despite the lack of refreshments, the men appeared in high spirits. Occasional bouts of laughter erupted from the table, and more than once the boss slapped Franco on the back. Once in a while someone would look back to make sure the captives were behaving themselves, but generally the three were left alone.

"Are you hurt?" Iskra whispered to Damir.

"I'm fine, thanks. He just caught me by surprise," Damir said, not looking over at his friend. "The boss said they're taking us to Dubrovnik. Why? He wanted to turn Orhan over in Korčula for a reward."

"I don't know." Iskra looked at the men. A lantern on the table cast a menacing glow on their faces. They were now playing some game with dice, and at intervals the boss would slam his fist down on the hard wood. She heard him say something about buying a bark and sailing to Senj where "a man like me can make his fortune." Karlo, apparently, was marked to join his crew.

Orhan sat close to them, quiet was usual. He flinched whenever the boss' hand slapped against the table.

"Can you get your hands free?" Iskra asked Damir.

"No. The Spaniard tied them very tight."

"Me neither. I don't think there's much we can do tonight, except rest. We need to look for a chance tomorrow to run, but we can't leave Orhan behind." She looked over at the Turkish boy. In the fading light he looked very young and fragile to her. "I hope Niko is all right."

The men at the table played their dice game late into the night, with the boss getting more irritated with his luck as the hours wore on. The game ended when the boss slapped the dice across the table and against a wall.

143

"It is just a game, señor," Franco laughed. "We're not even playing for coins."

"Well, that's because we've pretty much given all our coins to filthy watchmen here and in Korčula." The boss stood and walked around the hut, clearly agitated. "This had better be what you say it is or I'll figure out a way to get my money back from your Spanish hide."

"Señor, there is no need to worry." The Spaniard stayed on his bench while watching the boss intently. "My hide, as you say, is worthless compared to the riches that await us in Dubrovnik. Trust me. It's been a long day for all of us, and we can all use some rest. Perhaps we can send young Karlo into the village to get some wine."

"Too dangerous," the boss snapped. "And we don't have the spare money to get wine even if we sent him."

"One doesn't always need money to get wine," Franco suggested. "I thought you were the kind of man who understood this."

"I'm the kind of man who wants to gets this business behind him as soon as possible and be done with you and this whole country!" the boss yelled.

"Patience, señor." Franco's calm tone only irritated the boss more. "Not long ago, I served on a galley that was part of the Ottoman fleet laying siege to Malta. The captain was a hot-headed fool. Señor, it was a most beautiful fleet. Thousands of warriors waiting aboard two hundred of ships for a chance at glory. The world had never seen such a sight."

"Just put a cork in it," the boss interrupted. "No one here needs a bedtime story."

"But, señor, there is a point. One evening, hours before the battle was to begin, the watch saw a light in the horizon. Thinking it might be a Maltese patrol, the captain ordered the galley to close on it, ignoring sage advice from his janissary captain to signal other ships to join him. He rushed forward and found not one, but two small galliots! Normally, this wouldn't be a problem for a galley such as ours, but these galliots veered in different directions. For a moment our galley continued forward as the captain couldn't choose one or the other to pursue. This was enough for these fast boats to approach from each side, delivering twin salvos that

crippled our ship and took it out of the battle. A mc
patience would have saved the ship and captured the en

"Touching, but as I said, save us your stories. It's
boss grumbled. "Let's get some shut eye." He took a plac ....
back against the door, while the other two made themselves as
comfortable as possible, stretching out on the dirt floor. Damir,
Iskra, and Orhan huddled together, and eventually they all drifted
into fitful sleep.

Early the next morning, a slight noise drew Damir from his
slumbers. He opened his eyes to find Franco rummaging quietly
through the shoulder bags lying on the table. Occasionally how
would look up to see that everyone was still asleep. In the end, he
pulled out a whet stone, stank into one the chairs, and started
sharpening his blade. The rhythmic scratching of the steel blade
against the smooth stone lulled Damir back into sleep.

He awoke again later to find the Spaniard still at the table with
his sword, and now the boss and Karlo were stirring as well.

"Everybody up," the boss called in his raspy voice. He took a
loaf of bread from one of the bags. He tore off three chunks of
various sizes and threw them at the captives. "Eat up, darlings. You
never know when the next meal will come."

Iskra shook off the last threads of sleep and held up her hands.
"Can you untie us?"

The boss laughed. "I'm sure you'll manage. Hurry, my child.
We're going to leave soon."

They ate quickly, the men at the table with the same fare. As
they gathered their gear to leave, Karlo brought water over for
Damir and others.

"Just do what he says, and everything will be fine," he said
softly.

"Karlo, get over here," the boss ordered. "Check to make sure
no one's outside and get the horse and wagon ready. Let's get this
done. If we leave now, we should reach Dubrovnik in four or five
hours. If our friend Franco is right, we'll be rich by nightfall. If
not, hellfire, we can always sell him back!"

The boss laughed riotously at his joke and slapped Franco on
the back. The Spaniard laughed along and busied himself getting
their things together. He examined his sword once more and
sheathed it in the scabbard on his belt. Before long, they were all

in the wagon and heading south along the road toward Dubrovnik, the capital of the Republic of Ragusa. The boss took the reins, with Iskra, Damir, and Orhan, their hands still bound, sitting in the flat bed immediately behind him. Karlo and Franco lounged further back, leaning against the rear gate.

"Have you ever seen Dubrovnik, children?" Franco asked. "It is a most magnificent city. Not as beautiful, of course, as the grand cosmopolitans of Constantinople or Tripoli, but it has a provincial charm with its high walls and stone palaces. They say the women there rival even those of Spain. But, I'm sorry to say, I would not know, having seen it only from the portholes of my galley and, even sadder, having never been back to my beloved Spain since I was much younger than any of you. Too bad I will still not be able to walk the marble streets of Dubrovnik on this occasion as well. I'm afraid my tattoos could raise embarrassing questions among the knowledgeable."

"Your markings? Don't all galley sailors have tattoos?" Iskra asked.

"My young lady, these are special," Franco answered, running his hand across his forehead, where five diamonds drawn with thick lines stretched from temple to temple. "For those who can read them, these say that I have upset my former masters enough that they would pay dearly for my return if I were ever to escape."

"You *upset* them?"

"I had a disagreement with one of the guards and was overly aggressive in proving my point. I would have been hung immediately if I were not so valuable to the captain. Instead, I was beat and marked for a lifetime of slavery with no opportunity to ever gain freedom."

"Then why risk going to Dubrovnik at all?" Iskra asked.

"Excellent question, señorita. There is a risk. That is true. But if you want to sell a fine wine at the best price, you must find buyers who are most thirsty."

"I don't understand," Damir joined in.

Franco looked at the captives and smiled broadly at the foreign boy.

"Can it be that you are unaware of the value of your young friend here?" Franco asked. He looked mischievously at Orhan and spoke rapidly in a foreign language. Orhan held firmly to his mute façade and showed no sign of understanding.

"Well, my young friends, allow me to introduce you to His Excellency Orhan son of Mehmed Mustafa, the recently crowned pasha of Tripoli. He is the youngest son, and perhaps not as valuable as his older brothers might be, but he will still command a small prince's ransom if we can get him to the Ottoman emissary unharmed. The pasha, I'm sure, will be very generous to anyone who saved his precious son from this barbaric land.

"Indeed, I could not believe my ears when my new companions here approached me in my cell and asked about ransoming a young Turkish boy. When they described that blot on his wrist, I could only dream that your friend here was really the pasha's son. Of course, I agreed to help only if they got me out of my own captivity. When I saw Orhan in the wagon by the woodmen's shed, I had no doubt Allah ... or the saints had smiled upon us. The pasha and his brood were on my very ship, and I had seen them often. But how did he get to your rustic island?"

"You really do talk too much," the boss called from the front board. "A man can't hear himself think. And you better be right about your Turk's ransom. It wasn't cheap to pay off all those guardsmen. I better get my money back and then some or maybe we'll need to cash in some of those diamonds."

"Ah, señor, do not worry. The elçi in Dubrovnik – the Sultan's eyes and ears in the Republic – will be most eager to gain favor with Mustafa Pasha. The Ottoman courts are greased by relationships and money flows most swiftly where..."

Franco's defense was cut short when the boss suddenly pulled the wagon to a halt. Saplings had been cut and laid across the road, blocking their path. The boss and Franco drew their swords as a group of burly men stepped from the forest that bordered the road. One grabbed the draft horse's bridle.

A man with long wavy black hair and a wild beard stepped forward. He wore a leather jerkin and pointed a weathered musket at the wagon. The others – five not counting the one holding the horse – fanned out behind him.

"Put your swords down and get out of the wagon" the bearded man called. "It's ours now. The horse, too."

Franco motioned subtly for Karlo to stay in the wagon. "Guard the Turk," he said softly as he stood and sheathed his sword. He

147

jumped down to the right side of the wagon and walked forward, showing his empty hands.

"That would be like a brother taking from a brother, friend," Franco said as he ambled toward the bandits. "I'm sure there's another way we can work through this problem where you're happy and, well, we keep the wagon and horse."

"Stop where you are. I'm not looking to strike a deal. The rest of you, out of the wagon. Now!"

The boss lowered his sword and stepped down on the left side of the wagon. The Spaniard continued to do the talking, stepping wide so he could see around the man holding the horse to the man with the gun.

"Where are you from, friend? If you were from this area, you would know that this is not a wagon that can be of much – what should we say? – use to you. In certain circles, the ownership is quite obvious and any transfer of ownership would be viewed as highly suspicious. I, myself, am from *Malta,* and it took only one painful lesson for me to learn this. I now have patience in my dealings with all. Right, captain?"

Franco looked over to the boss to see if he understood.

"There are some kids in the back. They're tied up!"

One of the bandits had advanced close enough to see what the wagon was carrying.

"Children?" the bearded bandit called. "What's going on here?"

"As I was just explaining, friend, these children, well they're almost adults really, but they were caught taking bags of salt from the warehouses of Ston. It is truly unfortunate how early some people fall astray of the authorities, if it not?" Franco kept slowly circling wide of the man holding the horse. He was pleased to notice the boss also edging forward on his side of the wagon.

"The magistrate of Ston has been commanded to deliver these children to Dubrovnik so their punishment may be a lesson to others who suffer from similar temptations. If they do not reach the walled city by sunset, their presence will be horribly missed and patrols will be dispatched."

"Stop!" the bearded bandit demanded, swinging his arquebus between the boss and Franco.

His order had the opposite of its intended effect. Immediately,

148

Franco drew his sword and charged the bearded bandit, letting loose a high-pitched war cry. On cue, the boss rushed from his side of the wagon and joined in the shouting. The charge caught the bandits by surprise, and the leader, with one shot in his musket, wavered between his two attackers.

He wavered too long.

The boss and the Spaniard were on him in an instant. The boss grabbed the arquebus' barrel and pointed it skyward just as the bandit recovered enough to press the firing level. They were enveloped in a cloud of blue gunpowder smoke, and before it cleared Franco thrust his sword through the man's chest, unimpeded by the thin leather shirt. The bearded man fell to the ground.

The boss and Franco's advantage of surprise had worn out, though, as the other bandits recovered their wits and maneuvered to join the fray. They quickly surrounded the two and began parrying for position. At the wagon, the bandit who had discovered Damir and his companions drew a long knife and was skirting around the side boards to get an opening to Karlo.

"Karlo!" Damir called. "Cut me loose, and I can help! Cut me loose, and I can help! Hurry, Karlo!"

Karlo crouched and danced around the wagon's flatbed, trying to keep his distance from the bandit near him. He looked at Damir and over to the boss and Franco, who despite being outnumbered had reached a stalemate with the men who around them. The bandit at the wagon made a feint at jumping onto the bed, which startled Karlo enough that he stumbled to his knees.

"Karlo!" Damir pleaded.

The young Korčula man looked once again at the group in front of the wagon. He was frozen with indecision.

"Karlo!"

As the bandit circled the wagon once again, Karlo dove across the bed toward Damir. For an instant, he looked desperately into his neighbor's eyes, and cut the ropes that bound Damir's hands. He turned back just as the bandit vaulted the back gate and landed in the wagon bed. Karlo tried to dodge as the bandit ran forward. The bandit's knife caught Karlo's arm and sent him spinning to the floorboards. The bandit turned to deliver a second blew, and was caught off balance when Damir pushed him from behind and sent him toppling over the sideboard.

Damir seized the moment to rifle through the carry bags lying in the wagon bed. He found a small knife and began cutting Iskra and Damir free.

Meanwhile, the deadlock at the front of the wagon had broken in a swirl of swishing blades and long knives. The boss and Franco had sidestepped the bandits until the two stood with their backs against the horse and their combatants arrayed in front of them. A second attacker was already on the ground, and a third had blood pouring from a deep wound in his cheek. Karlo, a trickle of blood flowing down his sword arm, was back on his feet and again facing his own bandit.

"Run into the woods," Damir told Iskra as he finished cutting the foreign boy free. "Keep Orhan close. If we get separated, I'll find you. Remember, 'Chuke!'"

The three leapt over the side of the wagon and started toward the woods on the right. Iskra grabbed Orhan's arm and disappeared into the foliage first.

"Dado!"

Damir looked back at the wagon. Karlo was again at a disadvantage. He was on his back on the ground next to the wagon. His face was covered with blood from a gash on his forehead. The bandit was kneeling on his chest, and Karlo has clutching with both hands the bandit's knife arm, trying to keep him from delivering another blow, his strength slowly waning.

Without hesitating, Damir rushed to help, raising his own small knife high above his head. The bandit rolled off Karlo when he saw Damir racing toward the melee. The bandit braced for the new fight and then seemed to look past Damir. Panting and drenched with sweat, the bandit backed up a few paces before turning and bolting down the road.

Damir reached to help Karlo to his feet. Instead of accepting the help, Karlo grabbed Damir's forearm tightly. Karlo opened his mouth to say something, but his energy drained noticeably, and he released the boy's arm.

"Go," he said.

Damir stood and took a final look at his neighbor before dashing into the woods after Iskra and Orhan. When he pivoted to flee, he ran straight into the broad chest of Franco. Behind him, three bandits lay in the ground, including the bearded leader, and the others had disappeared. The boss had the horse by the bridle, calming the animal.

Franco grabbed Damir's arm with a grip strengthened by years on a galley. He gave no indication of letting go.

200 gold ducats

After the storm of clanging steel and furious shouts, the roadside was eerily calm. Even the constant chirp of morning cicadas seemed to still. Three dead bandits lay sprawled in pools of blood near the front on the wagon, where the boss stood shushing the Ston horse. Karlo slouched near the back wheel, the blood on his face and arm drying, and Franco stood next to him, holding Damir tightly. The rest of the bandits had fled down the road, and Iskra and Orhan into the woods.

The first movement to interrupt the stillness was Franco kicking Karlo fiercely in the ribs.

"You son of a Persian fool!" the Spaniard shouted. "You let them go! You let go the rewards meant to be ours, the destiny that awaited me!"

"Leave him alone," the boss ordered.

Franco turned toward the boss, his body trembling in anger, and then back to Karlo. He reared his foot for another powerful kick and seemed satisfied when Karlo flinched and gasped. Franco stepped away without delivering the blow, dragging Damir along with him. Then he pulled Damir onto the flat bed of the wagon and surveyed the trees surrounding them.

With one muscular arm holding Damir tightly against his chest, Franco brought his bloodied blade against the village boy's neck.

"Girl! I know you're watching!" Franco called, turning Damir effortlessly to the left and right. "Come back, and bring your little Turkish friend or else today will not end well for your *Dado*. No one will be hurt if you come back now!"

The woods around them gave no response. The boss looked at Franco and nodded his approval.

Franco angled the sword more threateningly and tried again. This time he shouted in foreign language. Damir caught Orhan's name in the outburst, but nothing else.

The cicadas and an odd bird answered. As he scanned the woods, Franco regained his calm demeanor. He turned Damir in slow, tight circles on the wagon bed and looked into the trees and underbrush. Rustling in the thickets several yards above them might have been an animal or the children.

"This is your last chance, girl!" the boss shouted, startling the horse.

"You see, señorita, it is time for you to decide," Franco called matter-of-factly. "On the one hand, we can kill this young señor now and hunt you and the prince both down. How far do you think you'll get in this strange country? Or – and this is really the better option, señorita – you both come back, we return His Excellency safely for a small reward, and everyone goes home fat and happy." Franco punctuated his demand with another monologue in the foreign language.

"Run!" Damir shouted before Franco tightened his grip, knocking the air out of his lungs.

"That, señorita, would be the bad option," Franco said in voice that was just a little more than loud. When there was still no response, the Spaniard shrugged his broad shoulders slightly and shifted the blade deliberately against Damir's throat.

"*Dur!*" Orhan stumbled from the undergrowth behind the wagon, dropping to his knees as he lost his balance.

Iskra rushed out of the woods close behind the boy. "Stop! Stop!"

"Welcome back, Your Excellency," Franco saluted with a mock bow that was echoed by Damir, still held fast against the Spaniard's chest. "Please come forward so we might greet you properly."

Iskra helped Orhan to his feet, and together they walked back to the wagon.

"Tie them up, Karlo, and I'll let our tattooed friend loose on you if you let them escape again," the boss yelled. "And wash that blood off."

Franco lowered his sword, keeping a firm grip on Damir as Karlo rose slowly to his feet. Orhan and Iskra climbed into the wagon bed with Karlo pushing them slightly. Once on board, Karlo bound the three again, this time tying their hands and feet. He looked to Franco for approval and was met with a stony stare. He avoided looking at Damir altogether.

"You shouldn't have come back," Damir said as they again crowded into the front of the wagon bed.

"Quiet!" the boss shouted. With the situation under control again, the boss rifled through the dead bandits' clothes and found a small pouch of coins tied to the leader's belt. He took the loot, climbed back onto the driver's board, and shook the reins. The wagon jerked to a start, throwing Franco and Karlo against the back board.

"So, again, we're one happy group!" Franco crooned, wiping his blade with an oily cloth his took from his bag.

"I said, 'Quiet!'"

Franco looked at the boss' back and smiled broadly. He contented himself with the task at hand, rubbing the rag methodically along the length of his sword until it shone a bright silver again. Everyone else in the bed was still and silent. Only Karlo emitted a small moan whenever they hit an especially grueling bump.

The road to Dubrovnik kept near the coastline, staying clear of the Ottoman-controlled hinterland that was only a few miles inland. While treaties with Venice and tribute to Constantinople kept the region in a tense peace, the danger of more bandits was always present. Yet the odd company travelled the remaining miles toward the great walled city with no further threat. Even as they passed through a handful of villages, their progress drew scant attention.

Progress was smooth until, just as they reached the last leg of their journey, they came to a deep, narrow bay that stretched miles inland. None of the company had expected this obstacle, and the option to take a ferry across the bay exposed the growing tensions between the boss and Franco. The boss favored the ferry, even though it would cost most of the coins he took from the dead bandit and they would have to wait an hour or more before their turn came. He even offered to barter his carving blade for ale at a nearby inn to pass the time and stymie any challenge.

Franco was adamantly against the idea. The Spaniard was

visibly anxious around the crowd of people in line for the ferry, and he argued with the boss that they should take the road around the bay no matter how much time it added to their travels. The boss prevailed only when Franco backed down abruptly, insisting instead that they wait out of sight until their turn on the ferry came and getting the boss to promise they would continue around the bay if they had to wait too long. With the compromise, the boss stayed with wagon in the line to the ferry while the others waited on a hillside behind the village.

After an hour or so, the boss signaled the others with a whistle and together they took their place on the ferry, a flat barge just large enough for two wagons and about a dozen people. Although their fellow passengers glanced at the children tied in the back of the wagon, the boss' glare was enough to dissuade the curious from asking any questions. The ferryman guided the boat along a rope that was tied across the narrow inlet, and soon the group was rolling onto a pier on the southern side of the bay.

The boss lost no time in driving the wagon forward, quickly pulling ahead of the other travelers who had shared the ferry. He followed a road that backtracked along the south side of the bay until it reached sea and turned sharply left toward Dubrovnik. By late afternoon the wagon rumbled into a clearing and Dubrovnik sprang into view as they crested a hill. The boss pulled the wagon to a halt, and even the captives turned in awe to take in the grandiose vista. The four from Korčula had heard stories of Dubrovnik, the city that had never been conquered, but none had ever seen it, not even the boss.

High gray walls and higher towers surrounded the city, while red roofs peeked over the parapets from the northern quadrant, lifted up by a steeply sloping hillside. To their right, battlements rose forebodingly from the sea, waves crashing against their foundations. A circular fortification on a rocky outcrop protected the nearest corner as the wall turned sharply inland, tramping off toward the hills in the north. Colorful banners fluttered along the walls and towers. Countless ships sailed in and out in the distance.

A massive, foreboding monolith rose just in front of them. The fortress, cut from living stone across a small cove from the city's the western gate, soared overhead menacingly. It commanded the approaches to Dubrovnik from the sea and the western approaches by land. Watchmen were visible on its upper reaches, and others patrolled the city walls.

While the Korčulans were dumbstruck by the size and splendor, Franco remained unmoved.

"The city will still be here when we are all rich, my friends, and when you are all rich you will be able to enjoy it more," the Spaniard laughed, breaking the spell. Indifferent to the spectacle of the great city, Franco watched up and down the road. As they got closer to the city, the road became busier and Franco more nervous. "For now, there is work to be done and preparations to be made. We must find a quieter place."

"He's right," the boss agreed reluctantly. "Let's keep going. We need a place to camp before nightfall. This has taken too long already." He forced his attention away from the walled city and surveyed the area. "Let's find a way to those hills," he said, pointing toward rounded slopes behind the city.

He shook the reins, turning the wagon around and away from the city. He and the other Korčulans kept glancing back at the gleaming walls of Dubrovnik until the wagon again dipped below the hillside. Each imagined different pleasures and entertainments that might be found within if one were rich enough.

They soon found a smaller path that cut northward through a copse of trees and eventually joined a road that twisted along the slopes just north of Dubrovnik. There were fewer people on this road, which seemed to bypass the city. After a hundred yards, the boss pulled the wagon to the side of the road.

"Franco, take Karlo and look around," he ordered. "There should be a trail up this hill, and maybe a place to camp. Be quick, I don't want to stay in the open too long."

After Franco and Karlo disappeared down the road, the boss pulled a flask from his bag and took a deep pull.

"Hellfire, it's hot," he said.

Damir shifted in his place so he was facing the man.

"Boss," he started, "you know, you don't really need to keep me tied up. Iskra either, really."

"Hold your trap! I'm not in the mood for conversation."

"But really, we all want the same thing, to get Orhan back to the Turks. If you make a profit, who cares? But, you know, why settle for just one reward when you can have two?"

156

"I said quiet," the boss snapped. "Why does everyone want to talk so much? I'll give you this, though, boy, you're smarter than you look."

The old man cut short any more talk, and the four waited in silence for Franco and Karlo to return. When they did, Franco reported that they had found a good spot just a little further down the road. He and Karlo jumped back into the back of the wagon, and Franco guided the boss to a path, partly overgrown, that struggled up the side of the hill. With difficultly, they forced the wagon up the trail until they came to the first switchback, which was partly washed out by a long-ago rain. They abandoned the wagon, hiding it as well as possible, and continued along path, kicking away prickly tendrils that attacked their legs.

"By hell, I don't see why we couldn't just to go in and get the money," the boss complained as he led the group through the low scrub. "You said this would be easy. Hellfire, it would be easier just to turn you in for the reward." He laughed loudly at his own joke.

Franco, holding fast to the rope that bound Damir, Iskra, and Orhan, glowered at the boss' back.

"That would indeed be easier, good señor," said Franco, whose cheerful tone contrasted his contorted face, "but the reward would be much smaller. I doubt it I could fetch a hundredth of what we can demand for the princeling here. And we will get nothing if we are not patient. Our meeting with the elçi must be on our terms, not his. Of course, if you prefer, we can always test our fortune with His Excellency surrounded by his house guards."

The boss grunted a reply.

Any more complaints were curtailed when the path opened onto a wider, flat area that overlooked the main road. From the front edge of the plateau, sight lines were reasonably clear in both directions, while anyone at the far side remained invisible. Even though small paths led off in both directions along the hillside, a steep slope separated the plateau from the road, about six yards below. The boss was satisfied with the site, and the group settled in away from the ledge, tying the horse nearby.

"Nothing to do but wait for the morning," the boss said, clearing stones from a small patch of ground. "Someone should stay awake to watch. We'll take turns."

The six settling in as the lights of Dubrovnik flickered on in the distance and the sun dropped toward the sea on their right. That night, the sun chose long streaks of vibrant reds and oranges for its closing act. The colors filled the sky until the sun the slowly disappeared under the horizon and the approaching darkness squeezed the colors into narrow bands. In silhouette, the distant islands became lumbering sea monsters drifting out for their nightly hunt. Their prey, it seemed, was a school of scattered lantern lights bobbing in the waters beyond the city.

A cool breeze blew away many of the frustrations of the journey, and the group, including the captives, relaxed as the boss doled out water and bread that he bought at the ferry stop.

"So, how do we do this?" he finally asked, sitting down in the dirt and stretching his legs in front of him.

The growing moon was still hidden behind their backs, and a blanket of stars replaced the sun's fading hues above them. The murky path of the Milky Way stretched clearly overhead. Sailors had a name for each pattern of stars, Damir knew, and Father Anton once recited a number of them, animals and mythical heroes. For farmers, though, the stars were simply familiar points in the sky. Only their absence or presence suggested the next day's weather. Directions were an easy matter of knowing the mountains and the valleys and the trails.

"Nothing could be easier, señor," said Franco, who knew the stars and could find his way to Spain from the slightest glint in the night sky. From the plateau in the early evening, his attention was held by Arcturus, which the Ottomans called *al-simāk,* as it floated toward the unseen horizon. "In the morning, you go to the elçi's palace, let him know we have found their lost prince, and guide him here with the reward. He will want guards, but not too many. And, no bowmen. A child could do it."

"If it's so easy, maybe you should do it, Franco. I'll stay here and watch the treasure, make sure no one leaves. You speaking his language and everything."

"Gladly, señor, except, the tattoos. Dubrovnik is a welcoming city, but I would not get three steps inside the gate before someone decided that I, too, was a gift from heaven, their ship to a comfortable life. Anything I say from that moment would be held suspect, a ploy for securing my own release. I do not think I would be allowed out of the city once I received its hospitality."

The group sat in silence. As the moonlight reached over the hills, the boss studied Franco closely. The Spaniard's vigil never left the western horizon. The others were also lost in the slow dance of lights spread before them.

"I can go," Damir volunteered, surprising everyone.

"You would run at the first chance, *Dado*," the boss objected. "I'll send Karlo."

Franco looked quizzically at the boss. No further argument was needed.

"I can go," Damir persisted. "We all want to get Orhan back safely. Why would I run? Where would I run? I can meet the Ottoman, bring him here, and we can be finished with it all quickly. You all can take your ducats and disappear."

The boss was quiet as he considered the options.

"Damir, then," the boss said at last. "He's a bright boy, and he cares about what happens to our foreign friend here. You won't let us down, right, Dado? And if he does, we still have the Turk."

"That is true, señor," Franco interjected. "The boy is no idiot, but he is naïve. He has barely left his cozy village. Can we trust him not to get lost – or worse – as soon as he enters the great walled city? Perhaps the girl, the lovely Iskra, is a possibility, but who would believe a girl would be sent on a task such as this? Would the elçi even accept a meeting with her? I am afraid, you are our best choice, señor, if we want to complete this business quickly and profitably."

"Listen, *friend,* I am not leaving you alone with the treasure chest," the boss snapped.

"I would not be alone. Karlo would be with me."

It was the boss' term to offer an incredulous glance.

"You can trust me, señor."

The boss stood and paced in small circuits along the ledge. The moon had meandered overhead. He looked at the dim faces of his companions on the plateau, and then at the undulating lights of Dubrovnik. A peasant man and a girl with a vegetable cart passed on the road below, lost in murmured conversation. He watched as the cart rattled away to the west. The two showed no sign of noticing him, just a few yards above them.

"Damir and the girl will both go," he declared. "She will make sure he doesn't get lost."

"Señor, they are but children. You would be…"

"It's decided," the boss interrupted. "You said yourself this would be so easy a child could do it. The only question is, what's the ransom?"

Franco seemed about to argue more, and then thought better of it.

"Yes, the amount of reward is a delicate matter," Franco offered, acquiescing to the decision. "If we suggest too little, the true identify of our prize would come into doubt and, not to mention, our purses would suffer. Too much, on the other hand, and the Ottoman could refuse or insist on a larger guard. I have given the question much thought during our arduous journey across your lovely island.

"One hundred ducats seem an appropriate amount."

"One hundred?" the boss shot back immediately. "You said this boy was worth a king's ransom! Once we take out what I've had to pay to get us this far and split the rest, it wouldn't last a year!"

"His Excellency is a princeling, not a king, not even a pasha, and not even an eldest son," Franco returned. "I do understand your quandary, however, señor. We could risk asking for two hundred ducats, shiny and bright. Even the youngest son of Mehmed Mustafa should be worth such an amount to the Ottoman representative here."

"Two hundred? Spaniard, you filled me with stories of riches. My share of two hundred ducats, no matter how shiny, won't satisfy my dreams." The boss' pacing around the plateau quickened.

"Then you should have found one of his older brothers, señor."

"Let's go for three hundred and be done with it."

"Three hundred," Franco considered. "That's possible. It would require some negotiating to convince the elçi that His Excellency Mehmed Mustafa and especially his lovely wife, the beautiful Ayse, would see that as an appropriate price for the return of their youngest son. It would be a task beyond the persuasive skills of mere children."

"Hellfire!" the boss fumed. He stopped pacing and glared toward the lights of Dubrovnik.

"Señor," Franco continued, "I'm as eager to have this business over and return to my blessed Granada as you are to take a company to Senj. If it speeds a conclusion, I would take a smaller share of the reward, say thirty percent instead of the forty percent that was our agreement. My dreams are much more modest."

The boss turned toward the Spaniard, numbers slowly making their way through his calculations. In the end, he sighed heavily.

"Two hundred gold ducats it is."

The rest of the evening was spent telling Damir and Iskra what was expected of them and how to find the elçi's palace. The lessons were spiced with several warnings of what would happen to Orhan if they did not succeed. Slavery was outlawed in Dubrovnik, they were told repeatedly, but there were other markets. The orders lasted well beyond midnight, and once they were understood completely, the group lay down to sleep, with the boss, Karlo, and Franco taking turns at watch. The night passed noiselessly, except during Franco's watch, which Damir noticed was marked by the scrapping sound of a sword being sharpened.

Dubrovnik

"Be back by sundown," the boss shouted from the edge of the plateau. Franco stood next to him, holding Orhan by the arm. Karlo watched from a few feet to the side, the gash on his face red and angry. "Get this done, and everyone will be fine."

From the roadway, Damir and Iskra stopped to look at the four looming above. The morning sun lit half their faces in a yellow glow, while the other half remained in deep shadow. The pair waved acknowledgement and started walking along the road, turning left toward Dubrovnik at the first large trail they found.

They talked very little as they gradually joined the leisurely current of tradesmen and others flowing toward the city gates. Both Damir and Iskra understood implicitly that there was no question of defying the boss. What could they do? Alert the city guard? The boss and Orhan would disappear as soon as they saw troops marching down the road.

And besides, there was no real reason to disobey their instructions. In the end, Orhan would be with the Ottomans, which is what Iskra and Damir wanted. Did it really matter to them if the boss got his two hundred ducats in the bargain? Orhan would be safe, and Iskra and Damir would be heading back to Korčula, probably never to see the boss or Franco again. Karlo would have to choose his own fate.

Such considerations didn't linger long with Damir and Iskra. Guilty excitement about seeing Dubrovnik eclipsed their immediate concerns. The allure of entering the storied city grew stronger with each step. Part of the silence was that they were ashamed to admit it, even to each other. Streets paved with polished marble, shops selling wares from the furthest reaches of the seas, and people from every land awaited them.

Soon, the woods opened, and the two found themselves on a road that traced the path of the western wall along a wide moat. Homes, workshops, and warehouses clustered along one side of the road, growing more frequent as they neared the gate. Across the trench, twin walls rose from living stone, interrupted by a series of rounded towers. The nearer wall, somewhat lower than its twin, tapered away from the defensive ditch and stretched higher than anything the two islanders had ever seen. In comparison, Korčula's walls were mere playthings, little more than the walls Damir built among the olive groves.

Ahead on their right, the massive fortress they had seen the day before towered against the sea, more threatening than before now that Iskra and Damir were alone. In an instant, dwarfed by these stone fortifications, they were overcome by the seriousness of their mission. They stopped just before reaching the stone bridge that led to the western gate. Iskra noticeably took a deep breath.

"In this dirty, torn frock, I look like some poor peasant girl, right? Not like a kidnapper demanding ransom?" Iskra asked quietly as they watched a parade of people – most on foot, some on horseback – ramble without a care across the cut-stone roadway and onto a wooden drawbridge at the far end. A group of three guards stood just in front of the gate, an arched entryway barely wide enough for three people abreast. They seemed entirely indifferent to the procession, and the patrols on the walls showed even less interest in the comings and goings at the gate.

"We look just like everyone else," Damir assured her, taking Iskra's arm and nudging her toward the bridge. "Maybe a little dirtier. Remember, if anyone asks, we're brother and sister looking for work."

The pair was almost to the drawbridge when their progress was halted. The guards had taken an unusual interest in a passing cart, stopping it and everything behind it. They looked through the gourds being brought into the city, picked through the melons, and asked the woman driving the cart several questions. Damir and Iskra couldn't hear the exchange, but after a few minutes the guards laughed loudly among themselves. They let the woman and her produce pass, and the line began moving forward again.

When Damir and Iskra's turn came at the gate, the guards were once again preoccupied with their own conversation. One glanced over at the two islanders or perhaps at the man beside them. Damir reflexively put his arm around Iskra, but there was no challenge. They passed unquestioned under the statue of Saint Blaise, the city's patron saint, who watched the procession from a niche above the arched gateway.

Instead of marble streets beyond the gate, Damir and Iskra found themselves in an enclosed courtyard, facing a second gate. It was like being inside a giant stone box surrounded by featureless stonework. The second gate was just as narrow as the first and also protected by another effigy of the patron saint. Along with the others entering the city, they descended a winding ramp toward the archway. Unlike the first gate, however, there were no guards at this entrance, and the train of people progressed steadily into the city.

A rush of noise and activity greeted them as crossed the second threshold. They entered into a large square with vendors on all sides selling food and drink, cloth and tools, the exotic and the mundane. Buyers and sellers in a colorful array of costumes negotiated lustily over the price and quality of the wares. A huge, circular fountain dominated the interior of the square, and sweet water poured from the mouth of grotesques that defended its circumference. Damir and Iskra allowed the crowd to jostle them toward the fountain, where they refreshed themselves greedily and took their bearings.

A broad avenue stretched directly in front of them toward the city's far gate. From the Franciscan monastery at the foot of the avenue onward, shops opened onto the main thoroughfare. Merchants waited at doors whose upper halves were swung open and pawned a gamut of crafted products, from medicines to finely embroidered kerchiefs. Tall stone buildings stood shoulder to shoulder along the avenue, an unnatural canyon created by armies of unstoried masons.

Men and women bustled over the marble pavement, precisely cut stone that gleamed from the passage of countless boots. Some disappeared into narrow side streets, while others emerged to take their positions in a continuous dance of commerce and busyness.

"By the saints, where do we start?" Damir moaned.

Iskra looked around at the chaos that surrounded them. Nothing offered any help. She climbed onto an empty crate that had been discarded next to the fountain and turned full circles.

"I'm not sure, Dado," she called from her slightly elevated perch. "Maybe we should find a watchman and ask him? ... Wait!"

Iskra jumped from her perch and grabbed Damir's hand. She pulled him behind her as she hurried down the main avenue.

"Come on, you lazy mollusk! Keep up!"

Damir trotted behind his friend obediently. They dodged around others on the hectic street, shoppers, merchants, traders, workers, and nobles. As they neared the far gate, the shops lining the street shifted into elegant palaces. Just as they entered a square at the end of the avenue, Damir spotted what Iskra was chasing: two dark-skinned men, wearing turbans and deep in conversation.

Their quarry slipped through the crowded streets almost effortlessly, while every obstacle slowed Iskra and Damir's progress. With great effort, they closed in and Iskra shouted out.

"Excuse me, sirs! Excuse me."

But the men either didn't hear or didn't care. They continued without notice.

"Please, sirs, excuse me," Iskra repeated, reaching out and grabbing one of the men by the sleeve.

This time the turbaned men stopped and turned. The taller looked beyond the pair for an instant before giving them his attention. Iskra and Damir stood before them, sweaty and slightly out of breath. A thin strip of cloth at the hem of Iskra's torn skirt hung loose, and both wore clothes stained by their long journey. The contrast with the rich clothes and easy demeanor of the men was stark.

"Thank you, sirs," Iskra began after a pause to gather her breath. "Please, we are looking for the Ottoman palace. We need to speak to the emissary, the ambassador, the ... *itchy*? We have an important message. Can you help us?"

The two men listened intently and spoke quietly together in a foreign language. The taller one smiled awkwardly, and the smaller one gave her a silver soldi that he pulled from his purse. Then, the two men rushed away.

"Wait! Wait!" Iskra called to no avail. The men had already folded into the crowd.

"Well," Damir suggested, "at least we can get some food while we look for the palace."

After the fruitless chase, the two found themselves in a market square much larger than the one at the western gate. Public palaces with elegantly carved stone facades formed the boundaries. The north edge was dominated by the newly built Sponza Palace, where traders brought their wares to be weighed, judged, and taxed. The colonnade on the ground floor was crowded with laborers and merchants fighting to move their goods through as quickly as possible. Next to the palace, bordered by a soaring clock tower, the eastern gate opened to the docks, where longshoremen rolled barrels and lifted bales onto and off of awaiting ships.

The square itself was another sea of trading stalls with narrow channels flowing between them. Among the roar of bickering and haggling rising from the colorful waves of fabric awnings, a church dedicated to the city patron saint rose like a rocky island in a tempest. Nearby, Orlando's Column, a singular peak offering orientation to the masses, honored a storied French knight said to have saved the city from Saracen pirates almost a millennium earlier.

"We're no better off than when we started," Iskra complained.

"Let's just go through the city," Damir proposed. "It's not that big, really, and we're sure to find the Ottomans eventually."

"Not that big? You're crazy, Dado." Iskra looked around at the people and stalls and buildings that surrounded them. Nothing she saw offered any hint of what they should do next. "Follow me."

Iskra led Damir on a rambling circuit through the market square. She tried to ask directions from the buyers darting from one stand to another and was ignored. She tried the sellers. As soon as it was clear that she wasn't buying anything, they too ignored her, barking touts to persons whose purses had more jingle. It seemed she had approached everyone in the market, a few more than once, before finding a rotund man pawning small fish fried in pig's fat at the edge of the madness.

"The Ottoman Palace? I've never heard of it. Here, you look hungry. Have a couple. They're really good." The man ladled a few of his fish onto a chunk of bread and handed them to Iskra. "No charge. No one's buying today, and they'll just rot. I love these little fishies."

Then in a softer tone, "It's day-old bread. I get it from a friend in a bakery." He gingerly took a fish straight from the pan with two fingers and, after shaking it a bit, nestled it in a hammock of bread, and popped it into his mouth. He watched as Iskra and Damir ate the fish and greasy bread, and glowed happily when they complemented him appropriately.

"Great, aren't they? It's a simple fisherman's meal. Just the thing for a simple fisherman like me." The man laughed and ladled a few more up for them. "Now, the Turks have a villa in the southern district ... more like a large house, I'd say. I don't think anyone would call it a palace. It's much smaller than the rector's palace here." He pointed to the massive edifice behind him with arched windows and imposing columns. "They used to store gunpowder there. After it blew up twice, they moved the powder somewhere else. Funny that they needed two explosions to get the point. That's government for you."

Iskra and Damir listened politely to another tale of the city's architectural history before gently steering the topic back to the Ottomans.

"Oh, yeah, the Turks. They have a house they use to entertain and for official business. From what I hear, though, their parties are pretty dull, not like the ones that the Hapsburgs throw. Those are something. I don't think the Venetians throw any parties at all. They're pretty tight fisted."

"So, sir, where is the house?" Iskra asked, trying to keep the conversation on track.

"Whose house?"

"The Turks."

"That's right. They don't make a big display of it, so it's easy to miss. I'm sure you'll find it, though. Go down to the cathedral. It was paid for by the English King Richard centuries ago as a gift. We saved his life, they say. Go right onto the street behind it, behind the cathedral. The Ottoman house is toward the end of the street, on the left just before you reach the big granary that they just finished building. If you get to the granary, you've gone too far. I don't go that way often, but you should be able to find it by the crest over the door."

Iskra and Damir thanked the man quickly before he started on the history of another of the city's buildings. They found the cathedral easily enough, with its high, domed tower, and headed down a side street on their right. Almost immediately, they were lost in a warren of twisting, narrow streets. Many of the buildings had family crests above their doors, and the two quickly realized they did not know what an Ottoman emblem would look like. The stone buildings began to look alike, and churches and chapels appeared randomly, with Saint Blaise judging them from slender niches at every turn.

They circled the southern district at least twice and avoided wandering into the higher northern areas only because the wide avenue between the two was an obvious boundary. They quarreled about whether they had already searched specific streets. They asked for directions, but few people had time for them. Those who did pointed down different streets. By mid-afternoon, they found themselves again at the big fountain near the western gate.

"Franco said this would be easy. We don't have much time left," Damir said as he refreshed himself at one of the carved spouts.

"We have to be smarter," Iskra said. "Why is no one helpful?"

Damir pondered the question. "Maybe they think we're beggars, like those men in the turbans. Maybe they don't like beggars."

The day was again hot and only the slightest breeze dared breach the walls of Dubrovnik. The mass of shoppers in the square had thinned since the morning, while the crowd around the fountain had thickened. Many were impatiently awaiting their turns at the cool waters flowing from the spigots. A short, bearded man in a richly embroidered jacket pushed past Iskra and Damir, knocking them back among the emptying stalls.

"Here, you're welcome to drink your fill, and then you have to make way for the next," he grumbled.

The man who spoke was not much older than Iskra and Damir, perhaps in his mid-twenties. He wore a scarlet coat with a matching, flat-topped cap.

"Thank you, sir," Iskra replied, irritably, and started to pull Damir away.

"You're most welcome, young lady," the man said, bowing slightly. He stepped forward and kept pace with the two islanders as they moved away from the fountain. "You are visiting our fine republic?"

"Yes, we are, thank you." Iskra answered tersely as she

continued to drag Damir back into the southern district. "Come on," she prodded quietly between clinched teeth.

"Have you enjoyed your stay? Our food? Our wares?"

Iskra gave up on escaping the persistent gentleman and turned toward him. He, too, stopped and smiled.

"We have neither the time nor resources to enjoy the comforts of you fair city, sir, as you might have surmised." Iskra spread her hands in a gesture than embraced their general haggardness. "So, please, if you would allow us to continue. We have business."

"Forgive me," the man said with another habitual bow, "I was merely trying to be friendly."

"If that's true," Damir muttered, "you would be the first friendly person we've met in this *fine republic*."

"But this is a very friendly city, sir, I assure you," the man replied, "if you are not ... spies."

"Spies?" Iskra and Damir exclaimed as one.

"Please forgive the assumption, but your accents give you away." The man smiled broadly, exuding cleverness. "You are clearly from the lands of His Serenity, are you not? We are a very welcoming city, and we have many traders and merchants arriving from Venetian lands. The visitors from the north, however, tend to be more ... prosperous – better dressed, lovely hairstyles, and ... washed.

"Yet here you both are in tattered clothes and unwashed, appearing as poor peasants lost in a wicked world. How, if I might ask, would such poor peasants afford such a long journey from the domains of His Serenity to our gates? Why would they bother?"

Iskra took a breath to start to answer and thought better of the idea.

"To gather information, of course, thinking their disguises were ingenious," the man continued, breaking the brief silence with a tone twice as clever. "These are tense days, and rumors of war fill the air. And – *ecco!* – two misplaced puppets with northern accents arrive on our streets ... asking questions about the Ottomans, of all things. Most people would see that as quite suspicious. The people of Ragusa are quite sensitive to political intrigue."

The man stopped to watch Iskra and Damir's reaction. The two Korčulans looked at each other, eyes wide. Their first instinct was to bolt through the gate and flee. The gate was yards away, though, and they would have to scramble past the man, the crowd, and the guards. And, that would mean abandoning Orhan. Iskra looked back at the man and after several false starts took a deep breath.

"But, sir, we are not spies."

"Young lady, I do not believe you are," the man said triumphantly. "If I did, you would not be talking with me, but with my two colleagues standing near the gate." He waved vaguely at two uniformed men with spears hovering at the edge of the crowd. Neither Iskra nor Damir had noticed the guards before.

"Indeed, if you are spies, you are very bad spies. You've been walking in circles around the city for hours, making no secret of your intended goal, which by the way you passed several times. Your longest conversation was with the old fish monger on Luža Square. That man is happy to talk with anyone, is he not? But he has no secrets.

"Of course, at first we thought you were common thieves preying on those poor silver merchants. It's a good thing you weren't. We like keeping our business interests safe within these walls. When you merely asked questions about the Ottomans, they brought me in. The mystery remains, however, who are you? And I suggest answering ... truthfully."

The lie Iskra and Damir had planned about seeking work in Dubrovnik fell apart before they had a chance to use it. The man is the red cap was right. They had spent the day roaming the streets of Dubrovnik and had nothing to show for it. From one perspective, they had done nothing wrong: they were the messengers, not the kidnappers. It was getting late, and the boss wanted them back by sundown. Perhaps it was time to take a risk.

The elçi's interview

Iskra studied the man in the red coat and cap. His face and hands showed no scars, no signs of a life more demanding than a bureaucrat's pampered existence. He carried no weapon, not even a dagger. His expression was the embodiment of patience and caring, even as his eyes betrayed constant vigilance.

She looked at Damir, who nodded slightly.

"I am Iskra from the island of Curzola, and this is my companion, Damir, who is also from the island," Iskra began, trying to gauge the man's reaction. "We need to speak to the Ottoman emissary or envoy or whatever his title is. Some men are holding a boy. They say he's a Turkish prince. We were sent – ordered really – to seek an exchange."

The man in the red cap listened intently, his countenance unchanged. He allowed Iskra's pause to expand until she rushed to fill the silence.

"We found him on Curzola and were trying to bring him here. But these men grabbed us, all three of us. We don't have time. They said they want us back by sundown. Please, sir, we need to speak to someone."

"And ... how did this *prince* arrive in Venetian territory?"

"We don't know," Iskra replied. "He showed up a few days ago, after a battle at Curzola town. He doesn't speak our language. Please, sir, we are running out of time."

The man considered Iskra's story. After a moment, he turned to Damir.

"Is this all true, young man?" he asked. "And remember, there are people here who believe you could be Venetian agents."

"Yes. Every word," Damir responded, stepping forward slightly.

171

"Well, we shall see!" the man almost shouted, bringing his hands together in a prayer-like gesture. "We shall see."

The guards who that had been lingering at the borders of the square had moved up behind Iskra and Damir unnoticed. Their grim demeanors were a sharp contrast to the ready smile of the man in red.

"Come with me … well, with us," the man said and started walking back into the southern districts. "My name is Miho Bunić. I am what we call a *dragoman*. I have been trained for years to represent the interests of the Republic to the Sublime Porte. I even spent some time in Izmir. On the Aegean Sea."

Miho glanced over to Iskra and Damir to ensure that they were suitably impressed.

"We are going to see the elçi at his residence. He's the high representative for Ottoman interests in Dubrovnik. The elçi is usually a most gracious gentleman, fair and even-tempered. In these tense times, however, he has shown that he does not suffer fools gladly, and he is quite busy. I have already discussed your presence in Dubrovnik with him, and he has agreed to an audience if I deem it an appropriate use of his valuable time."

The news that they had been talked about in hidden consultations caught Damir and Iskra by surprise. While they were drifting blindly through the narrow streets and climbing endless steps, their movements were marked and the information fed into the city's mechanism of intrigue, like grain into a flour mill. The result come could have gone badly for them, as evidenced by the two armed men who kept close behind them. And all the while, they were oblivious, two flies that had wandered into a spider's nest and didn't even see the webs.

Miho led his contingent of five confidently through the jumbled streets, passing many buildings that had become familiar to Iskra and Damir. They quickly found a modest compound that abutted the wall facing the sea. The building was indistinguishable from dozens of others, except for a crest, partly hidden by shrubbery, that presented a glyph that looked to Iskra like a bird's head with some lines running through its beak.

"That's the tughra of His Most Excellent Sultan Selim, son for the great Sultan Suleiman the Magnificent," Miho explained helpfully when he noticed Iskra's interest. "We are here. Best behavior, now."

Miho rapped on the door. Immediately a servant opened it and ushered Miho, Damir, and Iskra through a small room and into a courtyard.

As the door closed, Damir looked back and saw the armed men who had accompanied them were already walking away. In their place were two other men, mirrored images standing on each side of the doorway. They were motionless, carved into the stone walls like chiseled twins. Both had heavy dark beards and deep, dark eyes. Both wore a long dull blue coat and white pantaloons, topped by the same complex headdress: a metal crown with a feathered plume and a tall white cap that folded over and cascaded down their backs. Both carried a large curved sword hung from a green sash. And both were marked by the same tattoo under their left eyes, a square off center within a square.

"Please come in," someone called from the far end of the courtyard. "It's a lovely day, and I thought we would have coffee here in the yard. Thank you for bringing our guests, Mr. Bunić."

In a corner of the yard, under the shade of a spreading fig tree, a table stood encircled by four heavily cushioned chairs. Two men, one in a broad white turban and a flowing silk robe of many colors and the other in a simpler robe and a tighter headdress, stood next to the setting.

"May I introduce His Excellency, the elçi in Ragusa to His Most Excellent Sultan Selim, Mohamed Hamid Pasha," Miho announced with great flare, and the man in the white turban nodded. "Your Excellency, Iskra and Damir of the island of Curzola of the territories of His Serenity."

"Please, do sit down, my guests," the elçi implored. The elçi sat first. The other man, an aide by appearances, stood behind the Ottoman official attentively. With no signal that Damir or Iskra noticed, servants fluttering around the courtyard bringing trays of figs, pitchers of water, and small urns made of hammered copper with matching cups and bowls. They poured rich, dark coffee from the urns and opened the bowls to reveal squishy, sugary cubes. "Now, tell me your story. From the beginning, please."

Aware of the hour, Damir and Iskra rushed through the narrative. Damir began, describing how he found Orhan in the woods and the journey to Korčula town. They took turns telling how they made their way from Korčula to Dubrovnik, sometimes talking over each other in their haste. They described the boss and the galley slave, Franco.

"And they want two hundred ducats as a reward for returning Orhan safely," Iskra concluded, somewhat confidently. "We need to hurry. They said to be back by sundown. And, they said, no bowmen or musketmen."

"The days of summer are long in Ragusa. We have time," the elçi replied gently. "So, tell me, please, how did this boy get to your island, and so far from the field of battle?"

"We don't know," Damir said. "As I said, we haven't been able to talk with him. He was hiding from those men on the bark. Maybe they chased him to my end of Korčula, um, Curzola."

The elçi considered this for a moment, and then asked, "And why do you think he is a prince among the Ottomans? It would seem very fortunate for you and your colleagues that such a prince would wash up on your shores."

Under the questioning, it occurred to Damir and Iskra that they really knew little about Orhan. Their story was filled with assumptions and guesses, and they grew more nervous with each question and answer.

"He is obviously a foreigner, his dark skin and unusual clothes," Iskra pleaded. "He doesn't understand our language … or doesn't seem to. Franco said he saw the boy on his galley with the pasha."

"A galley slave saw this young prince from the confines of his rowing bench?"

Damir and Iskra nodded meekly.

The elçi stood up and walked around the courtyard in thought. Near the entrance, the guards grew more alert at the sudden motion.

"Mr. Bunić," the elçi said after reflection, addressing the dragoman who had listened quietly throughout the interview, "I want to thank you for bringing these children to my attention. Their story is quite fascinating, and I am pleased to have had the opportunity to hear and to judge it myself. And, of course, I understand why you wanted me to pass final judgment. The topic is quite intriguing. Unfortunately, I find the children's tale unconvincing. I suspect they are merely clever brigands whose accomplices will be waiting somewhere along the road."

The elçi gave an order to the two guards, who moved toward Iskra and Damir.

"My men will escort the children to the city watch and explain the circumstances. They are now the Republic's concern," he explained. "Now, if you will excuse me, my work is always calling."

Damir and Iskra protested, but the elçi merely waved them off. He pulled Miho aside and spoke softly to him and his aide as the guards helped the Korčulans to their feet and guided them toward the door. Servants quietly moved to clear the table, and one opened the outer door for Damir, Iskra, and their two escorts.

"Wait! Wait!" Damir called. "There is something else I just remembered."

The elçi looked up irritably.

"A mark," Damir called. "Orhan has a birthmark on his wrist, a large white birthmark that circles his whole wrist. That's how Franco said he knew he was the son of the pasha. I don't know why I didn't remember it before."

Another order was given to the guards, and they stopped at the door. The elçi's expression changed from annoyance to interest.

"A white birthmark on his wrist?" he asked. "Which wrist?"

Damir hesitated, unsure for a moment, and Iskra jumped in.

"His left wrist, sir," she answered. "It covers nearly half his forearm. He pulls his sleeve down to try to hide it."

The two looked pleadingly at the Ottoman official as he circled around the courtyard toward them. He furrowed his brow and pursed his lips as he approached.

"This changes matters, my friends," he said when he reached them. "Guests from the Levant have spoken of the new pasha of Tripoli and mentioned a son with such a mark. Some gossips say it denotes where Allah, my He be praised, grasped him at birth, helping him into this world. A sign of divine blessing, they say. You might have heard a similar tale, of course, but why then wait so long to reveal this telling detail?"

"I apologize. There appears to be more truth in your story than I originally concluded."

"Then, you will get him?" Damir asked, relieved.

"That is not decided yet," the elçi said. "Two hundred ducats is not a trivial amount, even for the son of a pasha. Please have a seat again. You will have my answer shortly."

The guards brought Iskra and Damir back to the table, where a bowl of figs and pitcher of water materialized instantly, almost by magic. The elçi took Miho and his aide aside. The three spoke rapidly in hushed tones. Iskra and Damir watched the debate impatiently from their places under the fig tree. When Iskra started to stand, Damir touched her shoulder, drawing her back into her seat. They had made their case, and now the decision was beyond them.

Shadows were already starting to fill the courtyard when the elçi returned to the table with Miho. The aide had vanished.

"We will pay for His Excellency's return," the elçi announced. "We must move quickly because the city gates will be closed soon. I have sent my aide to gather the ducats and arrange for horses at the gate. I warn you, however, if this is indeed a trap, the city watch will never have the pleasure of your company."

The exchange

Damir and Iskra fidgeted nervously in the courtyard as preparations were completed. Having nothing to do only added to their impatience. The elçi had retreated to the inner rooms of the compound, and Miho had left on his own errands. A servant hovered near the two, ready to produce more coffee or water or figs, and the guards remained near the entryway, standing somewhat relaxed.

At last the aide returned and rushed through the courtyard and into the inner chambers. Instantly, the elçi emerged from his rooms, dressed less formally in a multi-colored vest made of heavy cloth and dark blue pantaloons. Now, he, too, had a curved sword hanging from the sash tied around his waist.

With few words, he led his entourage – the aide, two guards, and the two Korčulans – hastily through the city and out the western gates. The city watch obligingly opened space amid the crowd jostling to leave at the end of the market day. Miho was waiting at the foot of the stone bridge, standing beside an unadorned open carriage with a driver. Two saddled horses were tied nearby.

"Damir, if you will, you're beside the driver to show the way," the elçi directed. "Everyone else with me in the carriage."

The aide handed the elçi a heavy leather pouch, and the elçi, Miho, and Iskra climbed into the carriage, while the guards mounted the two horses.

"Just two guards?" Iskra asked, her tenor suggesting she expected more.

"My young lady," the elçi grinned, "these are janissary. You can tell by the unique tattoos on their foreheads. I assure you, each one is worth at least ten common brigands in this country. You and your friend said we only have to worry about three."

The elçi secreted the pouch into a box secured under his seat and ordered the driver to set off. The carriage and two guards behind it moved in a quick trot along the road that followed the west wall. It turned north briefly before finding a broad trail that cut through the scattered houses toward the highlands. Sooner than Damir expected, the group was on the road that traced the foot of the hills.

The procession slowed, and everyone became more watchful. The guards, in particular, were tense and alert. It was very late in afternoon, almost dusk, and no one else was in the road. From their low vantage point, the five in the carriage could not discern any ledges or plateaus in the hillside. The lowering sun cast heavy shadows and intermittent scrub hid any sign for where the boss and the others were waiting.

Damir worried that they might have passed the plateau or, worse, the boss and Franco had changed plans. He looked back at Iskra, who only shrugged slightly.

"Stop right there!" It was the boss' raspy voice, although he remained unseen.

The driver halted the carriage immediately. One of the guards edged past the wagon and reined in his horse a few yards ahead, while the other remained behind. Although both reached instinctively for their hilts, neither drew their swords. Everyone on the road scanned the slopes in a vain effort to spot the boss or the others.

"Damir, Iskra, is everything arranged according to plan?" the disembodied voice asked.

Damir looked at the elçi, who nodded.

"Yes," he called back. "We can finish this now."

"You have the ducats? Two hundred?"

The elçi nodded again.

"Yes."

"There is a path a little further east, the same one you left on," the boss shouted. "Bring the reward up. If the gold is all there, I will send the boy down."

Damir rose, but the elçi signaled for him to stop. Instead the elçi stood in the carriage and surveyed the hillside. He held his hands wide by his side, and looked for the source of the voice for a moment longer.

"You will soon have your reward and the eternal gratitude of the Porte for the return of one of his noble children," the Ottoman began, smiling. "And, indeed, we are all very grateful. Of course, first we must have proof that the boy is safe and unharmed and that he is who you claim him to be. I am sure you can understand."

There was no immediate response from the upper slopes. Then, the boss stepped slowly to the edge of the plateau with Orhan beside him. His hands were tied behind him with a rope that the boss was holding. The Turkish boy was dirty and his clothing torn, but he looked unharmed.

The elçi called to Orhan in a foreign language, and the boy began to struggle against the ropes. The boss jerked the rope and held him tight.

"Franco!" the boss yelled. "What's he saying?"

"No fear, señor," the Spaniard replied, still hidden beyond the ledge. "His Excellency only wishes to see the boy's left arm, the one with the mark."

The boss turned Orhan around gruffly so his bound hands faced the group on the road. He pulled up the long sleeves of Orhan's shirt, showing the stark mark that circled his left wrist, pushing the boy precariously close to the ledge. Even in the fading light, the mark of Allah was unmistakable. After a minute, the boss pulled Orhan back yelling down, "See it?"

From the ground, the elçi shouted rapidly in his own language, and Orhan replied. The boss let the exchange go on for a few moments, and then ended it by putting his hand over Orhan's mouth and pulling him a little further back.

"Franco?" he called to the man behind him.

"His Excellency was asking the young princeling some questions about his father and Tripoli, which the boy seems to have answered satisfactorily. His Excellency added that he should stay calm and he would be safe soon," Franco said, adding, "I suggest we conclude our business here rapidly, señor. The guards appear to have moved a little further from the carriage and may be seeking a route to our little haven here."

The boss, who was focused on the carriage with the elçi, only then noticed that the two armed men on both sides of the wagon had fanned out slightly. He drew his sword, still bloody from the encounter with the bandits, and waved it at them.

"Call your guards back," the boss shouted, "and tell them to dismount!"

The appropriate orders were issued, and the guards complied.

"That's better. No more Turkish, now. There's nothing more to say to the boy, just to me. Everyone out of the carriage, and give Dado, give Damir the gold."

The elçi, Miho, Damir, and Iskra all rose and stepped down from the carriage. The driver stayed on the wagon board holding the horse. Before the Ottoman official stepped from the wagon, he pulled the leather pouch from the box. Once on the ground, he gave it to Damir. The pouch was about the size of a small melon. Damir was surprised by its weight and fumbled it briefly when the elçi handed it to him.

"Damir, is it all there?"

Damir opened the pouch and found it filled with coins. He had never seen gold ducats before, so he took a handful and showed them to Iskra. She recognized them from her family's inn, where on rare occasions travelers who spent weeks in Korčula would use one to pay for their lodgings.

"The bag is full of coins," Damir shouted up. "I don't know how many, but there are a lot. Do you want me to count them?"

The boss hesitated. He didn't want to be cheated of his ransom, but he also didn't want to waste time. His dilemma was solved when a new voice called from the road.

"Sir! Sir!" Miho shouted, stepping forward a half pace. "I am with the Ragusan government, a liaison with the elçi, if you will. A trusted individual. I was there when they counted the ducats. There are, indeed, two hundred as you have requested for your services. It is all there."

"Who is this man?"

"He is from the city. He is like a negotiator with the Ottomans," Damir said. "We would not be here if he had not helped us convince the elçi that we were telling the truth."

There was silence from the plateau as the boss considered the next move. Those on the road kept still as they awaited a reply.

"We're good, then," the boss finally answered. Those on the ground were visibly relieved and awaited the next command. "Dado, bring the money up. Use the eastern path. Franco, take the boy down. You can let him go when you're almost to the road. No one else move. This will be over soon."

Damir closed the pouch and looked up just as Franco appeared behind the boss to take Orhan.

Without warning, a gleaming blade erupted from the boss' chest. The boss stiffened, his eyes wide and mouth gaping. He stood unmoving for a moment, a statue of betrayal. Then his body slid from the blade and tumbled over the ledge. His sword, free of his grip, clattered down the stony slope and came to a rest at the feet of the group below. In an instant, the guards by the carriage drew their own swords, ready for any attack. Everyone else froze in place and looked up.

Smiling broadly, Franco towered above them. He stood next to Orhan, taking the space where the boss had just stood. He yanked the rope holding the boy to show that he was now in control.

"Ekselanslari," he announced, "there has been a change in plan. Before we discuss that, though, please tell your henchmen to drop their weapons." Franco waved his sword casually at the armed men, his blade made more scarlet by the colors of the setting sun.

The elçi protested in Turkish, but Franco cut him off.

"No, no, no, Ekselanslari," he said in an overly gracious tone, "the local language, please. I see you are adept. It would be rude to our local friends otherwise. And I would like them to understand what is about to happen and, more importantly, why. Now, the weapons, please."

With a word from the elçi, the guards dropped their swords to the ground. Everyone waited for the Franco's next move. For his part, the Spaniard patiently wiped the fresh blood on his blade onto Orhan's shirt. He moved in small circuits along the ledge, pulling the boy along with him and looking pleased with himself.

"*Dado,*" he shouted, pronouncing Damir's nickname with a slight edge, "do you think you can throw that pouch up here? It is not exceedingly high, so I'm sure a strapping young lad like yourself can do it without problem."

"First the boy," the elçi called.

"Do not give me orders!" Franco yelled. "The boy will follow our unfortunate, greedy friend down there unless you simply do as

I say. Did you know he was planning to turn me in for a reward after the matter with the young Excellency was complete? He discussed it with his young accomplice thinking I wasn't listening. The fool. A bad decision." Franco moved the blade to Orhan's throat, much as he had held Damir the day before. "Now, Dado, if you please."

Damir began swinging the pouch of gold by his side, gathering momentum. When the elçi didn't stop him, he launched the bag of gold with an underhanded lob onto the plateau. It cleared the ledge easily and landed with the sound of coins jangling onto the ground.

"Excellent." Franco glanced back at the coins. "Karlo, gather all the ducats back into the pouch. We might need to leave quickly," he said with excess charm. "Be careful, young sir! I'll be counting them later, and you better hope that our dear dragoman was correct when he said the tally was complete."

Franco relished the moment. He again walked along the edge of the plateau, keeping Orhan close. He alternatively scowled and smiled down at the Ottoman and his entourage, soaking in his dominance.

"Now, Ekselanslari, as you can see the arrangements have changed," Franco oozed. "Where do I start?"

The Spaniard paused and paced some more, as though he were contemplating the question and enjoying each possible answer before settling on a favorite.

"Many, many years ago, when I was even younger than our princeling is now, the Porte snatched me from my mother's breast. It's a common story, of course. He brought me to his lands, where he trained me to fight and punished me when I failed. He stole my childhood and my home. Indeed, my only knowledge of my beloved Granada is from the beautiful stories I heard in foreign taverns from drunken seamen. He sent me into battle when I was born to the pleasant life of a fisherman like my father and his father before him. I dreamt of a peaceful sea with no greater enemy than the weight of a full net."

Franco stopped and listened to himself in his second ear, the echo of his monologue. He exploded in laughter.

"Ha! Have you ever heard a worse ballad ... at least while sober? Forgive me if I have bored you. It seems so many years under the thumb of the Porte have instilled upon me a melancholy slant," Franco brought his blade against Orhan's throat. "Please, do not move or the story will end sooner than it should."

The guards had begun drifting away from the carriage again. They immediately returned.

"To bring this miserable tale to an end, I knew there was no chance to reclaim what was stolen from me, to regain a reckless youth, but on the pasha's galley during the battle at Curzola I seized my chance to balance the ledger for my lost years, trading one lost youth for another. An eye for an eye, as the Christians say. The pasha's son was on the quarter deck, and during the height of the battle I charged at him with my sword. At the last moment, he saw me and stumbling backward and over the gunwales.

"I thought that was the end of it until I noticed that a lieutenant had seen the whole affair. Rather than face what I knew would be a particularly harsh judgment, I chose to follow the young princeling into Mother Sea. I had failed, but Fate, it seems, had chosen not to finish the story there. Now I find myself again with opportunity to avenge my stolen youth and, with gratitude to the generosity of Ekselanslari, to return to my home a rich man."

Franco arced his blade to slash across Orhan's throat.

"Stop!" the elçi shouted. "This boy is not to blame! I can bring more gold!"

Franco just laughed, blood lust in his eyes and his cackle. Then a cry from behind Franco mingled into the laughter. Karlo rushed the big man from behind, knocking into his back. The tackle barely nudged Franco, who pivoted swiftly to face Karlo with his sword. In spinning, however, the Spaniard stepped on loose rocks. His foot slipped just over the edge of the plateau. He tumbled a few feet down the slope before catching himself.

"You miserable wretch!" Franco cried as he elbowed himself back onto the ridge. "You'll be joining your beloved boss soon!"

On the road, Damir was the first to react. He grabbed the boss' sword from where it had fallen on the ground and raced toward the trail to the plateau. He darted past a guard, who was looking to the elçi for orders, and turned up the hillside. The trail twisted in a switchback before it opened onto the plateau.

Damir reached the table in time to see Karlo disappear among the scrub and scamper toward the summit. Franco, who was getting to his feet next to Orhan, saw Karlo vanish as well and Damir emerge. The giant Spaniard took Orhan's rope in his left hand, and advanced toward Damir, who waved the boss' long blade awkwardly.

"You can leave now, *Dado,*" the Spaniard said, waving his own blade effortlessly. "Your hand begs for a shovel, not a sword." He looked at the teen and smiled. "Once we start, it's over."

Damir wavered. Franco was right. The sword felt heavy in his inexperienced hands. He looked over to the Spaniard and saw broad shoulders, arms like tree limbs, and a sword wet with fresh blood. Behind Franco, Orhan was being pulled awkwardly backwards. As Damir weighed his option, Karlo's call of "Death to them all!" echoed in his ears. In an instant Damir knew he didn't want to be Karlo.

The Korčulan olive grower found his balance, took a firm grip of the boss' sword, and charged the galley slave. Damir screamed wildly as he ran forward, the blade waving high above his head. Franco seemed surprised, or perhaps amused, by the attack. He held fast as Damir approached, pivoting at the last moment. Damir's momentum carried him past Franco until he stumbled and toppled onto the ground.

As Franco turned to press his advantage, Orhan dropped to the ground as well, becoming an anchor to the huge man. Franco lost half a step as he let go of the ropes that bound Orhan. The boy's maneuver was enough to give Damir time to get back on his feet and face the Spaniard again.

Franco was no hurry. He stepped deliberately toward Damir, holding his sword loosely at his side. Although Damir sidestepped and tried to delay the attack, the plateau offered little room for dancing and even with his leisurely stride Franco was soon on the boy. Damir blocked a half-hearted diagonal slash. A quick follow-through caught the Korčulan off balance and sent him to the ground again. He hacked madly at Franco's legs, swings that were too easily evaded. Franco started to move in for a final thrust. As Damir tried to roll out of Franco's reach, one of the elçi's guards came through the scrub and onto the ledge, calling out something in Turkish.

The Spaniard found himself facing two adversaries, including one who was skilled with the sword. He repositioned himself, moving toward the back of the plateau and keeping Damir and the guard in front of him, although on different sides. The guard lost no time joining the battle, advancing into Franco. After a couple of exploratory swipes and parries, the two found themselves with locked swords, pushing against the other. Franco swiftly overpowered the guard and threw him against the slope just in time to meet Damir, who was coming from his right.

Franco disarmed Damir easily with a twisting thrust and shouldered him away to focus on the real challenge. Franco and the guard re-engaged in a series of strikes. The guard was outmatched and was retreating slowly just as the second guard arrived from the eastern path. Franco released a fanatical laugh and charged into both of them.

With the Spaniard occupied, Damir took the opportunity to get to Orhan and untie him. He made quick work of the ropes. The sword fight continued on the far edge of the plateau, so he and Orhan scurried to the western path. Once they reached it, they raced downhill as metal clanged against metal behind them.

Damir and Orhan got as far as the first sharp curve when their way was blocked by the Ston wagon, which was overturned in the path and draped with freshly cut branches. The boss and Franco wanted to make sure there was only one way for the elçi's guards or anyone else to get to the plateau. The wagon and branches were piled high and tight across the path, and after pulling at a few boughs experimentally, Damir decided they couldn't waste the time to get past the roadblock. He and Orhan turned around and crept back to the plateau.

They stopped as soon as they came into sight of the narrow table. One of the guards was on the ground, motionless, lying next to the pouch and a few gold coins that has spilled out. Franco was bleeding from his side and still engaged with the second guard. Despite his wound, the Spaniard clearly held the advantage. While the guard fought loyally, he recognized his odds. He retreated and dodged at each of the Spaniard's advances. The guard was skilled enough to parry Franco's attacks so far, but it was only a matter of time before a fatal or crippling thrust found its mark.

Damir and Orhan watched, crouched at the edge of the plateau. The fight moved in circles around the small landing, the guard taking a step or two back whenever Franco approached. When the sword dance reached the far end of the plateau, Damir made his move. He grabbed Orhan's arm and pulled him across the clearing to where Karlo had disappeared toward the upper slopes. After a moment, he found a small gap that opened to a narrow trail up the hill.

They had just started up the slope, when the second guard cried out from the plateau. Damir urged Orhan to climb faster. The path twisted and turned as it rose up the hillside, folded upon itself, and eased parallel to the steep slope. After one switchback, they saw Franco, a cut across his face and his side soaked in blood, laboring up the trail after them. At one point, he paused just a couple of yards below them along the serpentine path.

His face painted with blood and sweat, Franco looked up at Damir and growled, "You should have run when you could have, boy."

As the trail crested onto the summit, the scrub thinned. Damir and Orhan scrambled toward the hill's spine, and with every stumble they could feel Franco gaining on them. Damir pushed Orhan ahead of him and urged the boy to climb faster. No prompting was necessary as Orhan rushed up the hillside, sometimes using his hands to keep his balance. Damir was right behind him, and they reached the top of the hill with Franco just a few paces further back.

"Run! Run!" Damir yelled to Orhan. "Just run!"

Orhan sprinted along the crest toward a low structure in the distance. Damir had little time to prepare. He picked up a thick, sun-bleached branch from the ground and held it in front of him as Franco mounted the summit. The Spaniard was breathing heavily, but still managed a grin, unleashing a new trickle of blood from the gash in his cheek. He paused and shook his head slightly as he scrutinized Damir, holding the bough in front of him with both hands.

"You lost with a sword, little Dado, what do you plan to do with a stick?" Franco chortled as he sliced his sword cleanly through the branch in Damir's hands.

Damir dropped the remaining bits of wood, and took a step back, a move echoed by Franco. As the Spaniard raised his blade for a final blow, Damir looked past him and saw Orhan rushing up with a large rock in his hands. The furtive glance, however, betrayed Orhan's attack. Franco stepped easily aside and tripped the boy as he passed.

Orhan fell onto Damir, throwing them both onto the ground.

"Ekselanslari, this makes it all that much easier." Franco stood towering over the two on the ground, waving the point of his blade from one to the next as though deciding who to kill first. Then, he unhurriedly raised his sword for a backhand swing.

"Franco, please don't," Damir pleaded.

The Spaniard grinned and lifted his sword a bit higher. "I have no time for this, Dado. It's over."

"Wait! It's just the three of us," Damir tried again. "There's no one here to see your triumph."

Damir took Franco's delay in killing them as a sign to go on.

"It is over. Well, it can be over for you, Franco. You can leave here now. It will be dark soon, and there's no one here to follow you. Go over those hills and find a way back to Spain. But if you kill us – if you kill Orhan, the elçi will be after you, and not only him, but all of Ragusa. You are a tough man, but as you said, with those markings anyone can recognize you. And with a bounty on your head, you won't get far."

As Damir talked, Iskra came quietly over the crest behind Franco. She held a long dagger in her hand and stiffened as she prepared for her one chance to catch the Spaniard by surprise. Iskra took a careful step toward the three, still hidden from Franco's view.

"Iskra, don't!" Damir called.

The girl froze in her place, her face a mixture of puzzlement and betrayal.

Franco looked back and found the girl behind him. He pivoted and took a step back, bringing Iskra into full view. He lowered his blade into a more defensive position as he judged the new situation. Then, his shoulders sagged and he let a sigh escape as he took a reluctant step toward the girl.

"Franco," Damir called, trying to regain the Spaniard's attention. "This can be over. It can be, but not if you kill us. You wouldn't have revenge. You would, you would just be what they made you to be. A fisherman would walk away ... run way; a janissary would kill us all."

Franco took another step toward Iskra and stopped. He looked at the girl, the dagger trembling in her small hand as she held it high in front of her – an amateur stance, he couldn't fail to notice – and at the two boys still lying defenseless on the ground. In the fading light, he became visibly smaller, as though deflated of his rage. The burly swordsman stepped back indecisively. Then he took another step back.

"Damir, no one has ever been able to change the mind of Franco of Granada before with just words."

He spoke a few lines to Orhan in Turkish, turned, and started walking along the ridge. As the three Korčulans watched, Franco veered left, away from Dubrovnik and down the hill.

Once the Spaniard had disappeared, Damir stood and walked over to Iskra.

"Are you OK?" Iskra asked, looking only into Damir's blue eyes.

"Um, yeah." Damir stopped just beside the girl he couldn't stop thinking about. "Bruised, but Franco never cut me. I don't think he wanted to."

"You didn't have to stop me. I had him by surprise."

"He would have killed you."

"Maybe. Maybe not," Iskra offered. "But everything's better this way."

"Not maybe, Islić," Damir said, for the first time using the nickname Niko called his sister. "He was a janissary."

"A janissary?"

"Yeah," Damir said, relishing the familiarity of using the nickname. In an instant, Damir thought of all the things he wanted to tell Iskra. Instead, he said, "Now, that would have been hard to explain to your mamma."

The quip was enough for Iskra to throw her arms around his neck, at least until Orhan joined them a second later. Together the three took a moment to watch the sun sinking low toward the sea. As they caught their breaths and concealed their thoughts, an explosion of colors spread across the horizon. A bit closer, the lights of the Dubrovnik were flickering warmly within its walls.

"We need to go before it gets too dark to climb down," Iskra announced, again practical. "The elçi will be happy to see Orhan safe."

The trio passed easily down the serpentine path to the plateau, where they found one guard dead and the other with a deep cut in his leg. Damir and Iskra helped the wounded guard to the road as Orhan gathered the pouch of gold and brought it with them.

Late coffee

They put the wounded guard into the carriage and started back to Dubrovnik. The elçi and Orhan spoke animatedly in Turkish throughout short trip, while Damir and Iskra rode behind on the horses.

When they reached the city gate, it was closed and the drawbridge raised. Miho muttered something about the rector making a big ceremony of locking the gates each night to assure the citizens that they were safe. He called for the sergeant of the watch, and after a brief discussion and a longer wait the gate was opened and the bridge lowered. Some men came out to help carry the wounded guard into the city, and the elçi's aide was with them. The elçi spoke to his aide briefly, sending him off on unknown tasks, and Turkish diplomat and his company walked leisurely through the darkened city to the Ottoman compound. The west gate closed noisily behind them.

"I'm afraid you will have to endure our hospitality tonight, my friends," the elçi said over his shoulder to Damir and Iskra. "I've already ordered rooms prepared in my home, and my staff will find clean clothes for you. We'll eat after you have had time to wash."

The wounded guard was carried down the main boulevard, while a watchman escorted the elçi, who was holding the gold pouch tightly, and his entourage through the streets. As they preceded along the polished pavement, the bustle that marked the city during the day had settled into the quiet conversations of people sitting on benches and low walls, reviewing events, gossiping, whispering, conspiring.

Once at the compound, servants took Damir and Iskra to their rooms, where fresh clothes and wash basins filled with cool water were waiting. Before long, a servant arrived to announce dinner.

Damir wore a fresh white shirt with baggy sleeves and green trousers that were surprisingly tight. He was out of his room instantly and waited at Iskra's door. Minutes passes before the Korčula girl emerged, her dress a pale yellow gown with a long, dark blue jacket, curving shapes in lighter blue thread frolicked from shoulder to hem.

Damir could not find words, even the most casual ones, which made Iskra smile.

"I guess this was the best they could find in a hurry," she said, pivoting just enough to swirl the skirt. When Damir remained speechless, she added, "We should go. They're waiting for us."

The servant led them to a small private dining room decorated with ornate tapestries. The elçi, Orhan, and Miho – all dressed brilliantly – were already sitting at one end of a large table. They all rose as the Korčulan pair was escorted in.

"My dear, you look stunning," Miho declared effusively as Iskra came through the door. "Don't you agree, Damir?"

Damir shyly muttered in agreement as the elçi motioned for everyone to take their places around the table.

"What an adventure," he began, as waiters filled goblets with fruit juices and sweetened water. "His Excellency has told me all about it. He said he always trusted you, Damir, because of your blue eyes. In my land, the blue eye is a potent talisman to ward away evil spirits. May Allah be praised that you found our dear prince when you did."

The Ottoman then begged his guests to enjoy a small feast to mark the return of the lost boy. Plates were brought laden with steaming fish, squid, and prawns, accompanied by tender vegetables and fragrant breads. The elçi explained that the pasha of Tripoli and his three sons were travelling with Uluj Ali to Constantinople when a messenger arrived and they suddenly turned northward into the Adriatic.

Orhan wasn't clear why, but before long the fleet was in battle at the walls of Korčula. The young prince fell overboard when Franco, called Mohammed on the ship, charged at him. He clung to some flotsam until scavengers who had been following the fleet found him and brought him on board. There was arguing among the raiders, apparently over what to do with Orhan, but eventually they decided to chase after the fleet again. By then, the fleet had moved on and they had lost it. As they searched for the fleet, their barks came close enough to land for Orhan to flee during an unguarded moment.

"But I don't understand," Iskra said, as a waiter scooped prawns sautéed in garlicky tomato sauce onto her plate, "Damir says Franco wasn't a galley slave, as he claimed, is that true?"

"My dear," the elçi sighed heavily, "Franco, as you called him, was no galley slave. He was a janissary, a fighter. I saw that immediately from the markings on his face. And, as you witnessed, his skill with a sword was much greater than that of a galley slave. I had heard stories that Uluj Ali had problems with the janissary just before he embarked. Perhaps your Franco was among this mutinous group. We will never know now. But before he disappeared, Franco told His Highness that he was left alive only because of the persuasive skills of your young Damir here."

The rest of the evening passed amicably, with the elçi and Miho asking questions about life in Korčula and under the Venetians. They were entertained by the tale of the town's brave, small band of defenders against the pasha's fleet and had the two repeat the story several times, devouring each detail. For his part, the elçi peppered his inquiries with stories from his own home, Solun, and how the Adriatic Sea reminds him so much of the Aegean. The hour was late when the servants cleared the main dishes and brought the copper urns and cups for coffee, as well as a pastry made of nuts and honey that the elçi called *baklava.*

"You must pour slowly," the elçi instructed gleefully as he decanted the dark liquid from a small urn into his cup. "My friends here would say that it's too late for coffee, but in Solun, we say it's never too late for coffee!"

After coffee and dessert – Damir had two slices of the baklava – the group prepared to retire to their rooms. Before they broke up, however, the elçi gave Damir and Iskra each twelve ducats for the efforts in helping Orhan. Iskra protested, but the elçi insisted.

"His Excellency thought you should get all the two hundred ducats," the elçi laughed, "but he is still young. What would you do with two hundred ducats on that tranquil island of yours? And here, have another ducat for your friend – Karlo? – if you ever see him again. Fair payment for his well-timed shove on the plateau!"

Passage to Korčula had been arranged on a Ragusan galley for the next morning, the elçi said before announcing it was time for everyone to retire for the night. A servant led Damir and Iskra back to their rooms, where fresh water and night clothes had been set out for them. Damir waited in his tight green pants until he thought sufficient time had passed for the hallway to be empty.

He closed his eyes and took a deep breath before opening the door. As he stepped into the hall, a servant jumped up from a chair near the landing. "Coffee? More Water? What may I bring you?"

"No, thank you," Damir responded formally, stepping backwards into his room.

The next morning, Orhan was waiting for Damir and Iskra in the courtyard when they came down to leave. He handed each a small, folded handkerchief, and motioned for the two to open them. In Damir's was a small gold ring with symbols etched along the surface, and in Iskar's a gold pendent with a similar design.

"For good fortune, prosperity, and blessings," a servant explained.

Orhan hugged them both in turn, and watched as they left.

Epilogue

The next year, the Feast of the Assumption of the Blessed Virgin Mary in Korčula was a splendid success. No ships appeared on the horizon, and no Ottoman footmen threatened Revelin Gate. Indeed, the only threat came from low, grey clouds that gathered along the western horizon just as the morning bells were calling the community to mass. Even they cleared by midday.

Damir's mother and father both travelled to the town that year, bringing extra casks of olive oil to commemorate their son's safe return from his unexpected adventures. They promised Father Anton even better oil next year, once they harvested and processed olives from a small tract of grove they bought from the Nikoničić estate over the winter. Father Anton praised all the saints endlessly as he ate the oil sopped by bread baked that morning by Iskra's brother, Nikola, in his new oven.

The day, as it should be, was an endless stream of mass, pageantry, theater, and food.

As the sun set, Father Anton, Damir, and Iskra walked together along the eastern wall, looking toward Badija Island where the galleys were first spotted a year earlier. Already the horizon was dark with scattered points of lights, far off flecks of gold twinkling from the island and the peninsula across the dark waters.

"We were blessed," Father Anton said, breaking the transcendent silence. "Whether it was our walls, the Bura, or our piety, Curzola was spared the destruction that Uluj Ali brought to Hvar after he abandoned his battle here. Whole villages burned. May God have mercy on their souls."

"And has anything changed?" Damir asked.

"Almost," Father Anton answered, resting against the wall as he watched distant lights sputter on and off. Sounds of late festivities drifted over them from the courtyards of Korčula behind them. "Just after he attacked here, Uluj Ali joined a great battle off the Greek port of Lepanto. Ottoman fleets faced warships from Spain, Venice, and the Holy See. The Papal allies won, helped by Venice's new giant ships. Among the Ottoman fleets, only Uluj Ali's escaped. The first dispatches we heard said this would mean peace at last in our sea, but ships were rebuilt and new battles engaged. Now we have a new pope, and the European alliance is said to be weakening. So, no, Dado, in the end nothing has changed."

Iskra took Damir's hand. "Well, maybe nothing in the lands of kings and sultans." The two started to stroll off, but Father Anton, somewhat flushed, caught up with them.

"Did Karlo ever return?" he asked them.

"He never did," Damir said. "His parents are heartbroken. I never told anyone the story, except for you and my parents. Maybe I should, but I don't think the village would understand why we went to so much trouble to rescue a Turkish boy. I wish I would have told Ivan the cartman, though, before he died. He would have understood. There are rumors in Blato that Karlo went off to join the Uskoks. People are willing to believe that even though he doesn't seem the type. Others think he might have drowned at sea sailing with the man he called 'the boss.'

"I still have the ducat promised him, if he ever comes back."

The three walked quietly until All Saints Tower, where Father Anton had led the town's defense against the attackers. They turned back and retraced their steps along the eastern wall. All the color had left the sky and the world beyond the wall was a blanket of black with no obvious horizon separating sky from sea. Pin points of starlight above were mirrored weakly by random lantern lights along the Pelješac hills. They stopped as the wall bent around the northern edge of the town.

"Good night, father," Iskra and Damir said, almost in unison.

Then Iskra added, in hasty explanation, "Damir's parents are staying at our inn. We need to return before the conversation turns to unwanted themes."

Father Anton smiled in understanding and embraced the two. He watched them descend the stone staircase and disappear down a narrow street. The old priest started to follow them down into his familiar town, but changed his mind. Instead, he walked back to the wall facing the sea and watched the stars for a moment. A light streaked across the sky for an instant creating a long line pointing nowhere knowable. A moment later, two others. He watched as others came as well and went in a twinkling.

"The tears of Saint Lawrence," Father Anton said to no one.

Made in the USA
Las Vegas, NV
20 December 2020